D0394012

The CARNIVAL OF LOST SOULS

A Handcuff Kid NOVEL
BY
Laura Quimby

Amulet Books
NEW YORK

Cataloging-in-Publication Data has been applied for and may be obtained from the Library of Congress.
ISBN 978-0-8109-8980-1

Text copyright © 2010 Laura Quimby
Book design by Maria T. Middleton

The text in this book is set in 11-point ITC Garamond.
The display typefaces are Fantail, MONA, Ringlet, and Templar.

Printed and bound in U.S.A.
10 9 8 7 6 5 4 3 2 1

Amulet Books are available at special discounts when purchased in quantity for premiums and promotions as well as fundraising or educational use. Special editions can also be created to specification. For details, contact specialmarkets@abramsbooks.com or the address below.

THE ART OF BOOKS SINCE 1949
115 West 18th Street
New York, NY 10011
www.abramsbooks.com

TO

Steve Muchow

Contents

The boy wove through the crowds of the carnival, shoving his way to the sideshow tents. Darkened pathways swarmed with fire-eaters, sword-swallowers, and contortionists, but the boy would not be tempted from his mission to see the legendary and most feared of them all: the Amazing Mussini.

Whispers pulsed around the tent like the lightning bugs filling the dark summer sky with tiny bursts of light. The line quickly thinned; the boy's body tingled as an Asian girl, her neck covered in tattoos, escorted him to Mussini. He stumbled toward the great magician. His throat tightened as he made his request, eyes heavy with awe.

"I've come to hear the secret."

The magician waved him closer.

Mussini grinned from under his black top hat. He offered the boy a deal, for the secret he wanted to hear was the most expensive of them all. The boy tried to steady his hand as he signed the contract. Thick ink oozed from the tip of the pen like tar or blood. The aged paper, cool to the touch, held the sour stench of death. The boy squinted at the contract, the words swirling fast—a contract on his soul to be collected in fifty years, time to enjoy his secret, time before Mussini would return and collect his price.

A dark web of words spooled from Mussini's lips. The boy stared into the black pools of his eyes, caught in the ebb and flow of his voice. And when the story was over, the secret told, only then did the boy realize what he had done. The mistake fresh in his mind, the boy pleaded for mercy. But the magician roared with laughter, his contract ironclad. No room for second chances. The raucous crowd around Mussini drifted toward the boy. Fearing for his life, he burst out of the tent.

The night rang in his ears; the air stung his lungs. A sudden burning on his flesh brought him to his knees—a tattoo appeared on his wrist, the mark of the magician himself. Mussini. It was then, through the pain and fear, the boy decided he would study the strange ways of the magician, learning everything he could about the world, science, stars, and magic, anything to combat the wicked curse laid upon him.

The only thing the boy was sure of, clutching his wrist, was that when Mussini came back in fifty years, the soul he took would not be his.

1

Jack Carr

Suspension was just another word for "vacation." Jack
Carr dug his hands into his pockets and strode right out
of the principal's office, past the receptionist's desk, and
out the front door. He could use a little time off from
the sordid hallways of McDovall Academy, crowded with
misfits and delinquents. Reform school was having a bad
influence on him. A rusted Buick idled in front of the
school, and a cloud of cigarette smoke drifted out when
he opened the door and climbed in.

Mildred Crosby, his social worker, had been courting
retirement since she met Jack. He wasn't sure why she
didn't kick back and start collecting her Social Security
checks, but Mildred just wouldn't quit. Once she told
him it was to keep him from raining terror on poor

unsuspecting foster families, but Jack had a feeling she had a soft spot for him, despite his bad behavior.

A cigarette dangled precariously from Mildred's lips. A thick coat of rose lipstick clung to the filter. Her right eye was clenched shut to avoid the upward flood of smoke rising from the bright cherry tip. Mildred told Jack smoking was a disgusting habit, but it was her one vice, and overall, one vice wasn't too bad. A ribbon of smoke curled in the air. Jack pictured the Nile River and the way the water flowed northward, not south like most rivers, the muddy, silt-filled river gushing upward against the sag and pull of the heavy earth, trying to drag every-thing down.

He rested his head against the back of the seat and glanced over at Mildred, her hair a football helmet of white curls. Every once in a while she would leave a pink sponge roller in her hair way in the back where she couldn't see it, and he would have to fish it out while she screeched, "Get it out! Get it out before someone sees!"

Jack didn't know what the big deal was. It was just a hair roller; it wasn't like her fly was open—but she was old-fashioned, always wearing dresses. When he thought about it, he was just thankful she didn't have a fly. She glanced over and motioned to his seat belt. He dutifully put it on.

"Well, mister, you're lucky the principal owes me a favor. This is your second suspension in two weeks.

One more and you get kicked out for good." Mildred clicked her tongue and shook her head. "What were you thinking, hitting your gym teacher in the fanny with a dodgeball? That could seriously hurt a man."

"He's lucky he turned around when he did," Jack said, rolling down the window to let in some cool air. "Because I wasn't aiming for his fanny."

"Young man! You can't solve your problems with violence. Did you try taking deep breaths and counting to ten like I told you?" Mildred put her cigarette in the ashtray and gripped the steering wheel in both hands. She probably wanted to strangle him.

"No, but I didn't throw the ball that hard." Jack squirmed in his seat. "Plus, he deserved it. He makes me do extra push-ups and run the track three more times when the other kids get a water break. He says it's character building. But that's not fair."

"I know it's not fair, but we talked about that. You certainly got shortchanged in the fair department, but you have to get over it. *Life* isn't fair," Mildred said, reaching over and brushing the hair out of his face. "If you get suspended again, I don't know what I'll do."

"Sorry, I'll try harder next time." Jack glanced out the window, avoiding her gaze.

"Well, when you apologize, at least try and sound like you mean it."

"*Sorry,*" Jack said in a sappy voice, then burst out

laughing. Mildred had him *so* figured out. "Hey, at least you got to leave your office to come pick me up."

"Actually, the timing was perfect." She pressed her lips together and smiled widely—too widely. That smile was a sign Jack had grown accustomed to, and it was the sign of oncoming, lightning-strike change. She continued: "I was going to wait and tell you after school today, but since I'm here, I have some good news for you." She beamed. Emotionally, Mildred could turn on a dime, disappointed one minute and happy the next. "I found a new foster home for you."

"Are you serious?" His stomach jumped. He knew she was, because Mildred rarely sugarcoated the truth, life-altering as it might be. "You could have warned me."

She stopped at a red light and glanced over at Jack, ignoring his comments. "You won't be spending another night in the group home. I know that will make you happy," Mildred said, patting his knee.

Jack shrugged. He didn't mind the group home that much. He thought of it like the pound, just for kids. Everyone wanted the puppies, and he was an old dog.

"I packed all your *stuff* for you." Mildred twisted up her mouth in disapproval of Jack's hobby. "We're going to your new home right away." She paused, picked up her cigarette, took a drag, and exhaled slowly. "I know it took a while to find you a place this time, but this one will be different. I promise." She nodded confidently.

"Yeah, I guess." Jack tried to smile. As tough as Mildred was, he knew she went easy on him, and he was grateful. "I'll give this foster home six months," Jack said, reaching for the pack of cigarettes that poked out of Mildred's purse. She slapped his hand and stuffed the pack deep into the chasm of her handbag.

"I thought I told you never to go inside a lady's purse."

"They were hanging out the side." Jack grinned. On the first day they met, Mildred warned him that she had an alligator in her purse, and if he ever went inside, it would take his arm off. He believed her.

"Six months. You're optimistic. I'll go with four," Mildred said, playing along.

"Four months is good."

"I meant four *weeks.*" Mildred's laugh was gravelly, and a long stream of ash fell from the tip of her cigarette and scattered across the burgundy seat. She and Jack had been together for five years now. Five years of strange homes, strange people, and their strange ways. He sighed, trying to relax. He could only imagine what kind of place he was about to walk into.

Mildred eased the Buick up to the curb in front of the latest foster home, and, boy, was it a doozy. "It's the Victorian one right up there," she said. She'd scraped the tires against the curb, and Jack rolled his eyes, because she always did that. Before getting out of the car, Mildred flicked her cigarette butt through the open window, leaned her head back, and exhaled a lungful of gray smoke. "Ready, baby?" she said. Jack pulled his duffel bag out of the trunk and slammed it closed. "Do you have your *book*?" Mildred asked the way she always did.

Jack's book had been given to him by his first foster parents, an old priest and his lilac-smelling wife, many years ago. It was a good-bye gift. In Jack's opinion, reading was pointless unless it was for school, and then it was simply pointless with consequences if he didn't do it. But this book was different. The man on the front cover had on old-fashioned bathing trunks, and his muscles bulged like a wrestler's. He was wrapped in chains with thick padlocks dangling from his arms and legs. The chains forced him to bend over from the weight as if an invisible ceiling pressed down on him and he couldn't straighten up.

The book was about magic. Not *real* magic, though, but trick-of-the-eye magic. The man in chains was not a prisoner or a slave, but a magician. And his name was Harry Houdini.

"Yes, I've got my *book*," Jack said the way he always did.

They walked the long, steep path up to the house, which loomed atop the scraggly lawn. The path was made of slabs of broken slate positioned like stepping-stones across a weedy ocean of grass up to the front door. The house resembled a witch's dollhouse with elaborately carved trim that looked good enough to eat, but would surely kill him with one bite. Tall, pointy spires pierced the still, blue sky. The house could use a good paint job, but it had a lot of windows with tall shutters and a porch surrounded by spindly columns. "This house is right out of Nathaniel Hawthorne," Mildred said, craning her neck and shading her eyes against the sun as she squinted up at it.

"Who's that?"

"A famous American author—remember that. The man who lives here is a professor. This could be your big chance of having a real mentor. Someone to look up to." Mildred squeezed his shoulder. "Need I remind you you're running out of chances? This could be your last one. We got lucky. The professor asked for a boy who liked magic, and I knew you would be perfect."

"OK, so what did this Hawthorne guy write?" Jack sighed, bracing for the inevitable lesson on famously boring writers he couldn't care less about.

"*The Scarlet Letter.*"

"What's it about?"

"Lust, adultery, and impure thoughts, and poor Hester Prynne had to wear a scarlet letter pinned to her bosom." Mildred clutched at the front of her knit cardigan.

"Bosoms!" Jack wrenched his neck, jerking his head toward Mildred, and burst out laughing. "This was your first choice of places to leave me, a house that reminded you of bosoms?"

"I'm not *leaving* you." She grasped his sleeve. Her eyelashes fluttered, her watery blue eyes brimming with tears. Jack had made a critical error. Mildred was a crier.

He squeezed her hand in his, her skin a soft bruised peach. "Don't cry, Millie." She loved it when he called her Millie. Last time she cried, half her makeup ran down her face, and it was *not* pretty. He had had no idea that women put a skin-colored layer of makeup over their faces. (Jack was learning that women were highly layered, and it was not a good idea to get them wet.) Mildred dabbed at her eyes with a wad of crumpled-up tissue.

"Just give me a ring if he turns out to be a murderer, and I'll be back in a flash." Mildred tried to pat down his light brown hair—it was a little too long all over, but it didn't go all the way to his collar. She licked her thumbs and pressed on his temples.

Jack swatted her hands away. "Millie, stop. Why don't you just spit on me?"

"Don't say 'spit,' young man. And when we get inside, don't say 'booger,' 'loogie,' or 'fart.' And don't talk about any other bodily functions in front of your new foster father. Please try. *Please* try to let him like you."

Jack stared into Mildred's eyes as she inspected his face for any microscopic filth that might still be visible. "Mildred, we all fart."

"Not necessarily. I was married for thirty-five years

and never once expelled gas in front of my husband." Mildred held her chin high, as if the suppression of one's bowels were an admirable quality in a woman.

Jack scrunched up his face and asked, "What'd you do when you had to fart?"

"I would run into another room and sit on a pillow," Mildred said, revealing yet another layer of her complicated female persona.

"Fine, I won't fart. I'll probably get some intestinal disorder, but I'll hold it in."

"Good boy, Jack."

She kissed his forehead, and held his head in her hands like she was sending him off into the Wild West. Jack liked to think he lived his life like a cowboy with nothing behind him, riding into that big sky country, dodging arrows and Indians. Mildred smoothed her hands over her dress and pushed the doorbell.

Ehrich Weiss

He isn't born Harry Houdini.
The exact day that Ehrich is born is lost,
like many things left behind.
Sardined into the belly of a steamer ship,
his journey begins by boat,
miles of wild Atlantic stretched out in front of him.
He arrives on a sweat-soaked July day
in the New World,
leaving everything for a chance at a life in America.

Opportunity lands him and his family in Appleton.
In a metropolis of empty fields and small-town ways,
they do not last long.
Sometimes the first place isn't the right place.

Ehrich wants to be an acrobat.
Sailing through the air, flying from slim bar to slim bar,
for a brief second the acrobat is airborne.
Nothing is impossible, for Ehrich is the prince of air.

The family moves to New York City.
They struggle to make ends meet,
beg for a bucket of coal,
for small dollars earned on street corners,
working odd jobs: shining shoes,
selling newspapers, running errands.
Always running,
striving to be enough.

The whole world is ahead of him,
sparkling on the slim horizon
as the sea presses against the sky,
where dreams live with room to run.

From the heaven of a high wire,
he sees the world in possibilities,
squinting against the glare of the sun,
dancing on the surface.
It's all a trick of the eye.

One day the world will turn around and take a look at him,
but Ehrich Weiss will be gone.

2

Professor Hawthorne

"Good afternoon," the professor said in a baritone voice as he swung open the front door.

"We made it." Mildred exhaled deeply and fanned herself with her hand, as if making it across town was as treacherous as a journey across the Atlantic. The man at the door stepped back and swept his arm out, welcoming them into his home. In the entrance, a glass chandelier dangled from the ceiling on a thick chain. Long velvet drapes hung from the windows. Jack held on to the sleeve of Mildred's jacket as he followed her into the Nathaniel Hawthorne house. Mildred had said the guy's name, but he didn't catch it. Professor something or other. He knew it wasn't Professor Hawthorne, but that's all he could think.

To call his new foster father old would be an understatement. The guy was an antique, and not the expensive French kind either, more like the kind of chipped and battered old armchair (with an afghan thrown over it) his grandmother (well, if he had a grandmother) would've had. His tweed blazer was so threadbare it could have been a hand-me-down from Nathaniel Hawthorne himself. Plus, the professor had the most unusual facial hair: two enormous lamb-chop sideburns and a long mustache. Though his naturally wavy hair was oiled down, the ends frizzed out. He shook Jack's hand and lowered his face, so they stared eyeball to eyeball.

Jack let his canvas duffel bag, which he had picked up at an army surplus store, slip to the floor. There was a loud clank. It was the distinct, slightly muffled sound of metal hitting the wood floor through the thin canvas bag. Mildred wrinkled her nose and narrowed her eyes at him. Over the years, Mildred and Jack had developed a secret way of communicating with their expressions whenever they went into a new foster home. The look Mildred shot him was not the happy look. His handcuff collection had slipped to the bottom of the bag, which tended to happen since all the rest of his worldly possessions consisted of jeans, T-shirts, socks, and underwear. He grinned at her and shrugged.

The professor grabbed the duffel bag and threw it

over his shoulder. "Let's take this up to your new room, shall we? We'll commence with a little tour."

Mildred eyed Jack. "Sounds lovely."

"I'll lead the way."

They dutifully followed the professor, his daddy longlegs taking the stairs two at a time. Mildred ran a finger over the highly polished wood banister as they walked up the staircase. He must have seen her do it, because the professor cleared his throat and said, "I won't pretend to insult your intelligence, Ms. Crosby. I must confess that I am not the domestic type. I have a housekeeper who spoils me rotten by doing all of my chores."

Jack beamed. No dirty toilets to scrub or stupid cat figurines to dust or ugly shag carpet to vacuum. He wagged his tongue in glee at Mildred, who rolled her eyes and pushed Jack up the stairs after the professor. The house was surprisingly sparse, almost empty, and very clean. Mildred would like that. Despite its haunted house exterior, the inside was unexpectedly normal, even nice. No wonder the guy was a little eccentric, living in this big old house by himself. It was so big Jack got his own room, and he probably could have had two rooms if he wanted.

This wasn't the first time he got his own room, but that was only if he counted the walk-in closet he slept in for six weeks back when he was nine; that was in some creepy duplex where the father rolled out a sleeping bag and told him it would be like camping. The mother always gave him the evil eye since his being there meant she no longer had a place to line up her pointy-toed shoes. Jack slept under a burned-out, bug-filled light fixture. He pretended he was camping in the wilderness and that the darkness was alive with small creatures, he among them. Technically, this was his first *real* room.

"Here we are. It's not much, I'm afraid," the professor said, watching for their reaction. But Jack and Mildred knew better. It was quite a lot. There was a bed, a dresser, a nightstand, and a closet filled with rows of wooden hangers. There was even a desk, a chair, and one of those bendy gooseneck lamps. Navy blue curtains hung in the window and matched the blue bedspread. The professor eased the duffel onto the floor while Mildred pirouetted around the room, inspecting the glorious normalness.

Both Mildred and Jack edged themselves tentatively down on the bed as if testing cool water, still slightly uncertain the whole thing wasn't a mirage. "Not like that," the professor said, staring at Jack and Mildred. "You must give it a good bounce." Suddenly, the professor whirled around like a skinny tornado, flopped down on the bed, and bounced up and down on it, sending Mildred careening over backward into the pillows. Jack got on his knees and bounced on his new bed. He tried to make eye contact with Mildred, but she just stared at the ceiling and laughed. They didn't have a look practiced for this occasion.

After a quick tour of the rest of the house, they made their way to the parlor, which was a small room with a fireplace, a sofa, and a few chairs. Displayed on a round coffee table situated in the center of the room was an assortment of small cakes, a teapot, cups, and saucers. This guy had pulled out the big guns. Jack wasn't sure he trusted the professor, but still, he was surprised Mildred hadn't fainted dead away.

"Please, sit here on the settee next to me, Ms. Crosby," the professor said.

Jack made a mental note that in fancy English, "settee" meant "sofa." Mildred settled down next to the professor. Jack sat on the floor next to the coffee table.

The professor poured a stream of tea into three cups. Jack leaned his face down toward the hot, minty liquid and sipped at his tea without lifting the cup. Next, the professor extended a plate covered in tiny chocolate cakes with baby rosebuds on top to Mildred. "May I offer you a petit four?"

Mildred smiled and placed two of the tiny cakes on her plate. Jack had no idea what a "petty four" was, but it was working like a charm on Mildred, who stared dreamy-eyed at the professor.

A scruffy, black, dust-mop creature scurried into the

room and bumped into Jack's knee. He ran his hand through the dog's tangled fur.

"Everyone, meet Little Miss B." The professor motioned his hand toward the animal, whose hair was pulled back from her face and held up into a sprout on top of her head with what looked like a red twist tie taken from a loaf of bread. Her eyes were cloudy and dull.

"She loves people, but she is blind, so I must ask you to watch your feet around her."

"Well, hello there, Little Miss B." Mildred's voice rose to a scratchy high pitch. Baby talk was not her forte. "What's the 'B' stand for?"

"The 'B' stands for 'Beatrice,' my third wife. Rest her soul."

"Why do you pull her hair up out of her eyes if she can't see?" Jack asked.

"Because, Jack, a lady always likes to look nice." The professor took a long slurp of tea. His mustache hung to either side of the cup like a walrus's.

"Aren't you excited?" Mildred asked Jack, then turned to the professor. "Jack always wanted a pet."

"Yeah." Jack shot her the *are you serious* look. When he said he wanted a dog, Little Miss B. was not exactly what he had in mind. She proceeded to sneeze, lick him, and bump into the coffee table. (Obviously her other senses had not been heightened by her lack of sight.) Jack scooped up her slim, black body and carried her over to a chair, resting her in his lap. With his hand around her middle, he felt her tiny heart beating rapidly under her rib cage. She was probably a little scared, too. Mildred ignored Jack's look and went back to admiring the professor.

"What exactly do you teach, Professor?"

There was a dramatic pause. The professor inhaled deeply as if sucking in all the oxygen from the room through his gigantic nostrils. "I have many vocations. Darwinian philosophy, cranial psychology, intercontinental anthropology."

Jack snorted. Sounded like bull to him. This guy was getting weirder and weirder by the second. Mildred shot him the *stop being a brat* look, and the professor continued. "But I teach organic composition." He set his cup down and crossed his legs. "It's a freestyle, earthy writing technique that I developed myself."

"Fascinating," Mildred said.

Not really, Jack thought, but he kept his mouth shut. "Can I go to the bathroom?" he asked, setting the dog down.

"Certainly, my boy. It's right down the hall." The professor rose from his seat and patted Jack on the back. Mildred licked the icing rose right off the top of another petit four, not noticing when Jack shot her the *make him stop calling me "my boy"* look as he walked out of the room.

Jack was used to the routine. The first day was always the best, which was surprising to some, but it was the day when both parties were still pretending. The thin veneer of love, family, and the good-boy routine had yet to fade.

Jack wandered down the hall until he found the bathroom. He didn't actually have to go; he just needed to think. He tried to imagine himself living in the house with the professor, because he would have to stay; he knew that already. Mildred liked the guy, and she was right. He wasn't so bad—a little weird, but at least he wasn't boring. Jack reached into his pocket and pulled out a black-and-white picture that he had torn out of a library book, which certainly was a stain on his character. Santa would be ticked off, so would God, but they were miles away—one in his snowy wonderland, one in his sky kingdom. Jack had to have the picture, so he took it. The world owed him this tiny treasure, even if he did have to steal it.

Harry stared back at him, showing off his handcuffs. Seven metal bracelets trailed up his muscular arms. The first handcuff was the Russian manacle with its two tight-lipped looping cuffs and heavy heart-shaped lock; then there were two Darby cuffs with long cylinder locks; then the Bean Cobb; the simple, smooth-rounded Romer; and another Bean Cobb, which was attached to one of Houdini's arms and then attached to the final cuff: the Berliner, which looked like an enormous steel ice pick had bitten his arm. The vintage cuffs encased Houdini's wrists, but the look on his face was coy. Houdini could slide right out of the cuffs in his sleep if he had to. It only *looked* impossible.

Staring at the picture calmed Jack down, made him feel less lonely. He could handle this, and like Mildred said, it would probably only last four weeks. Jack folded up the photo and slipped it back into his pocket. He flushed the toilet, turned the faucet on, and let the water run for a few seconds. Before leaving the bathroom, Jack casually pulled out the spare pair of handcuffs he kept in his back pocket and attached them to the leather strap of his belt. The cuffs jangled by his side. Mildred was going to be furious, but Jack thought it was only fair the professor knew up front what he was getting into. No secrets.

Mildred immediately spotted the handcuffs when Jack walked back into the room. She cleared her throat and said, "Tell the professor a little bit about yourself, Jack."

Jack eased back down into the chair. A deafening silence filled the room—a clock-ticking, throat-clearing, ringing-in-the-ears silence. He hated it when Mildred made him do this. What was he supposed to tell people? He sucked at school. He sucked harder at sports. Or worst of all: He was an orphan. Should he tell the professor his sob story: that he had been left, bundled in a blanket, on the steps of Saint Michael's Episcopal Church when he was a baby? His father left before he was born, and his mother was just a girl—that's what the priest's lilac-smelling wife would whisper into his ear. Jack was lucky to be alive, she would say, widening her eyes so that the white part made the blue part look like a small planet. *Lucky to be going on a journey.* And for a long time, that's where Jack thought he was going, on a journey to another world, a small and perfect planet.

Sharing was not his thing. Jack stretched his legs out in front of him and crossed one black sneaker over the other. Silence ensued. Mildred sucked in her cheeks but didn't look at him. Jack unhooked the handcuffs and started opening and closing them.

Mildred was not above playing a little hardball. "Jack just loves Houdini. He has read all about him, his life and his magic. I don't know what it is about boys and magic. But he just *loves* Houdini." She picked a morsel of cake off of her plate and placed it on her tongue.

Jack clenched his jaw. Why did she have to tell people that he loved Houdini? (But he knew why: It was a safe subject, and Jack had very few safe subjects to talk about.) He spun the handcuffs around on his finger, and the professor pretended not to notice.

"Ah." A spark of interest flared in the professor's eyes. "Magic, yes, illusions. I myself love magic and have cultivated quite an interest in the occult."

"Ooooh," Mildred cooed. "Spooky. I went to a séance

once when I was a young girl. The spirits never did come that night, but it was exciting just the same. I fell asleep and my girlfriends inked a mustache on my face. Isn't that funny?" Mildred nibbled on a tiny cake.

Bafflement filled Jack's face. *Was she serious?* Didn't she just hear the guy say he was interested in the occult? He probably had voodoo dolls and shrunken heads stashed in a closet. Four weeks—he wasn't going to last four *days* in this place.

"You know, Houdini was called the greatest escape artist." The professor had a way of raising and lowering his voice as if talking to a crowd, announcing some great feat and holding their fragile attention with a word or a whisper. He rubbed his chin and continued. "Technically, the term is 'escapology': the study and craft of escape, an undervalued art form, my boy. It's nice to see we are academic brethren."

Mildred let out a loud hack as she choked on her petit four. Jack had been called many things, but "academic" was never one of them. She took a swig of tea and cleared her throat while the professor continued.

"Houdini was a master escapologist. No chains or locks could hold him. But I prefer his other moniker. Do you know it?" For the first time, the professor looked down at Jack's handcuffs, the twinkle flaring in his green eyes.

Jack smirked, not answering. Houdini was *his* idol.

The professor didn't have a clue, and Jack had nothing to prove.

"During his show, Houdini challenged anyone to bring in handcuffs, and he would escape from them," the professor continued. "Sometimes it took him seconds, sometimes it took much longer, agonizingly longer, but he always got out. That is how he took the name the Handcuff King."

"Jack knows a little too much about handcuffs." Mildred smoothed her skirt.

"Really?" the professor said. "Well, how much can a boy like you know?"

Mildred pursed her lips and begged Jack with her eyes to say something nice. A hooked smile pierced Jack's cheek. "I can get out of any handcuffs you've got."

"That's a tall order, my boy."

"Anything," Jack said, overstating his abilities, but he sure wasn't about to back down from this guy.

"You know, Houdini was famous for something else, too."

"What?" Jack asked, waiting to hear what this guy thought.

"His belief in his own destiny, his own greatness. Do you believe in destiny, Jack?"

"Yeah. I've got one of those."

"But you're too young to be a king. No, that wouldn't do at all. Let me think." He tapped at his temple with one of his long fingers. The professor stood up in one swift motion, threw his arms in the air in an act of grand bravado, and yelled, "Jack Carr, the Handcuff Kid!"

The petits fours were devoured. The teacups were drained. Mildred clapped furiously, a genuine smile spread across her face. Jack and his handcuffs had found a home.

Heroes

Heroes are not born,
springing to life ready to save the world.
They are made from dirt and water,
as clay or metal bends,
they are forged with fire.

Ehrich starts at grimy cement bottom with nothing
but muscle and steadfast solidity, less lank or willow,
and a face that holds a boyish charm.

The sweat-soaked grind is not his way.
He is hungry to make a name,
drawn by the hypnotic lure of the stage.
His hero is the father of modern conjuring,
Robert-Houdin.

Ehrich is told that in French if he adds an *i*
to the end of a word it means to be like someone.
That is how Houdini is born, by becoming like his hero,
to stretch toward that speck of greatness.

The elusive silvery sand that loses itself in small spaces,
holding what cannot be held.

Magic is hope made beautiful,
made unbelievable in a believable way.

He will be a hero. One of his own.
A guild of magical believers.
A breakout sensation, breaking out of any jail cell,
handcuff, tight squeeze.

No lock or chain will hold him.

A hero for all the world that is ground down to its last,
for all who need to believe that the unbelievable I, is you.

The Magician

Jack had almost two entire weeks of living in the professor's house under his belt when a strange feeling started to creep in. He'd just returned to McDovall Academy after his brief suspension, and at first he suspected that he was having a heart attack. Either that or a bad case of indigestion. It was spaghetti day in the cafeteria, and he had wolfed down his lunch, including two slices of garlic bread, in, like, five seconds. He considered asking his geometry teacher, Ms. Turner, to call the paramedics, but then he pictured her giving him mouth-to-mouth resuscitation. Grooming was an extracurricular activity Ms. Turner didn't participate in, as her she-stache proved. After a minute he reminded himself that he was only twelve, and probably not having a heart attack. He realized he was feeling excitement—a feeling he had never before associated with going home. No wonder he mistook it for a heart attack.

As soon as he got home, Jack ran into the kitchen to help Concheta cook dinner. Concheta was more than a housekeeper; she was the professor's caretaker, who came to the house every day. Jack suspected that the professor liked having other people around, and so Concheta kept coming and cleaning the already clean house. She was such a tiny woman that Jack thought he could pick her up and twirl her in a circle—she was that small.

Donning his apron, the professor joined Jack and Concheta in the kitchen, where he pulled fresh vegetables and meat from the refrigerator. Dinnertime was an event in the Hawthorne household. None of the food came out of a box, not even the mashed potatoes.

More than once in his life, Jack had gone to bed hungry. He used to dream of Chinese takeout in those cool little white fold-up boxes, or steak cooked just right, not too bloody or too burned. And he loved birthday cake with his name written on it in squiggly icing. He never dreamed of neon orange powdery cheese and macaroni, which he had eaten so many times in his life that the instructions on the box were ingrained in his memory. The professor was a risk-taker in the kitchen, giving the recipe a quick glance and shutting the book.

Recipes aren't written in stone, he'd say, someone made them up, and the best recipes are created when the chef adds his own signature. Jack liked the idea of adding his own signature to things.

"It is very important that you learn how to cook," the professor said, opening the oven. A wave of hot air drifted over Jack's skin. He closed the oven and placed a hand on Jack's arm. "Fate dealt me a terrible blow, my boy. None of my three stunningly beautiful wives— Matilda, Claudia, or Beatrice—knew how to cook." He shook his head and brandished a stalk of celery in the air. "It was as if their beauty had exhausted any and all domestic skills."

Jack laughed. "At least they were beautiful."

"Ah, the view, my boy. The view was intoxicating."

Jack stirred the milk with scallions floating in it so it didn't scald. Then the hot cubes of cooked potato went in and the whole mess got mixed up with beaters. Jack pulled out the beaters prior to slowing the speed, sending hunks of potatoes splattering all over the stove, his face, and his shirt. Concheta howled with laughter from where she sat at the kitchen island shucking the last of the fresh peas. She hopped down off of her stool, walked over, and wiped a blob of potato from Jack's cheek. Then she licked it right off her finger and said, "*Mi chico* tastes delicious."

Jack beamed. He was a mess, and he had never been

happier. He didn't mind it that much anymore when the professor called him "my boy," and he really liked it when Concheta called him "my boy" in Spanish, "*mi chico.*" It wasn't so much the *chico* part, but the *mi* part. No one had ever thought of him as *theirs* before.

As the professor spooned heaping piles of mashed potatoes onto the plates, Jack saw a flash of dark blue on the professor's wrist. He squinted, focused on the color, and leaned over the professor to get a better look, but the professor's gigantic gold watch blocked his view. Poking the professor with the end of the potato spoon, Jack casually tried to nudge the watch back, causing the platter of steaming potatoes to teeter in the professor's grasp.

"Settle down, my boy. Dinner will be ready in a minute. What's gotten into you?" The professor set the plate down. His arm fell to his side, out of Jack's view.

"Nothing. I just wanted to help." Jack maneuvered to the professor's other side. Looking quickly, he saw a flash again—the midnight blue stain. He knew it! Unable to get a good look by stealth, Jack took the direct approach. "What's that on your wrist, Professor?"

The professor grabbed his watch and pulled his arm close to his body. "Oh, this? It's nothing." He turned his back, creating a wall between himself and Jack while he continued with the dinner preparations.

Jack's eyes lit up. He had seen marks like this before,

but never on a teacher, and he never imagined he'd see one on the professor. He grabbed the professor's arm and tried to push his sleeve up. "No way! Let me see."

The professor slipped out of Jack's grasp and shoved a steaming dinner plate in his hands. "Take this to the table."

Jack took the plate grudgingly. Maybe the professor was embarrassed and that was why he didn't want to show him what was concealed beneath his watch.

"Can I see it?" Jack asked, and then whispered, "I won't tell anyone."

The professor moved around the kitchen, tense and quick. "Very observant of you, my boy. You have discovered my little secret." He reached behind his back to untie his apron, yanking at the strings. "A folly from my youth. I wasn't much older than you when I got it."

"Please, I just want to take a look at your wrist." Jack rested his head against the professor's arm and stared at the watch.

"See." The professor held up his palms and wiggled his fingers, finally showing Jack the wrist without the watch.

"The other wrist," Jack said, nodding at the watch.

The professor flitted around the kitchen, collecting hot used pans like an anxious bird. "Oh, yes. *This* wrist." The gold watch shone in the light of the kitchen as the professor shifted his wrist from side to side. The shiny reflection winked up at Jack, hiding a secret.

Jack latched on to the professor's arm, unable to contain his excitement any longer. "Can you take the watch off, please?" If the professor didn't hurry up and take the watch off, Jack would yank it off for him.

At last, the professor relented, unhooking his wristwatch and slipping it off. Jack wrinkled his nose and pressed his face to the professor's bony arm as he examined the mark closer. An inky, round outline bled into the professor's skin. A thrill cascaded over Jack, because he was right. He stared down at a stunning work of art—a tattoo! The professor had no reason to be embarrassed. An impressively detailed drawing, the tattoo portrayed the face of a clock divided in half by a moon and sun, with stars surrounding the outer circle. There were tiny, swirled graphic symbols for noon, three, six, and nine o'clock, with an hour hand pointing to the symbol for twelve. Solemn expressions on the faces of the sun and moon reminded Jack of the drawings on old maps.

"I never thought you'd have a tattoo," Jack said, wondering what else he didn't know about the professor.

"Sometimes people confound your expectations. I'm not such a boring old goat." A feeble smile drifted across the professor's face.

"This is a good one. I like that you got it on your wrist, too. That's not a typical place for a tattoo." Jack rubbed his finger over the surface of the tattoo to make sure it was real.

"I wanted it on a place my mother wouldn't see. But I think she caught on to my ruse, as from then on I bathed with my watch on."

Jack laughed at the image of a scrawny young Professor Hawthorne sitting in a bathtub, wearing just his wristwatch. "Where did you get it done?"

"It's a long story. I'm sure you have better things to do than listen to me prattle on." The professor leaned wearily against the counter.

"Not really," Jack said, persisting. "Tattoos are never boring."

The professor rubbed at the mark like it irritated him, a deep itch he couldn't scratch. He slipped on his watch, the tattoo vanishing beneath a flash of gold. He slowly rolled his sleeves down as he spoke. "Tattoos are painful, and sometimes so are the stories that brought them about. My story is an unpleasant one. It would be unwise of me to risk telling you."

"Risk what?" Jack pushed.

The professor glanced over at Concheta, who had been silently watching. "I can't." The professor shook his head. "I don't want my old story to give you nightmares."

"I've *got* to hear it now." Jack crossed his arms and dug his heels in. "We can hang out together after dinner and talk."

"Don't push the professor, *mi chico*. If he wants to keep his secrets, let him," Concheta said.

Jack frowned at Concheta's rational answer. "Sorry to pry, Professor."

The professor paused, briefly drifting in and out of his own memories. "This story is serious business. I would have to be certain that you realize what you are getting into." Behind the professor's eyes Jack could see his mind working, thinking, hiding something other than a tattoo. And Jack had the suspicious feeling his comment was less of a warning and more of a dare.

"I don't scare easily," Jack said, sticking out his chest.

"Well, you were going to find out about it sooner or later." The professor tapped the face of his watch. "If you insist."

"I insist. I insist," Jack said, beaming at Concheta. Pulling out that win was easy, maybe a little too easy, but he got what he wanted.

"After dinner I'll tell you the tale about the man who gave me this tattoo." The professor turned around and almost whispered, "It's a dangerous story I can never forget."

"Awesome! I love scary stories," Jack said, bounding over to the dinner table. "Can I get a tattoo?"

"No!" Concheta yelled. "Only hoodlums get tattoos. No offense, Professor," Concheta added quickly, smiling at the professor. She handed Jack a pile of silverware. "Now set the table, *mi chico.* And be careful."

After dinner Jack plunged his hands into the scalding dishwater and scrubbed as fast as he could so that he could hear the tattoo story before bed. The professor informed Jack that sadly, his beautiful wives hadn't done dishes, either. Another lesson to learn.

Jack hurried down the hall and into the office, which had previously been off-limits. The professor's office was creep city. Towering bookshelves, filled with thick, dusty books, lined the walls of the dimly lit room. A huge desk strewn with paper dominated the center of the office, and a collection of weird, yellowed animal skulls hung on the lone empty space on the wall above the desk. Jack grimaced, sickly fascinated by the skulls. It was like their hollow eye sockets were watching his every move. The professor was getting more interesting by the second.

"Concheta, come sit next to me. I'll hold your hand so you don't get scared," Jack said as he plopped down on the Oriental carpet, trying to ignore the skulls.

Concheta hurried in carrying two mugs of hot chocolate, her purse hanging over her arm. "No, I'm leaving you two to your ghost stories and going home," she said, handing Jack his cocoa. Concheta wrinkled her nose and ran her finger over one of the filthy shelves.

The professor walked up behind her, catching her in the act. "Thank you, my dear. See you in the morning."

"I don't see why you don't let me clean in here," Concheta said, setting the professor's drink onto the nest of papers on his desk.

The professor paused, his mouth twisting up, an eyebrow arching in contemplation. "Ah. Um," he continued, "I have highly sensitive academic accoutrements in here. Things that could get you in trouble. I wouldn't want anyone to touch them."

Concheta made a little *humph* sound and twisted up her mouth. "Well, your *accoutrements* are covered with dust."

The professor patted Concheta on the shoulder. "I know, I know, my dear. Have a good night."

When she had left the office the professor turned a serious gaze to Jack. "I need you to give me your word, Jack, that you will never touch anything in here. Is that clear?"

"Sure, I get it. I won't touch anything." Jack glanced around at the piles of books and was certain he wouldn't be touching any of those, ever.

"Do I have your word?" The professor leaned down and looked Jack in the eye and extended his hand.

"You have my word," Jack said, shaking the professor's sweaty hand.

"You don't want to face the consequences if you break your word."

"Yes, sir," Jack mumbled. "Consequence" was just

another word for "punishment," and the professor was right, because Jack didn't need any more consequences.

The battered leather armchair groaned as the professor eased back into the seat and sipped from his mug. He had slipped on a dark brown jacket that blended in with the surroundings, making his face look pale in contrast. He drummed his long, bony fingers on the armchair. He cleared his throat and a silence settled over the room, which suddenly darkened as Concheta clicked out the lights in the hallway.

"When I was a boy, I spent most of my time roaming around outdoors, building forts and exploring the woods around my home. I didn't have television and video games to entertain me. So you can imagine my excitement when one brisk fall day the carnival rolled into town," the professor said. "The entire town buzzed with anticipation as the carnival tents rose high into the sky. The smell of roasted peanuts and cotton candy floated on the air, and I wandered around all day, riding the Ferris wheel, playing games, and gawking at the attractions." The professor leaned his head back and closed his eyes, recalling the memory.

Jack's eyes drifted around the professor's office, seeking out the forbidden "academic accoutrements." "Mildred won't let me go to carnivals. She said the rides are rusty old death traps run by drunks and lowlifes." Jack smiled. "Sounds really fun to me."

The professor peered at him through half-open eyelids. "Ms. Crosby does have a point. I think some of the rickety rides from my youth are still barely in service today." The professor leaned forward in his chair and wagged one of his pale fingers in the air. "But I was more interested in the strange and macabre acts that filled the side tents: Siamese rattlesnakes, tattooed ladies, sword-swallowers, and the Dog Boy."

"Dog Boys! Cool!" Jack sat up on his heels. "That sounds like the good stuff."

The professor seized on Jack's wide-eyed attention. "But there was one man who was a legend in the strange carnival arts, who loomed and crept behind the scenes. A dark, massive conjurer, he was a jack-of-all-trades: knife-thrower, fire-eater, and magician. He captivated the audience with the grace of a snake charmer. His name was . . . *the Amazing Mussini*. In the dark recesses of the carnival, he performed the most magnificent tricks of all."

"What kinds of tricks?" Jack asked.

"Mussini had traveled all over the world and *beyond*. He knew things no ordinary man knew. That night, his amazing feat was selling *secrets*." The professor dug his fingers into the soft leather of his chair.

"Secrets? What kind of secrets?" Jack asked, thinking that was as good a trick as fortune-telling, which he didn't buy for a second.

"Mussini claimed to know *all*. He knew things that

you had done even if you'd never told a soul. Secrets big and small. He knew if your best friend was really a foe. He could tell you the secret strategies in school yard battles. Or what your teacher would put on a test. He could tell you anything for a price. Well, my boy, I was instantly hooked. I just had to buy one, but I didn't have any money. And as a foolish boy, I wanted the most expensive secret of them all."

"What's the most expensive secret?" Jack slurped down his hot chocolate, the liquid warming his whole body.

"I don't believe that when we die, we rot into nothingness, food for worms. I knew there was more to learn about the underworld, and I wanted a glimpse into this land. It is the secret of where we go and what becomes of us." The professor reached down and pulled Jack close, just for a second. His mustache twitched against Jack's ear as the professor whispered, "The most expensive secret of all is the secret of the dead, of course."

"The dead! You mean like spirits or ghosts?" A shudder cascaded through Jack, and he pulled himself up from the spell of the story.

The professor took a drink and licked the marshmallow from his mustache. "There is a land for the dead, for the poor souls who have not passed on—the ghostly ones that drift once they leave their cold boxes, roaming into a dark forest that awaits them."

"Like another world?" Jack asked. It sounded kind of like outer space, or time travel, or an undersea city. He could almost believe in a place like that, where stories were real in a made-up way.

"Exactly like another world, my boy." The professor's eyes darted from side to side. His voice deepened. "But a world that is rarely spoken of, a shadow world beyond death. It is the Land of the Dead, and it can be reached by the living."

"If the Land of the Dead is real, then how do you get there?" Jack asked, trying not to get sucked into the story. "I mean, besides dropping dead."

The professor held up his wrist, and the gold watch sparkled in the light. Jack's eyes widened, for while listening to the story, he had completely forgotten about the tattoo.

The professor curled his finger and motioned for Jack to move forward. "This tattoo is the mark of the Amazing Mussini, the magician. It is my passage into the underworld. It guides my steps out of the now and into the dark abyss of the dead."

Jack kneeled at the professor's feet, totally captivated. "How's the tattoo work?"

"Well, here in the land of the living, it appears to be just an ordinary tattoo. See?" He pulled his watch and sleeve up in one motion so that the tattoo faced upward. "But if you look at it differently, the mark points the way."

Jack marveled, because from his viewpoint on the floor the tattoo no longer looked like a clock. The hour hand was really an arrow. "It's not a watch! It's a compass!" Jack exclaimed.

"Exactly!" The professor held up his finger and ran it along the outline of the tattoo. "The mark of Mussini is a compass to the domain of the dead. It is the only way I know of to get into the world of Mussini."

Jack jumped up to his feet and paced around the room. "Wait," Jack said, his brow furrowed. He wanted to believe the story, to believe in a mysterious world of magic, but he didn't want to be a sucker for a spooky story. "If you didn't have money, then what did you pay him with?"

The professor's deep-set eyes and bushy brows made it look as though he were peering out of the depths of a dark cave.

"Mussini's a trader. And to receive the most valuable secret, a person must trade their most valuable possession. You see, Jack, where Mussini comes from, money doesn't mean much."

"What did you trade him?" Jack pushed, needing to know the answer. "Come on, tell me! What did you give him?"

The professor smirked. "I think that's enough for tonight." He stood up, collected his cup, and made his way to the door. "It's getting late."

"Wait, you can't stop now! That's cheating. It's not fair to tell half a story." Jack frowned but didn't move from his position, hoping the professor would come back.

"Then think of it as a puzzle. You're a smart boy. You will probably figure it out anyway. What would I trade to Mussini? What is our most valuable possession? What might a magician want?" And the professor walked out of the office, flipping off the light and leaving Jack in total darkness.

"A puzzle? Sounds more like a trick to me." Jack swallowed the chocolaty dregs of his hot cocoa. It was a good story, but he was still on the fence about whether he believed any of it or not. Either way, he was determined to figure out what a magician could possibly want from a kid.

That night, Jack sat up in bed; panic swept over him. He swatted at the air, the webby shadows of a dream clinging to him. He didn't know where he was. The wind rushed through the eaves, circling the house like an animal trying to get in, sniffing out every crack and crevice. His heart pounded wildly in his chest. A word escaped his mouth before he could stop it: *Mom.* It caught in his throat as the shadows of the room settled into familiar shapes and he realized where he was. Jack remembered the professor's story, remembered he was in his new bedroom.

Something stirred. He swung his legs over the side of the bed and let his bare feet rest on the wood floor before standing and walking across the creaky floorboards to the door.

Making his way down the narrow corridors of the old Victorian house, Jack crept down the hallway and paused on the landing. A strange noise filtered up from below: a heavy thud, followed by scraping. He inched closer and closer toward the light and peered through the bars of the stairs, down into the hallway.

The professor hunched over a large, dark mass on the floor. He bent down and pushed at it, as if the thing was too heavy to lift. A black canvas covered the top. The light in the hall was dim. The professor grunted, heaving the thing a few feet down the hallway. Stopping to rest for a moment, he sat on the top of the black-covered mass. The professor wiped the sweat from his brow and when he stood up, the drape caught his arm and slid off. Jack gasped. The sides and top of the object—it was the shape of a trunk—were painted with dull red and black diamonds like something from an old-time circus or a *carnival*. A shiny new padlock dangled from the latch.

The professor pushed the trunk toward his office. Then the dog, Little Miss B., who was walking down the hall behind him, suddenly stopped. She glanced up in Jack's direction and started barking. Great. She was as blind as a bat, but her doggy radar worked just fine. Jack leaped to his feet, ran back to his room, and shut the door. He jumped into bed and pulled the blankets up over his face.

His breathing was loud underneath the covers. He had panicked. The professor had to have heard him. Jack closed his eyes and pretended to go back to sleep, trying not to imagine what was locked inside of that trunk.

Bruiser

Early Saturday morning, Little Miss B. scratched at Jack's door. Jack threw on a pair of not-too-dirty jeans and a ratty sweatshirt. He clipped the thin blue leash to her collar, and the two of them headed out in the cool fall morning. As Little Miss B. strode perilously close to the mailbox, Jack tugged on the leash. She was a good dog, but Jack refused to call her Little Miss B. in public. He chose instead to call her B. or her new nickname: Bruiser. He admired the way she held her little head high and marched fearlessly out into the world even though she was blind. Although she probably had more than a few bruises under her fur from plowing into any and all stationary objects that crossed her path, still she was a tough girl.

The wetness from the dew-drenched grass soaked into his sneakers. Jack took the back way to the park, cutting through the trees that divided the houses and the park, which bordered a strip mall. As he wove through the trees, he noticed that a trail of paper, bright yellow scraps, caught on the wind like leaves. He chased one and snatched it up from under his shoe. It was an advertisement for a carnival. It would be in town for one more week. That was a strange coincidence. His stomach fluttered. He would have to tell the professor about it when he got home, and maybe they could go.

As Jack walked Little Miss B. through the park, he saw a few kids tossing a ball around in the distance. When Jack got closer, he realized it wasn't a ball at all they were throwing, but a roll of toilet paper. There were three kids total, one bigger and two smaller, in the process of TP-ing the jungle gym and the swing sets.

The prank reminded him of this time in the group home when the boys on his floor had a toilet paper fight in the bathroom. Every surface was covered in toilet paper, including this kid everyone called Rat, because he always ratted on anyone who took food from the cafeteria to hide in his bunk. Stashing food in the dorms was against policy. (Like a pack of Twinkies was gonna attract the mother lode of roaches or something!) For payback, Rat was mummified in two-ply, and the entire floor of B Group was forbidden to use toilet paper for a month. After wiping his butt with scratchy recycled paper towels, Jack had a newfound respect for sanitary products. Toilet paper became sacred. He smiled to himself at the memory and tried to skirt the edge of the playground, but the kids spotted him.

"Hey, I know you!" the big one turned and yelled over to Jack. "You're that new kid living with the mad professor." The big kid looked like a psycho Elvis with long black oily hair that waved back from his face. He swatted at one of the smaller kids and repeated himself. "Mad professor, get it."

They laughed on command. The sidekicks were fair-skinned and blond. The only thing remarkable about them was that they looked exactly alike, so much so that they *had* to be twins. The big kid tossed a roll of toilet paper up and down in his hands and looked at Jack sideways.

"Let me do you a favor, OK? That professor is into some weird stuff, like *crazy* stuff. There are a *lot* of rumors going around about him." He looked around and then said in a low voice, "Word is he's a grave robber."

"What?!" Jack said. "That's crazy. No one robs graves."

"Look, I'm just saying what I overheard my mom and Miss Julie talking about, and Miss Julie has all the dirt on everyone, and she said that guy isn't right. He's always hanging around at Crazy Grady's and over at Taylor's Funeral Home. Well-adjusted adults don't hang out at mental institutions and funeral homes. At least that's what Miss Julie said."

"He just has strange hobbies, that's all." Maybe Psycho Elvis had a point—thoughts of the trunk filled Jack's head—but Jack was willing to give the professor the benefit of the doubt. The professor had been nicer to him than anyone he could remember. Except Mildred.

"Yeah," one of the blond kids piped up. "I heard he has a pet cemetery in his backyard, except it's really for his dead wives."

Psycho Elvis kid rolled his eyes. "Shut up! I'm being serious here, doing a community service by warning this kid. I don't care if you don't believe me. I'm just saying that guy isn't normal."

"He's all right. You just don't know him." Jack picked up a rock, threw it at the belly of the slide, and watched it slip back down to the ground. "He's cool once you know him. He lets me do whatever I want."

"Aren't you listening? You're living in a *freak* house with a *freak* father, a total weirdo."

Jack felt a tinge of anger and a need to defend the professor. "No weirder than you."

"Who you calling weird, you loser *orphan?* Did your mommy and daddy not want you, so the only home you could get was with a kook?" The three all laughed in unison.

Jack narrowed his eyes. "Up yours, lard butt." The

words flew from Jack's mouth like a stone slung from a slingshot. Big mistake. Psycho Elvis balled up his beefy fists and threw a roll of toilet paper at him. The kid was not going to take the comment without a fight, like a silverback gorilla staking out his jungle gym territory by pounding his fists on his chest.

"You think you're funny?" Psycho Elvis's lip quivered like he was about to start singing, "You ain't nothin' but a hound dog," causing Jack to laugh.

"Yeah, I do."

"You're dead now, buddy."

Jack dropped the leash and hoped Little Miss Bruiser would make it home OK. "Go, B., go," he said, and pushed her away with his tennis shoe. The dog ran. Psycho Elvis smirked and nodded to the twins, who advanced one on either side of Jack, surrounding him. Jack clenched his jaw. His palms started getting sweaty. He tried to relax and stay loose, but Jack had never excelled in the art of butt-kicking. He had watched kung fu movies and tried to study the technique, but somehow whenever he got into a fight, the picture he had in his head of how it *should* go down never matched his actual movements.

Typically, he never started a fight, but he also never backed down, so he would take the hit and then have to regroup. Houdini could take a punch to the gut like it was nothing. He had a high tolerance for pain, unlike Jack, who was better at distraction, like throwing out a joke. Unfortunately, his stash of jokes typically referenced his lack of parental guidance, and that wasn't going to work here.

Once, Jack had met this boy who had been in and out of juvie at least five times. His uncle robbed houses for a living, and the boy had said that his uncle would always go back to rob houses if they were easy marks: no security systems or yappy dogs. It was the same with fighting. Like it or not, he had to fight back, because he refused to be remembered as an easy mark. Psycho Elvis cracked his knuckles. The first punch had to count, so he cocked his arm and plowed his fist into Psycho Elvis's nose. The rest of the fight was a blur of hitting and kicking, of elbows and kneecaps. The last thing Jack remembered was getting wrestled to the ground and Psycho Elvis sitting on his chest, forcing all the air from his lungs.

When Jack woke, he was staring up into the hairy caves of Professor Hawthorne's nostrils. As it turned out, Little Miss B. was a wonder dog—she ran all the way back to the professor's house and barked wildly at the door until the professor came out. He noticed the leash dragging behind her and went looking for Jack.

The professor pulled a white handkerchief from his pocket and dropped it, letting it float down to Jack like a wing. Blood dripped down Jack's nose, so he wadded the handkerchief and stuffed it up his nostril to help sop up the blood while Little Miss B. licked Jack's fingers. Jack stared at the grass and tried to forget the humiliating fact that he had just gotten his butt kicked.

"Never underestimate an old blind dog. I find that is the biggest mistake anyone can make." The professor helped him to his feet, and they walked back to the house. "Come on. I have a gift for you."

Jack followed the professor to his office, stopping just outside the door. The professor glanced back at him as he half-closed the door. "Give me a second, will you?"

Jack tried to peer into the room, but the door was in the way. The trunk was in the office. His arm nudged the door and it creaked open. There it was in the middle of the floor, big enough to fit a body. Jack's imagination raced. Maybe the professor *was* a grave robber. Jack stepped into the office and the professor turned around, not even noticing the trunk that sat in the middle of the room.

"Why the gift?" Jack asked, unable to take his eyes off the old trunk and the shiny lock that sealed it shut.

"Why not? I never subscribed much to holidays and proper gift-giving. If I see something I think a person might like, I get it. And I saw something I thought might interest you."

The professor turned and set a long, white department store box onto the trunk. Jack's stomach sank. Every birthday, Mildred handed him a similar box that never failed to contain some sort of terribly itchy sweater or a dreaded turtleneck. The professor seemed to notice the look, and the wicked smile that spread across his face made his mustache twitch like a caterpillar. "I'm not sure if you are aware of this, but we have a very prominent psychiatric facility in this town. I have a friend who works there."

Jack wasn't surprised at all that the professor had connections at Crazy Grady's psych ward—Psycho Elvis wasn't the first person to mention the professor's odd habits. To Jack, that just made the present even more mysterious. Jack lifted the lid of the box, pulled back the white tissue paper, and stared down at the contents. Definitely not a turtleneck, but very binding—it was the coolest gift anyone had ever given him. Mildred would not be happy, but Jack was ecstatic. "How did you know?" he asked, pulling the jacket out of the box.

"A little deductive reasoning."

Jack beamed. "I love it."

"I knew you would. You can't be a fan of Houdini and not have your very own straitjacket."

Jack lifted the heavy canvas into the air and held it up to his chest. It was a perfect fit.

The Trunk

When Jack woke up the next morning, his entire body ached. He hobbled into the bathroom and stared at his reflection in the mirror. Despite the pain radiating from his body, with a black crescent moon carved under his eye, he looked really cool, very butt-kicked. He liked it. But thinking of the fight reminded him of the kids in the park, which made him think of the professor, which brought him to the trunk. After seeing the professor's clandestine maneuvering of the trunk into his office, Jack suspected that the professor was hiding something. An investigation of the office and trunk was the only way to be sure.

The day started out pretty normal. Both the professor and Concheta were being extra nice to him since the incident the day before. They had no idea that the fight was no big deal, but he enjoyed the chocolate chip pancakes Concheta made and the *Star Wars* movie marathon he and the professor watched while sprawled on the settee, their socked feet propped up on the coffee table. Concheta came in every hour on the hour, bringing snack trays heaped with tiny egg rolls and pizza bites and filling up their drink glasses with frothy root beer.

After watching movies, Jack practiced his straitjacket escape, albeit painfully. Getting out of a straitjacket was really hard. (That was the point.) With his arms hugging his own body, a wave of claustrophobia cascaded over him. Jack's face flushed; his nose pressed into the hardwood floor. The professor observed, giving him tips.

"It's all in the arm, get it over your head," he said as Jack floundered around on the floor. "Slack, my boy, you need to make it more slack."

Finally, Jack got his head wedged under his arm and said breathlessly, "Got it." After he got his head loose, he went to work on the buckles, and he was home free.

"I made certain to get the correct size so as to not give you an unfair advantage if the jacket was too loose," the professor said.

For the first time Jack had a real coach, a mentor, just like Mildred said, only he didn't think getting tips on escaping from a regulation nut suit was what Mildred had in mind. Still, it was very cool of the professor. That made it harder for Jack to suspect him of keeping unsavory secrets, but he had to get more information to be sure.

Finally, at around five, Jack got his chance. The professor went to the university to get some work done. Jack strolled into the kitchen. Concheta slapped a meat loaf into a pan, popped it into the blazing oven, and set the timer. "I've got to take Little Miss B. to the vet. She ate something that made her sick."

"B. might have accidentally bumped into the platter of egg rolls earlier." Jack shrugged. "Sorry. She's fast when she wants to be. She scarfed down three egg rolls before I could grab the tray."

"Jack!" Concheta raised one of her thin penciled-in eyebrows at him. "Your dinner is in the oven. Remember to take it out when the buzzer dings." Concheta picked up a sluggish Little Miss B. in her dog carrier and headed out the door, leaving Jack with the whole place to himself.

Jack eased down the hall toward the professor's office. He stopped dead in his tracks when he noticed that the door to the office had been left open, just a crack. His first instinct was that it was a trap. It was just too easy for him to get in and snoop around. Then a wave of guilt rolled through his stomach when he realized that maybe the door was open because the professor trusted him. He touched the cool metal doorknob. For Jack, trust was earned, and the professor hadn't earned *his* trust yet.

He had given the professor his word that he wouldn't touch anything in the office, and if he got caught, the professor would probably kick him out for good; then where would he go? Mildred would be devastated if he screwed up again so fast, so for her sake, he couldn't get caught. Jack's fingers trembled slightly as he stared at the trunk; he wanted, no, he *needed* to know what was inside.

Jack crept into the office. The desk lamp cast a dusty halo of light across the carpet. Pulling the trunk away from the desk, Jack realized it was much heavier than it looked. A padlock dangled from the metal clasp. Jack slipped the lock pick from its usual hiding place in his shoe and made short work of the Home Depot special. The lock dropped to the floor with a thud. No turning back now. He heaved open the lid. A bone-chilling groan emanated from the box's rusty hinges. A flourish of goose bumps cascaded over Jack's skin when he peered inside.

Suddenly, a shrill buzzing rang through the house. Jack jumped, slamming the trunk shut. He skidded down the hallway to the kitchen and hit the timer and sighed with relief. He pulled the steaming meat loaf out of the oven. It was getting late. The professor or Concheta would probably be home soon.

Jack ran back to the office and knelt beside the trunk. A moldy smell rose up that he hadn't noticed before. The box was heaped full of dirt. Reaching down into the trunk, Jack dragged his hand through the rich black earth. The dirt was cold to the touch. Disgusted, he brushed his hand off on his jeans.

Jack inspected the cakey soil and shuddered. There could be human remains or mouse bodies or something really gross in there. He grabbed a pencil off of the desk and dragged it through the dirt. The tip of the pencil stopped, hitting something. Wedging the pencil deeper, Jack lifted a piece of what looked like cardboard to the surface. He snatched it up quick and brushed the dirt off. It was a card, like a birthday party invitation, with printing in bold black type:

Whoever dares open this box is cordially invited to be a guest of

The Amazing Mussini

KNIFE-THROWING, FIRE-EATING MAGICIAN

[LICENSED & BONDED]

Transportation to be provided

Jack dropped the card. It had to be a joke the professor was playing on him, probably trying to teach him a lesson not to pry into other people's trunks. He picked the card up again, but this time a new line magically appeared:

This means YOU, Jack!

He jerked his hand, and the card fell to the floor. Quickly, Jack grabbed the card and reburied it. This was definitely a trick, perhaps another gift, or more likely a trap to catch him snooping. He was so busted. For the first time since his arrival, Jack was afraid. He shut the box and fastened the lock.

In an effort to keep his mind off the card, Jack ate a thick slab of meat loaf for dinner and practiced with his cuffs. The metal bracelets called to him, and he could always count on them and their logic—a skill he could master and control. He twisted his hands behind his back like he had a thousand times before and closed the steel around his wrists.

As far as picking went, Jack was partial to the shim. He visualized the inner workings of the lock before inserting the slim metal tool. That's how doctors do it in the emergency room when they're trying to get a guy's windpipe open and slide tubes in so the guy can breathe. The doctors imagine the trachea with its soft pink walls and visualize the tube going in. The esophagus runs straight. Sword-swallowers really did swallow the sword. Jack visualized the lock mechanism in his mind's eye. He saw the ratchet—the toothed wheel inside the lock—the simple way it worked like a turnstile in a subway. He followed the shim going in and rounding the small metal corners of the lock, wedging its way in; overriding the catch, he pulled. *Click*. He didn't need to see it now to know that the lock had released.

Too antsy to stay cooped up, Jack had the sudden urge to go outside and run to clear his head. He didn't lock the door to the house. Jogging along, he was almost invisible in his black T-shirt and navy sweatpants, slipping in between parked cars and telephone poles, trading places with the dark. He made a game of it, trying to stay in the shadows, dodging a sudden flood of headlights. Throwing himself on the ground, he crawled on his belly till the car coasted by. He ran through the playground and through the small tangle of woods.

He felt alone, but alert, cautious. This was how animals must feel. People always liked to make it seem like animals had families, moms and dads and babies. But it wasn't true. Sure, they technically did, but most animals were left to survive on their own pretty early. Once, he saw a nest of baby rabbits that the mother had already left—and they barely had their eyes opened. If those baby rabbits could survive, so could he. They don't wait for their mothers to say good-bye to them. Jack kept running, like an animal in his leafy and tangled kingdom. He was a star in his own deep dark sky. His destiny was bigger and brighter than this journey of survival.

The card irked him—the strange invitation seemed so real, somehow feeling alive as it had trembled in his

THE CARNIVAL *of* LOST SOULS

hands. The words had moved. Was the invitation really from the mysterious magician Mussini? But the carnival was so long ago—when the professor was young. There was no way that Mussini was still around. The professor probably had a normal explanation for everything. Mildred would have never placed him with a dangerous guy. Weird was one thing, but not dangerous.

Still, Jack needed answers, and he would have to face the professor sooner or later if he wanted to get them.

An entire week went by. Jack was still as jumpy as a baby rabbit. He waited day after day for the professor to confront him for snooping in his office. Surely he had left some incriminating evidence behind—some dirt on the floor or on his clothes. But so far, the professor said nothing about his office, the trunk, or the card. Jack's deception was exhausting. His head ached. Regret spread through him more and more each day. Why did he break his word? Why did he have to screw everything up?

Saturday morning, Jack sat cross-legged on the living room floor, shoveling heaping spoonfuls of cereal into his mouth. The horrific moans of a violin oozed out from under the professor's office door, as on every Saturday morning the professor listened to classical music. Jack turned up the television, hoping that the high-pitched mania of his cartoons would drown out the screech of strangled cats the professor called masterpieces. Suddenly, the music stopped, and Jack jumped to turn the television down.

Jack slurped up the chocolaty milk-soup of his cereal while his eyes followed the professor walking around the room, circling him. The professor stared at him; the look of suspicion caused dread and guilt to roll around in Jack's stomach.

"When were you going to tell me?" The professor began gathering up pages of newspaper from the coffee table.

"Tell you what?" Jack asked, resting his cereal bowl on the floor. He tried not to panic; the less he said, the better. The professor didn't seem *that* angry; maybe he would let him off easy for sneaking into his office.

The professor glanced down his nose at Jack. "That's not a very good answer. Try again."

"I was never going to tell you," Jack said, hoping his blunt yet honest answer would at least gain a few points. He could still feel the cold earth slip between his fingers when he opened the trunk, and he could still see his name printed clearly on the card. *He* was the guest of the magician Mussini. He had opened the trunk when he knew he shouldn't. He broke his word to the professor and Mildred by sneaking into the office. And now he just sat there, pathetically waiting for his punishment. A lump formed in his throat.

"Never! But if you *never* told me, then we couldn't go." The professor stood in front of the television, focusing Jack's attention.

Go where? What was he thinking? Jack stared at the professor.

"I'm not sure I want to go." Jack wiped his mouth off on his pajama sleeve; his chin still ached from the fight in the park. If the kids were right, then Jack and the professor were off to the psych ward, which might not be so bad as far as punishments go, compared to where they *might* be headed.

"Well, as your legal guardian, I am insisting that you attend." Swiftly the professor wedged the newspapers under his arm and rummaged into his pocket. He pulled out a piece of paper and dropped the creased leaflet onto the carpet in front of Jack. "Concheta found this stuffed in the pocket of your jeans when she was doing the laundry."

Jack snatched up the yellow slip. It was the carnival flyer he found in the park! A wave of relief washed over him, and he jumped to his feet. He had forgotten all about it.

"All you had to do was ask." The professor smiled. "As you know, I love carnivals and was thrilled when Concheta showed it to me. I think you'll find we have many things in common."

"That's a relief," Jack said. "Um, I mean, I'd love to go."

"Tonight is the last night to attend." Jack grinned and the professor walked out of the room.

If the professor didn't know that Jack snuck into the office, then Jack wanted to keep it that way.

The Consequences

The professor decided to get some fresh air and walk to the carnival. They waited until after dinner when the sun was almost down to trudge through the woods and then maneuver a patch of tall, weed-choked grass. Concheta's long jean skirt kept getting snagged on the prickly weeds, and she cursed the grass in Spanish while simultaneously using Jack's head to keep her balance. Finally, they reached the gritty parking lot that had been transformed into a neon wonderland.

Before Jack could race into the crowd, Concheta yanked the hood of his sweatshirt, and he stumbled backward.

"Don't get lost," she said, handing him a fistful of crumpled dollar bills. "Now, go buy a candy apple and one for me, too." She smiled mischievously and pushed him toward a crowded alleyway of vendors selling loads of sticky sweets and fried food.

Jack darted into the crowd. The carnival was alive—a maze of rides and booths and games whirling and spinning all around him. Rides rose up out of the crowds like metal dinosaurs, roaring shrill music and blinking with millions of tiny lightbulbs. This place was better than he expected.

After devouring his candy apple, Jack and the professor attacked the arcade and the game alley, then jumped on a string of jarring thrill rides that spun their heads around and around in the fun chaos of the Tilt-A-Whirl and the Zipper. Concheta mostly watched, but she did take a few turns on the merry-go-round, sitting sidesaddle on a glittery pink horse. Jack looked, but he never saw any of the strange sideshow acts the professor had told him about. When he asked about them, the professor just stared off into space.

"Oh, those attractions are long gone." The professor put his hand on Jack's shoulder and directed him toward the center of the fair and an enormous glowing Ferris wheel. "Time for the last ride of the night."

Concheta planted herself a few yards away and waved them on. The professor and Jack didn't have to wait long; the crowds were thinning, as the night was growing late. Once locked inside the tiny swinging metal box, Jack jumped at the opportunity to talk to the professor alone. "I figured it out."

"Hm," the professor mused. "What's that?"

"What that magician, the Amazing Mussini, wanted from you. Your most valuable possession. It wasn't that hard, really." Jack figured the professor would respect him more if he solved the problem of what he sold to Mussini, and maybe even forgive him for opening the trunk in his office.

"Really?" The professor rested his arm on the back of the cart and twisted his body under the metal safety bar, turning his attention to Jack. "I've been anxious to hear what you think."

Jack took a deep breath. "I figured you're a smart guy, Professor, from all the books you've read and all the places you've been. You were probably a smart kid, too. You know a lot about everything, especially stuff that no one else bothers to study, like magic tricks and escapology. I think Mussini wanted a kid like you around, to help him create more tricks for his act." Jack eased back in his seat, not realizing that he had been tensed up against the safety bar.

The ride lurched, the box swung, and they were lifted high into the liquidy darkness. They both grasped on to the metal bar that rested across their laps. A rush of air blew over him, and Jack glowed with the excitement of soaring, as if he and the professor were escaping into the starry black sky as the simple magic of the ride carried them upward.

"That's a very good answer. But I'm afraid it isn't entirely correct."

"Then what did Mussini want, if it wasn't money?" Jack asked.

The professor's eyes anxiously darted over the crowd. "Mussini is a trader, and he travels between the lands of the living and the dead. He wanted my services, for sure, but that meant I would have to go with him."

"How does Mussini travel between the world of the living and the dead? That would be a cool magic trick."

"It's complicated." The professor twisted up his mouth. "Mussini is a powerful magician. He trades in *lives*. He wanted my soul." He spit out the words as if they tasted awful. "You don't understand the position that put me in."

"Couldn't you just work for him at the carnival?" Jack asked. "You could help him with his act."

"The deal doesn't work that way." Against the professor's pale face, his dark eyes gleamed like an animal's at night. He turned to speak into Jack's ear so that he could be heard over the din of the carnival. "I was around your age at the time. What did I know? I signed a contract, and I had no way out." The professor grabbed Jack's arm. "My only option was to figure out a way to escape the clutches of the Amazing Mussini and keep my soul."

"But you're here *now*. And that happened a long time ago. So you must've done it."

The Ferris wheel rounded the top of the circle, and Jack and the professor drifted backward on the ride. Jack's stomach dropped. He was falling with nothing but a slim metal bar to hold on to. He felt the same way about the professor's story. But the professor was still sitting right next to him, so it couldn't be true. The ride careened upward again, grinding to a halt at the top of the Ferris wheel, swaying above the world of the carnival. A wave of dizziness swept over Jack as he stared at the ground. Jack shook it off and listened to the professor.

"I haven't told you everything. The contract gave me fifty years to enjoy the knowledge of the secret." The professor jerked his long legs and the cart swayed wildly from side to side, about to tip. The ride began another circle, gliding up and around. "I had time to learn all I needed to know to escape Mussini. And that's why I asked for you! A boy who knew magic. It was my only chance to escape, and now it is *your* only chance."

Jack remembered that first day when he and Mildred stood outside of the professor's house, and she told him the professor wanted a child who liked magic. She thought Jack was perfect for the professor. She probably thought they could become friends and perform magic tricks. But the professor had his own plans for Jack. The ride ground to a halt at the bottom. The professor rose out of the box and stood on the platform, and Jack leaped out beside him.

"What's that supposed to mean?" Jack raced up behind the professor and pulled on his sleeve. He let go as a trail of ideas connected in his head. Magic, but not real magic—trick-of-the-eye magic. A strange answer clicked into place. "The trunk was a trick?" Jack whispered to himself, not entirely sure what he was saying. The professor had baited him with the trunk— the one he had opened. The fragile illusion of a home, family, and love was disintegrating right before his eyes, like a speck of stardust falling from the sky. Jack wanted to say something, but he was too stunned.

Concheta hurried over, waving frantically as if they had just arrived home from a journey to a far-off place. "You were so high up in the sky, like twinkling stars. I was afraid for you, *mi chico.*" Concheta ruffled his hair. "I didn't want you to fall and break into pieces on the ground."

"Me neither, Concheta."

When they got home, the professor went straight to his office, and Jack ran upstairs. He had to get away and think about what the professor said and what it meant. While lying on his bed, in the dark room, loud voices echoed up from downstairs. Then toenails clipped across the wood floor, and when he let his hand fall over the side of the bed, Little Miss B.'s wet tongue licked his fingers. The professor was shouting and Concheta wailed and screeched. On the Richter scale of domestic disturbance this was a 4.5, not bad. But still, he hadn't expected it, not here, and certainly not between the professor and Concheta. His heart jumped. Nothing good ever lasted long.

Without turning the lights on, Jack eased down the stairs. Concheta's voice filtered in from the kitchen. She made a little whimpering sound when she saw Jack standing in the doorway. "Oh, *mi chico*. You shouldn't be here. Go back up to your room."

"What's wrong? What's going on?"

"It's all my fault." Shaking her hands, Concheta looked up at the ceiling as if she was talking to someone above her. *"¿Qué? ¿Qué?"*

"It's 'cause I opened the box, right?" Jack headed toward the office. It was his fault they were fighting, not Concheta's. "The professor found out and now he's mad."

"No! Don't go in there. *He's* in there." Concheta pulled on Jack's sleeve.

"Who's in there?" Jack stopped in his tracks. She didn't mean the professor. Now *that* piece of information got his attention. "No way."

Concheta's lip quivered. "It's the magician."

The infamous, soul-stealing magician was in the house. Thrill-laced fear pulled Jack toward the professor's office. "I'll be right back." He broke free from Concheta's grasp. "I gotta check it out."

The door to the professor's office was shut. Jack eased down the hallway, kneeled outside the door, and pressed his ear close to the wood. He watched the slip of light under the door frame as shadows spun, and then he heard a dark, raspy voice. A tingle ran up his spine. A loud *thump* came from behind the door, then the rattle of a key being forced into a lock. A harsh voice boomed behind the door.

"Your plan worked, Professor. I must admit, no one has weaseled his way out of one of my contracts until you."

"The fact that our deal is done and the boy goes in my place is all I care about. I want this over with and quick. Take him and get out of my house." The professor was losing his cool, his voice quaking with a mix of anger and nerves.

"It will be my pleasure to take him off your hands. You never were father material." The sound of boot heels scraping across wood made Jack jump.

"Please give me a few minutes to collect him," the professor said. "No need to scare the boy."

"Hurry up. I'm anxious to get back to the forest."

Jack's heart skipped a beat. He jumped to his feet and ran up the stairs to his room. He snatched his duffel bag from the floor of his closet, threw open his dresser drawer, and stuffed all his clothes in his bag. His hands were shaking. He grabbed his Houdini book and his straitjacket and stuffed them in, too—everything he owned. A door slammed, followed by footsteps pounding up the stairs. He only had a few seconds before the professor reached his room. Panicking, Jack yanked his handcuffs out of the drawer, and they scattered across the floor. As he bent down to pick them up, the professor barged through the door.

The professor circled Jack like a tiger stalking a gazelle. "You broke your word. I told you there would be consequences." The once-kind professor stood before him now as a predator. His eyes narrowed, his expression hardened.

Jack backed away from him and said, "Yes! I did it, OK. I broke my word. What do you want me to say?"

"We are so much alike. I knew you would want to know the secret and open the box, just like I did. I baited the trap and you took it."

In that raw moment, Jack realized that none of it was real—his own room, the dinners, the games, and the presents—they were all part of the professor's plan. But worst of all, Jack had fallen for it. He broke the law of magic, and believed in the illusion. Shame and anger burned in his throat. "We're nothing alike. I'm not a liar. You were supposed to be my foster father and take care of me. But you're nothing but a con man."

The professor smirked. "It took me years to create the trick—one with consequences. We had an agreement—

just like a signed contract—and my idea was to lure you into my office with this magic box; if you opened it, you broke our deal. Now you will take my place."

"But you studied magic!" Jack pleaded, trying to grasp what was happening. "You had fifty years to learn how to escape the contract."

"Exactly. I finally figured out a way to beat Mussini." The professor raised his voice and glided closer to Jack, never taking his eyes off him.

"What did you come up with?" Jack stood trembling in the darkness of the room, wearing his faded jeans and favorite worn-out blue sweatshirt, but he already knew the answer.

"You!" the professor yelled.

"You traded me to Mussini to save your own skin." Jack's voice caught in his throat. "I thought you were my friend."

But really Jack had wanted more than a friend, like Mildred had said; he had hoped that the professor could be his mentor and protector. Jack didn't know what hurt worse, falling for the professor's trap, or the ache in his heart for believing—for the first time—that he had been loved. The professor never wanted him. He was just using him in his escape plan. Jack stared at the professor and finally the man looked up.

"You must go with Mussini into his world and pay my debt with your young soul. Now collect your things."

Jack shook his head and glanced at his duffel, trying to think about his next move and talk at the same time. "You can't just trade people's souls."

"Yes, you can." The professor balled up his fists. "It's done!"

"I'm not sticking around. I'll just call Mildred and get out of here."

"Don't argue with me." Ignoring his pleas, the professor grabbed Jack's handcuffs from his hands and shoved them into his duffel. "You will need all of your clever tricks and manacle dexterity where you're headed. Mussini lives in a dangerous land."

Jack's mind raced, seeking out an escape route. Glancing at the window high above the ground, he knew his only way out was down the stairs and out the door. "I told you, I'm not going *anywhere* with *anyone*." Jack tried to push the professor aside, but the professor grabbed him by the arm. "Get out of my way!" Jack broke free and took off, running down the stairs.

The professor chased after him. "You belong to the magician now!"

Jack darted to the front door, but when he grabbed the doorknob, it was bolted shut. He spun around, but the professor had already made it down to the landing. The professor held his arm tightly. He was trapped. Concheta paced back and forth at the foot of the stairs, tears streaming down her small brown cheeks. The tips of her fingers almost touched Jack's face as she looked at him like it would be for the last time. He had seen that look many, many times before. Then two words drifted clearly from her lips. *"Los muertos."* She almost whispered the ghostly words; he had to strain to hear her.

Jack's knowledge of Spanish consisted of "hello," "good-bye," and enough food items to order off the menu at Taco Bell. *Los muertos, los what? Los muertos, los muertos . . .* It sounded familiar. He remembered his sixth-grade Spanish class and the skeletons they made for Halloween. The class decorated the room with white cut-out bony limbs pasted onto black paper.

Concheta wiggled her way in between Jack and the professor and dug into Jack's duffel. Her small fingers snatched a pair of handcuffs from the bag and slapped them onto his wrist, securing the other end to the banister. "Let them try and take you now. Hide the key, *mi chico*! Hide the key!" Concheta made the sign of the cross, kissed the rosary that hung around her sweaty neck, and scuttled through the house to the back door.

"That's not going to stop them," the professor yelled after her. He turned to Jack. "Mussini and his minions are coming for you."

"Minions?" Jack's voice cracked. Jack yanked and pulled at the cuff. She had twisted the clasp so tightly that there was no give, no play between his wrist bone and the hard steel.

And then it hit him. Jack remembered the warning from the kids in the park: the occult, the grave robbers, and ghosts—*los muertos*.

The professor's dark gaze locked on to him and he said, "She's right. It is *los muertos*, my boy."

Jack's throat was dry. He could barely say the words. "The dead."

"Go with them to their domain. This is your destiny now." The professor let go of Jack's arm and vanished down the hallway, leaving the Handcuff Kid alone in the stairwell.

"Come back!" Jack screamed, yanking on the handcuff locking him to the banister. "Don't leave me here!" The house echoed with his voice. "Stupid jerk!" Hot tears welled up in his eyes. The front door slammed shut, and the house was suddenly quiet. "Stupid handcuff!" Jack coughed and punched the wall. Resting his forehead against the banister, he tried to calm himself down.

Jack thought about a show he saw on the nature channel about bear attacks. The worst thing a person could do was run, because bears are surprisingly fast runners, not lumbering Yogi Bear snatching a picnic basket. Curling up into a ball like a pathetic baby was a person's only chance. Jack heard heavy footsteps coming from the professor's office. A hundred tiny currents of fear rippled through his body, waiting for the swipe of the claws, for the bear to rip his guts out and miles of intestines to fall onto the floor. *Get a grip*, he thought. Whatever was coming for him, he still had a chance to get away. He had to try.

Jack snatched the shim from his shoe and went to work on the cuff attached to the banister, not the wrist one, so the cuffs would still be with him when they opened. He slipped the shim inside the lock, but his hands were sweaty and it was hard to get ahold of the slim piece of metal. The hallway disappeared as he stared into the small keyhole. He tried to think backward. He felt the groove, the small lip of metal. He pressed lightly as if touching delicate skin and then waited for it to catch, *shhhh*. He drove in the metal tip. It worked, like it always did for him, and now he could get out of there.

Jack unhooked the cuff from the banister. His arm fell to his side, the steel brushing against his jeans. He turned around and froze, unable to take another step. The dark figure of the Amazing Mussini appeared in the doorway of the professor's office. Darkness engulfed the hallway. Cold air wrapped around Jack as if encasing him in wet sheets.

Metamorphosis

Three seconds is a quick trick.

Wrapped in a dark black bag,
his wrists cinched, the trunk closes.

That's what being born must feel like,
being squeezed from the blackness,
suddenly shoved into the bright spotlight of life.

Wings unfolding, from amateur to pro,
the trick moves under a thin skin,
struggling larvae to pupa,
flying from the beautiful darkness,
diving into the sky,
the quick river that lives inside.

Houdini plays the dime museums
with their beautiful weirdos,
feeling the hard part of the road.

Destiny takes hold,
he plays the vaudeville circuit.

Not the big time,
but bigger than small-town, train stops to dive hotels.

It takes so long to break free. Time is slow,
then suddenly the curtain held high falls.
Harry stands on the trunk,
free from years of want and will.

Butterflies have to fight like hell
to break out of the cocoon,
the silky prison that holds them captive.

It is the way of the world.
It is Metamorphosis.

7

The Forest of the Dead

Jack collapsed to his knees, clutching his left wrist. Pain seared beneath his fingers as inky black marks sprung to the surface of his skin from somewhere deep inside him, forming into the same compass tattoo that the professor wore on his wrist—the mark of Mussini. Jack's head jerked upward. Soot-colored clouds poured through the floorboards and rolled down the hallway. It was too late to run, too late to hide. Freezing hands reached out of the cloud cover, squeezing his forearms, while icicle fingers laced a rope around, binding them together. A scratchy blanket, thrown over his head, shrouded him in darkness. He was lifted clear off the floor. His sneakers dangled. His legs thrashed. Viselike arms wrapped around him, folding his body in on itself, pressing his knees up against his chest.

Jack's heart caught in his throat—he couldn't scream. The front door opened, and he felt the vast emptiness of the night as he was carried outside. Since he couldn't see, he listened: muffled voices, hushed whispers, rustled leaves. Another door opened, and he was heaved inside a small dark box like he was a load of laundry thrown into the dryer. The door shut, and suddenly, he felt alone with his own desperate gasps.

Jack instantly went into recovery mode. Over the years, he had honed the craft of getting out of whatever dire situation he got himself into; this, he told himself, was no different. Where was he? The trunk of a car or the back of a van, except he didn't hear a motor running or smell any gas fumes, but whatever he *was* in jerked to a slow crawl. The rope burned into his wrists, but the knot was pathetic, telling Jack one thing: Whoever tied it had never been a Boy Scout. Then again, he thought as he gnawed at the rope like a desperate animal, neither had he.

Once his hands were untied, he yanked the stinky blanket, which smelled suspiciously like a horse, off his head. Jack felt around the small box-like compartment. It was just big enough to crawl in, so he inched his way to the back, or what he thought was the back. He felt a fabric curtain, and slid it open, revealing the dark night sky as cool air rushed over his hot face.

A thick fog clung to the trees alongside the vehicle, and he couldn't tell from his surroundings where he was, except for maybe the woods near the professor's house. Jack considered his options. If he waited to act, there was no telling where Mussini might take him. Jack felt like he was spinning wildly, trapped inside one of the rusty carnival rides. His sweaty hands grasped the edge of the cart. He had to make a run for it. They were gaining speed. He had to hope he didn't twist his ankle or get impaled by a tree limb as he leaped into the darkness. He swallowed the lump in his throat and glanced at the ground drifting by under his feet. *Jump now!* Jack flung himself over the side and hit the ground with a crunchy thud as he landed in a pile of leaves. He scrambled to his feet, clawing through the brush, trying to regain his balance while sprinting into the darkness.

A deep voice bellowed, half laughing, from behind him, "There goes a slippery eel! Grab him, Jabber!"

Branches slapped Jack's face and pulled at his sleeves. Quick footsteps raced up behind him. A knife sliced through the darkness, cutting into the bark of a tree only inches from his head, and he hesitated—*big mistake.* Instantly, Jack was tackled, thrown to the ground, and then yanked by his collar to his feet. He thrashed wildly when an arm wrapped around his neck into a headlock, choking off his breath.

"You're more trouble than you're worth," the one called Jabber hissed into Jack's ear. His hands were ice cold against Jack's flushed skin, and he had a weird musky smell like damp earth. Jack jerked out of his grasp, annoyed he had been caught so quickly.

"Is that Mussini?" Jack asked, motioning to the large man. "The coward who makes you do his dirty work?"

Jabber wrenched the blade free from the tree bark. "I warn you—call him a coward to his face, and it will be the last word you utter. He's obsessively fond of throwing knives, especially at deserters." Jabber shoved Jack back the way they came.

"We're almost to the wall. Gag him if he can't keep his trap shut," Mussini yelled.

Jack reluctantly climbed back up into what he now realized was a small black carriage drawn by a horse. Who traveled by horse and carriage? Had he been kidnapped by the Amish? The sharp smell of kerosene burned his nostrils. A match scraped across flint, then burst into flame. The man on top of the carriage lit a lantern that hung above his head and swayed with the carriage when Jack stepped aboard. He craned his neck to get a look at Mussini, but all he saw was the halo of light the lantern cast above the man's head, though this guy was no angel. A snakelike whip snapped in the air. Jack curled up on the floor as the carriage hurried on, straight for whatever this wall was.

Jack leaned against the back of the carriage and peered between the curtain folds. The bright white moon made the trees look wiry and foreign. Not long after they started moving again, the carriage slowed. Jack heard the gruff yell of Mussini and the snap of his whip, and then the strangest sound he ever heard erupted outside of the carriage—a deep guttural cry like a cross between a moan and a roar. He strained to see where the sound was coming from.

The carriage wheels rumbled and shook, passing over a rough surface before settling. That's when he saw an enormous stone wall covered in moss and vines. A beastlike figure with sharp twisted horns growing out of its head stood near the wall. The creature swung a towering metal gate shut behind them. It turned a metal key in a huge metal lock. A knot tightened in Jack's stomach. The carriage rocked back and forth. He closed his eyes and huddled down in a corner. *Los muertos.* The professor had traded him away, and the dead had taken him, snatched like a baby.

Jack must have fallen asleep, because the next thing he knew he woke up with his neck stiff and his jaw clenched shut. His face was burning up. He opened his eyes. Rough fibers brushed against his face and muggy air filled his lungs. He pulled at a ragged edge of cloth with his teeth, tasting bits of the burlap in his mouth. A sack was fastened over his head; his new warden wasn't about to take any more chances. He almost laughed—almost, because his hands were once again tied together with rope. Not a laughing matter.

Jack pictured Houdini inside the black sack, locked in the trunk for the metamorphosis trick, as he and an assistant switched places in three seconds. One second Houdini was trapped, and the next he was free. Jack wished he had someone to switch places with, so he could slip out of this bad dream. He shook his head violently. The muscles in his neck tensed and his breathing heaved in gasps, pulling the burlap into his mouth. The inside of the bag grew hotter and hotter. *Listen, listen, listen!* he yelled to himself, quieting his panic. He heard the swish of a tail and the neigh of a horse, air forcing through the soft snout.

"Ya!" He heard the yell of the angry man, the snap of a whip, the crack of wood, and then a wheel turned. Jack listened to the horse's hooves crunching through the leaves of the forest's floor.

"Ho, ho!" the voice called out. The horse neighed. The wheels groaned to a halt, followed by the heavy footsteps of someone landing on the ground. A fist pounded on wood. "Jabber! Water the horses!"

Metal rings dragged across a metal rod—a curtain

drawn back. Someone jumped down from the back of the wagon, perhaps Jabber, because he was lighter on his feet than the heavy footsteps of the angry man. Jack thought of Little Miss B.—now look who was the blind dog. He lay still on the floor of the carriage, trying not to move. A hand reached under his chin and untied the burlap bag, pulling it from his head.

Jack flinched. His eyes fluttered, adjusting to the punch of brightness. Leaning up on his elbows, he climbed out of the carriage and watched the world around him come into focus.

He was in the middle of a forest, but not the forest near the professor's house. Heaps of dead brown leaves covered the ground. An army of pale, tall trees surrounded him like ghostly sentries that went on for miles and miles. The tree limbs grew into a tangled net above him, obscuring the cloud-covered sky. Fog clung to the ground, and if Jack lay flat on his back, he might even disappear under the hazy carpet. The air of the place felt like ice-cold breath on his neck and made him shudder.

A large wagon stood in the clearing. Huge black wheels with long spokes supported the enormous wooden wagon, which looked like something out of an old-time circus. It was painted in the same dull red, black, and tan colors that the box in the professor's office had been.

Jabber, who looked about nineteen, give or take, kicked through the leaves and fog and kneeled down to untie Jack's feet. Jack was surprised when he saw Jabber. From the strength of the arms that held him in a headlock, he expected a much tougher-looking guy. His skin looked pale, an ashy blue color. A black hat rested on Jabber's head. His black velvet jacket, black pants, and black boots looked old, but not worn, more like vintage—as if he had been born one hundred years before Jack. His hands were wet, and his shirt was speckled with water marks. Jack gnawed at the rope binding his hands.

"You're going to want to ride up top," Jabber said.

"Huh," Jack said, spitting rope fibers onto the ground.

"Get a little air." Jabber motioned to the circus wagon. "You need it. You stink." Jabber gave Jack a good sniff, then stood, slapping him on the back.

"I smell as good as those horses. I was wrapped in their blankets."

Jabber ignored him and walked back to tend to the horses. Four speckled gray horses with long white manes stood in the clearing hitched to the gigantic wagon. One of the horses looked at Jack with somber eyes. He rested his forehead against her large body and stroked her soft coat.

"Who's this Mussini guy?" Jack asked, wondering what Jabber would divulge about the magician.

Jabber pointed to the side of the wagon. Painted in

swirled black script on the side of the wagon was the phrase: *The Amazing Mussini and His Traveling Players*.

"He's your new boss, and he runs the show," Jabber said.

As if on cue, a ferocious bear of a man came out of the woods and barreled past the wagon toward them. Enormous was an understatement. He was well over six and a half feet tall in his heavy leather boots. His thick, wavy black hair accentuated his bristly beard and black eyes. He snapped a long leather whip in the air. And when he spoke, his voice was deep and rubbed against Jack's eardrums like sandpaper.

"Hurry up, Jabber. It's a long ride to where we're headed, and we don't want to get caught in the forest at night."

Black crows erupted in flight through the treetops. Jack stumbled to his knees and then righted himself, trying not to look too freaked-out.

"Well, looky here. Sleeping Beauty is awake. Sorry about the rope and hood. I'm not a man of bondage by principle, but we couldn't take a chance you wouldn't try and leave without saying good-bye again." Mussini clapped a massive callused hand on Jack's back and his black eyes gleamed. "It was a show of spunk, I'll give you that. But if you try it again, I'll chain you to the back of the wagon like a beast of burden. Are we square?"

"I get the picture," Jack said, afraid to look Mussini in

the eye but more afraid to look away. Mussini smiled, but it wasn't friendly, more like a show of teeth, like a grizzly bear licking its chops.

"Good man. Then we won't have any more trouble before we make camp." Mussini stalked off, boarded the smaller carriage, and drove ahead of the larger, colorful wagon.

"Better do as he says," Jabber said as Mussini pulled out of sight. "You work for him now. You should consider yourself lucky."

"Lucky? Are you kidding?"

"You should be grateful Mussini took you on as a member of the troupe. I'd do my best to not screw this up. The forest can be a dangerous place for someone who gets lost or *accidentally* left behind."

Great, a slightly veiled threat, and we just met. Way to make friends. Jack looked around for his duffel. He saw it on the ground and heaved it up on the seat next to Jabber. He was so exhausted he could hardly think straight, but he had too many questions to fall asleep. "Where am I?" Jack asked as they rode through the forest.

"You aren't in your world anymore. You're in the Forest of the Dead," Jabber said matter-of-factly. He must have noticed the look of utter bewilderment on Jack's face, because he smirked. "Don't you believe me?"

"That's impossible. In case you hadn't noticed, I'm not dead," Jack said, rubbing his temples. He couldn't help but stare at the deep blue veins that spidered across Jabber's neck. Suddenly he realized why Jabber was pale, clammy, and smelled like dirt. "Whoa! No way, man! Are you dead?"

"Very." Jabber's eyes never left the road in front of them.

"Dead-dead?" Jack scooted away from Jabber.

"Is there any other kind?"

Head injuries caused hallucinations. Maybe Jack was actually in a coma, lying in a hospital bed, and this place was just a figment of his imagination. A weepy Mildred was probably on an all-night vigil, burning a candle at his bedside, yapping his ear off so he wouldn't get *lonely* in his coma state.

Jack rubbed the red rope burns on his wrists. This place felt a little too real to be a dream. Coma or no coma, this was getting creepy.

"The Forest of the Dead has its own rules," Jabber said. "The living are allowed in. But they don't last long here."

"What about heaven and hell?" Jack asked.

"Oh, sure. Heaven. Some people call it nirvana, paradise, cloud nine, a world-renowned place to spend eternity. And then there is hell or Hades, an ominous domain, a real scorcher, so I've heard, exactly where you don't want to end up. But we are neither here nor there. We're in the middle."

"Look, just to warn you, my social worker, Mildred, is going to be really angry when she finds out I'm missing. And she might look like a sweet little old lady, but she has the heart of a ninja. I wouldn't want to get on her bad side."

"Sounds formidable. You say your ninja guardian angel's name is Mildred?"

"Yeah, that's right. And she doesn't take crap from anyone," Jack said. "Being dead won't save you from her wrath. Once, I did something to get her girdle in a twist, and she pinched my ear so hard that I still have the scar." Jack pulled his hair back and showed Jabber his ear. "Since you haven't hurt me, I can ask her to look the other way. Just tell me how to get out of here, back to the professor's house, and we'll pretend this never happened."

"You can't leave. The professor traded you to the Land of the Dead, and now you are the property of the Amazing Mussini. You will work for him for one hundred years, and then you can choose to move on—if you are ready to leave the forest."

"One hundred years! No way, I'll be a hundred and twelve years old by then. I'll be, be—" But the sentence broke off in his mouth. He couldn't say it, so Jabber did.

"You'll be dead."

"This can't be happening. The professor didn't own me. You can't just go around selling people's souls. It isn't right." Jack was used to being forced into strange places, but this was ridiculous.

Jabber's hand suddenly snaked out and grabbed Jack's wrist. "Listen to me. You have entered the Land of the Dead—the underworld. Your soul has been traded, and it was a fair trade. Now do what you are told. Stay out of trouble and stay out of *my* way."

Jack looked down and saw the mark on Jabber's wrist. Mussini had marked him, too. "So, is everyone lucky enough to get one of these?" Jack pulled away from Jabber and finally examined his new ink. He gently rubbed his finger over the spidery lines of the fresh tattoo on his wrist. The pain was gone, but the brand looked pretty permanent.

Jabber looked away smugly. "When the professor tricked you into taking over his contract, you inherited his mark. And yes, we all have the mark of Mussini. But I'm the only one in the group who has ever figured out how the magic works."

"Magic?"

"The tattoo is a powerful illusion. It is a magical compass." Jabber pulled the horses to a stop and rolled up his sleeve to show Jack how the device worked. He squinted down at his wrist and said, "North Wall." The ink on his wrist began to bubble and twist as the lines warped to life. The dial spun and the arrow pointed behind them. "Last night we passed through the wall to the north. It's heavily guarded." Jabber pointed to the large *N* and a small image of a wall appeared to hover above his skin. "To the east and west is the Never-Ending Forest—masses of trees that are constantly growing outward. They are a maze, impossible to navigate. We are headed south to Mussini's base camp. From there all the towns are south until the Black River, and that is as far as the forest goes."

"Impressive." Jack ran his finger over the flat inked surface of his own tattoo.

"Impossible is more like it." Jabber snapped the reins. "Figuring out the magic made me Mussini's right-hand man. He trusts me and only me."

Jack didn't care about bonding with the Amazing Mussini. All he cared about was getting out of there, and figuring out the compass might help him do it. The image of the strange beast that Jack saw last night standing at the North Wall came back in an instant. He would have to bide his time until he could figure a way out of the underworld.

Compass or no compass, Jack didn't have a clue where he was. But he knew one thing, and that was there was always a way out. Even this forest had a trapdoor. He just had to find it. Jack looked on the bright side; at least he wasn't dead.

Yet.

A Gang of Minions

From his many foster homes, Jack knew the drill when it came to being thrown into new surroundings. He needed to blend in, stay out of trouble, and keep his head down while he plotted his escape. He was concentrating on an escape plan when the wagon groaned to a halt. Jack heard movement coming from inside.

Jabber nodded toward the wagon and said, "The others."

The others. These must be Mussini's minions. How was Jack supposed to blend into a group of minions? Jack took a deep breath and jumped down to the ground. A tiny hand slid the curtain open. He braced himself for whatever terrible creatures might suddenly appear from inside the wagon.

Jack expected a good freak show. Minions should

have slithery tentacles for arms, bulging, bloodshot eyeballs, and rows of sharp tiny teeth to gnaw on bones. He was seriously hoping at least one of them would have horns, so when they appeared from behind the curtain and began climbing down, Jack almost felt cheated. Talk about getting shortchanged in the weird department. They didn't look like minions: They looked like regular kids.

The first to climb down was a pretty girl. She wore a long dress and black button-up boots. Her clothes and manner gave Jack the feeling she was from another time, born long before he was, though she looked the same age as him. She jumped down the last foot from the back of the wagon and landed softly on the ground. Her long mahogany hair tumbled down her back as a hair comb came loose and dropped into the leaves. Jack picked up the comb. When he tugged on her sleeve to give it back, she just ignored him, so he slipped it into his pocket to give to her later.

A boy jumped down into the leaves and grabbed on to Jack as he stumbled forward. "T-Ray," the boy said with a salute. T-Ray looked about eleven, maybe twelve, but his clothes looked modern enough. He wore army-green pants and a long-sleeved gray T-shirt. His black hair was buzzed short on his head, accentuating his dark skin.

"Come on and give us a hand," T-Ray said to Jack. "I won't bite, but Runt might, so you better take these."

T-Ray shoved two quilted bundles into Jack's arms.

"Who's Runt?" Jack asked, but the question seemed to answer itself as a boy's head popped out of the wagon's curtain.

"I am!"

They all laughed at the younger boy with a tiny scowl on his face and blond hair poking up wildly all over his head. "And I was sleepin' till you all woke me up."

"No time for sleeping. It's time to get to work, my little Runt." The girl ran her fingers through the boy's hair and helped him out of the wagon.

After helping Runt, she started unloading the gear. The entire gut of the wooden cart was crammed with stuff. Even the ceiling had things attached to it to take advantage of every available space. Jack tried to help them, hoping someone would give him a little direction. It was better than just standing around dumbly, not knowing what to do. But beside T-Ray's salute, the kids pretty much ignored him and went about the business of making camp.

This was pretty typical behavior that Jack liked to call *new kid syndrome*. It was the norm when entering a new group of kids. No one wanted to get up close and personal on his first day. In the first phase, they ignored and acknowledged only when absolutely necessary. As a way of dealing with the cold shoulders, Jack peppered them with questions. T-Ray seemed the most eager to break down first.

"So, you a foster kid, too?" Jack asked.

"No. Better grab a bundle," T-Ray said, handing Jack a folded-up tarp.

"How'd you guys get here?" Jack asked the group, but the girl just added another tarp to his burden. "Have you been here long?" he continued, and his answer was a pile of bedding placed on top of the tarps. "I'll take that as a yes," Jack said, and the girl balanced a small crate on top of the growing heap in Jack's arms. For every question he asked, he received another thing to carry. She wasn't fooling around.

"He's a chatty one," Runt said to the girl as Jack stumbled over to the clearing where they were piling up the gear. He knew they wouldn't be able to hold out for long, so he just kept going back for more stuff and more completely ignored questions. The girl didn't even look at his face. She was good. He dumped his third load to the ground and rested for a minute.

An enormous boy heaved a trunk out of the wagon and carried it over to the clearing that was starting to fill with gear. T-Ray elbowed Jack and whispered, "That's Boxer. He's the strongest kid alive."

Boxer wore a white tank top that showed off his massive biceps and shoulders. With a plaid flannel shirt tied around his waist, Boxer looked like he had been carved from stone. He was a plow horse of a kid, probably raised on a farm.

Jack leaned against the back of the wagon and realized his hand was resting on the girl's shoe. "Oh, sorry," he said, jerking his hand away so quickly that he elbowed Boxer in the ribs. "Sorry." *Real smooth,* Jack thought. He doubted that he was making any headway getting on anyone's good side.

Boxer unloaded the heavy steamer trunks while Jack and T-Ray unrolled long bolts of crimson and burned-orange canvas. The three of them drove tall wooden poles deep into the ground. They attached a rope to the poles and threaded it through the canvas. They pulled the ends of the rope, raised the cloth, and suddenly, colorful tents sprouted up, giving a burst of life to the dreary surroundings. A light sweat beaded on Jack's brow. The cool air felt good in his lungs. Being with other kids made the forest seem less intimidating.

Jack held a wedge of folded canvas in his arms. Runt, who was lying across a row of bedding in the wagon, looked up and said, "That's a hammock. Take it inside the tent and hang it up." Runt seemed content barking orders while relaxing from a hard day of riding in the wagon.

After they made camp, T-Ray made a circle of large stones for the fire pit. Jack hadn't seen Jabber or Mussini all day.

"They scout out the area and make sure it's safe." T-Ray kicked one of the rocks closer to the circle.

"Safe from what?" Jack asked, pushing a stone into place.

"From the dead mostly. But there are other creatures, too, like wild beasts, tortured souls, and demons."

"I saw a demon once, lurking through the woods." Runt leaned up on his elbows from inside the wagon.

"That's just forest legend," Boxer said, tying down a tent flap. "How'd you know it was a demon?"

"'Cause of the long black chains dragging across the ground," Runt said, his eyes darting around the camp.

Jack felt sick to his stomach. He tried not to think about exactly where he was. He wondered what the professor and Concheta were up to. Probably cooking dinner. Oh man, it was Italian night, too. Concheta was going to teach him how to make lasagna with meat sauce. They probably ate bark here in the forest—if the demons didn't eat them first.

"Don't scare him, T-Ray. We're going to need his help. Once Jabber gets back, you boys will need to do a little hunting," the girl said as she carried a bucket of fresh water over to the fire pit.

"I hope they get back soon. My stomach's already growling," Runt said.

"All you do is eat and sleep," Boxer said, tossing a shiny red apple over to Runt, who caught it and sunk his teeth into the fruit. A stream of juice trickled down his chin, and he smiled, satisfied with the snack.

"Come on, Runt. You can help me gather the wood for the fire."

The girl pulled Runt to his feet, and they walked off into the woods. She picked up little sticks and bundled them in her apron, while Runt followed at her heels, holding on to her skirt and humming a little song.

"That's Violet," T-Ray said, noticing Jack watching her.

"Violet," Jack repeated. He liked it.

"Don't stare." T-Ray yanked on his sleeve. "She doesn't like it when people look at her. She's . . . ya know."

"What?"

"She's no longer breathing air." T-Ray grimaced.

"Wait, you mean she's dead—like Jabber?" Jack dropped the hammock he was carrying.

"Yes. From what I can tell, the living don't last long, and the dead tend to linger."

"So I've heard." What rotten luck. The prettiest girl he had ever seen was dead? He was starting to think that this place was closer to hell than it was to heaven.

"Hey, what about you, Boxer, and Runt? You're not dead, right?" Jack asked.

T-Ray snapped, a little *too* quickly, "No, I'm fine. Just fine, never felt better."

Jack paced back and forth, trying to understand what he had just been told. "No way I'm going to die here! We've got to find a way out."

T-Ray just shook his head. "Good luck. But if you ask me, we're doomed, too."

Runt ran back toward the camp, dumping an armload

of twigs on the ground. "They're back! They're back!" he bellowed.

Jabber rode up on one of the horses and quickly dismounted. "Time for some fun," he said, breathing heavily. He handed Runt the reins to the horse and walked up to Jack. "Are you ready for some excitement? We want to see if you were worth the effort."

Phase two of *new kid syndrome* was the test phase. Jack needed to prove himself to the group, and then they would either accept or deny him.

"Your job is to chase the pig," Jabber said. "Can you handle that?"

All he had to do was chase a pig, which seemed easy enough, but Jack was wary. The easier a test seemed on the surface, the more likely it was to have hidden pitfalls.

"It's just a pig, right?" Jack asked.

"You could say that, but we should warn you that it has spearlike tusks, razor-sharp claws, and horrific breath," T-Ray said. Jabber elbowed him, but he continued anyway. "And it's been rumored the pig's breath is so bad, it petrifies whoever it breathes on."

"That means turn to stone," Runt said.

"Yeah, I got it. I'll try not to kiss it on the snout," Jack said. "Are you sure this thing isn't a wild boar?"

"What do we look like, biologists?" T-Ray said.

"We didn't happen to have our scientific identification manuals handy," Boxer chimed in.

"This ain't a nature hike, boy." Runt punched his bony little fist into Jack's thigh. Jack knew the drill, but it was still a little annoying being called *boy* by a kid whose nose came up to his armpit.

"Can we count on you?" Jabber asked.

"I'm in," Jack answered. How hard could it be?

"The hunt is on!" Runt yelled. "Catch me a big fat pig, boys!"

The hunt was just what Jack needed to prove himself.

Boxer was not an intellectual genius, nor was he quick on his feet, but he was the strongest kid Jack had ever seen. He lifted fallen logs, moving them like toothpicks, as they all worked to build a small pen to trap the pig.

Jack's role in the operation would be just what Jabber said—he would hound the pig into the pen. Then T-Ray, who was perched on a tree branch, would toss down a net onto the clueless pig, while Boxer closed off the pen with a gigantic log, trapping the pig inside.

Jabber scouted out the pig's den in a small thatch of brush. The gang crouched in the bushes. Jabber nodded for Jack to get ready, and then he rushed the nest from behind and flushed out the pig. Through a flurry of leaves, a gigantic pale pink swine bolted out of the bushes. The pig took off like a chubby torpedo, sprinting out of the nest, heading right for Jack. Dodging the initial charge of the animal, Jack tore after the pig. In spite of their stumplike legs, pigs were really quick. Not cheetah fast, but still fast enough to get Jack racing through the trees, his blood pumping. He chased the pig toward the pen, but it took a sharp right turn and headed away from the trap. Pulling up and banking right, Jack tried to corral the pig back in a wide circle.

The plan worked. Jack went right and the pig went left. The pig's stubby little legs charged toward the pen. Jack had done it. Just a few more yards, and he was home free. Then the pig suddenly stopped running, skidding to a halt right in front of a clump of bushes. Raising its hairy snout into the air, the pig took a few big sniffs. Jack slowed down. He didn't trust that pig. Something was up. Why was the pig just standing there? If Jack wasn't mistaken, it seemed to be waiting for him, craning its neck back and peeking over its shoulder. Once Jack was in close range, the pig let out a deafening squeal.

It was a warning cry. The bushes erupted as three other pigs charged toward Jack. Nothing was worse than a pig with a plan. Jack skidded in the dry leaves, stumbled, and grappled on his hands and knees as he ran back toward the pen. Four angry, volcanic-breath swine were hot on his heels.

"The pig has friends!" he yelled. "They're coming! They're right behind me!"

Jack barreled into the pen and fell to the ground. Two of the pigs followed right behind. He sprang to his feet just in time for T-Ray to drop the net on him and one of the pigs. Jack grabbed at the pig, trying to calm down the animal's flailing hooves and mad squeals. Closing off the pen, Boxer tossed the log across the opening. Jack lay flat on his back, tangled in the net with the angry pig clutched in his arms. And though technically he had succeeded, he didn't feel like such a winner. He had fumbled his way to victory, and he knew it. Boxer picked up the other pig and tossed it over and out of the pen while T-Ray and Jabber clapped and cheered.

"Great job!" yelled T-Ray. "You did it, Jack!"

"If I hadn't known better, I would have thought you had done this before." Jabber bent down and helped Jack to his feet, untangling the net.

"You knew this pig wasn't alone, didn't you?" Jack wrestled to hold on to their catch.

Jabber placed his hat back on his head. "Of course."

"And you knew it would chase me, not the other way around."

"You made splendid bait." Jabber clapped him on the back.

"Pigs have very high IQs, so don't be ashamed that it got the jump on you," T-Ray said, picking a twig out of Jack's hair.

"Don't worry. You've got potential. A man can do great things with potential," Jabber said.

Boxer walked up. "Want me to carry that pig back

for you?" he asked, taking the squirming pig out of Jack's arms. While he held it, T-Ray tied a rope over the pig's neck, and they all headed back to camp together.

The final phase of *new kid syndrome* was complete. They played a trick on Jack and all got a good laugh at his expense. Jack was in.

Back by the fire, Boxer chopped the wood with an ax. Violet stoked the fire, blowing softly on the glowing flames. She still never looked at him. Jack turned away and scratched the chin of the pig that was now tied up behind the wagon, just like he had been. Violet walked over to him and reached her hand out to grab the rope attached to the pig, and as she did, she brushed her hand against the bare skin of his arm. Jack jerked his hand away suddenly, stupidly. He hadn't meant to, but her skin was snowy cold. She sneered, taking his reaction the wrong way.

"Let me help you," Jack said, taking the pig by the rope. He was stunned. Her eyes were a shockingly bright violet color. He gawked and sputtered, trying to think of something to say as the pig squealed.

"Bring it then, and stop staring. What? Are you a half-wit?"

"No, I just don't have a lot of experience with pigs." Could he have said anything more stupid? Who has experience with pigs, beside pig farmers?

"It won't come with you willingly. It knows where it's headed. You'll have to carry it." Violet rolled her eyes. Jack struggled to pick up the squirming pig in his arms and followed her.

"I suppose you want me to butcher it for you?" she asked.

"Oh. Um. I've never killed an animal before." He hadn't realized that the pig he was carrying was going to be their dinner, and his stomach rolled over.

"Can you?" she asked, looking into his eyes.

Jack never actually thought about it before. "I guess if I had to." As Jack set the pig down, Violet's hair comb fell out of his pocket and onto the ground at his feet, broken in two. He forgot that he had picked her comb up earlier. The comb must have snapped when he was chasing the pig. Jack panicked and tried to grab it before she saw it.

"What's that?" Violet asked, staring down at the comb and then reaching up and touching her hair. Her eyes opened wide as she realized her comb was missing.

"I'm sorry." Jack held the beautiful and broken hair comb in his hand.

"You stole my comb!" Violet bunched up her fists.

"No. It wasn't like that. I was going to give it back. I swear." Jack tried to hand her the pieces, but she wouldn't take them.

"You are a thief and a liar." She raised her voice, and the other minions looked over at them.

"It's made of shell, and it must have broken when I fell to the ground. I should have given it back right away."

"Beautiful things tend to break easily," she said.

"I'll get you a new one. I swear."

"Look around." Violet reached her arms out and let them flop to her sides in frustration. "There aren't any pretty things here."

"It's still nice." Not knowing what else to do with the pieces of the comb, Jack handed them to her again. Violet snatched up one of the pieces and threw it into the woods.

"No one wants something once it's broken."

"I promise I'll make it up to you."

"T-Ray, take the pig to the block," Violet yelled, anger and sadness in her voice.

T-Ray ran over and grabbed the squealing pig and carried it behind the wagon.

"I'll kill it. Our new *friend* Jack's had a long first day." Violet spun around and grabbed a long knife and headed for the block. Jack was glad he wasn't that pig.

All the kids gathered around the fire to roast the pig until it was crisp and juicy. Jack had never tasted anything so delicious and tender in his entire life. Grease rolled down his chin. With his stomach full, he rested his back against a tree and relaxed. The fire warmed Jack's face, and he felt comfortable with his new friends for the first time since arriving in the forest. Violet completely ignored him, but T-Ray assured him that she would forgive him, maybe in like twenty or thirty years. After dinner they roasted marshmallows on long thin sticks, dipping them into the flames. Jack toasted his marshmallow until it was golden crispy brown, and the hot gooey center almost burned his tongue.

"Mine's on fire!" T-Ray yelled, leaping to his feet. Waving his stick in the air, T-Ray tried to extinguish his marshmallow, which had erupted into flames. Mussini, hearing the commotion, threw the flap back and barreled out of his tent. He grabbed T-Ray's stick and waved the burning glob high in the air. With a showman's dramatic flair, he threw his head back and slowly lowered the burning marshmallow toward his open mouth. The fiery glob inched its way painfully closer until the marshmallow extinguished with a scorching sizzle in his mouth. Mussini stuck out his big pink tongue, completely unharmed, and took his bow. The kids cheered and talked amongst themselves.

No one was paying attention to him, so Jack took the opportunity to slip away. He hurried over to his tent and ducked inside, grabbing his duffel.

"Going somewhere?" Jabber asked, waiting outside of the tent for him.

Jack threw his duffel bag over his shoulder and tried to maneuver past Jabber. "I'm getting out of here."

"No you're not." Jabber crossed his arms and blocked Jack's path.

Jack pushed against him, but Jabber didn't budge. "Get out of my way."

"Keep your voice down. Do you want to get yourself killed?" Jabber raised his voice and yelled out, "Hey, Amazing Mussini! I think the gang would like to hear a bedtime story."

"Do they?" Mussini called back. "And what kind of story is that?"

"A scary story. One to keep them in line and hopefully alive." Jabber took the duffel off of Jack's shoulder and tossed it back inside the tent. Mussini raised his arms in the air and waved the kids closer.

"Gather round the fire, and I'll tell the tale of the Death Wranglers and why you will never escape the Forest of the Dead."

9

The Tale of the Death Wranglers

Jack didn't appreciate being dragged by the collar back to the campfire by Jabber. He got the hint. No need for Jabber to get pushy. He plopped down on a log and hung his hands between his knees. Darkness crept up around them. The glowing fire cracked and popped as the flames licked the black night sky.

The Amazing Mussini rubbed his massive hands together and waved them in the air over the fire. The flames danced under his fingers as if he commanded them. Mussini dipped his hand into the blaze, held a ball of fire in his palm, and threw it up into the sky, where it broke into a thousand single sparks that showered down on the gang.

"The Land of the Dead is a dangerous place. And a

dangerous place needs a guard who is fearless, heartless, brutal, and unkind."

Runt gulped, and a collective shudder rolled over the group. Mussini had them right where he wanted them.

"The Death Wranglers are neither men nor animals. They have the massive head of a bull with cruel spiraling horns and the Herculean body of a man. They are creatures bound to the earth. They are beasts of burden with only one task: to keep anyone from leaving." Mussini glared at Jack as he emphasized the last phrase and then repeated the word: *Anyone.*

"Patrolling the woods endlessly, they do not sleep. It is said they are the children of the Minotaur, beasts of myth. Burdened as the gatekeepers, they do not rest." With blazing eyes, Mussini rose up above the fire.

"You cannot escape them once they pick up your scent. They will hunt you through the Never-Ending Forest." In the light of the fire Mussini looked like a man ripped from the pages of myth himself, larger than a mortal man. Jack swallowed hard. Runt shuddered and clutched on to Violet; even T-Ray had a wide-eyed look on his face.

But Jack realized something and felt a small hope: If there were gatekeepers, then there was a gate—a way out of this place. It was as if someone had slipped him a note or whispered a secret into his ear. The gatekeepers guarded the wall. But they were just another obstacle, that was all. Jack leaned back and propped his feet up on a log, trying to shake out the nervous tension that had crept into his body.

"The Death Wranglers guard the only way out of the forest."

"The wall," Runt mumbled, his voice quivering.

"That's right. The wall is the only way out, and it's heavily patrolled. No one gets through the wall alive."

Jack remembered the night he arrived in the forest and how Mussini passed right through. He must be in tight with the Death Wranglers. If Mussini could travel back and forth, then so could he.

"But you cross through the wall," Jack said, deciding to give the bear a poke.

"You are correct. I made a deal with the Death Wranglers to pass through the gate." Mussini brushed his palms together, and when he did, Jack saw that they were blackened from the fire.

"What kind of deal? What did you trade them?" Jack asked.

"I traded them a magical gift. A special something just for them."

"Like what?"

"That's enough," Jabber said, kicking the log that Jack was sitting on.

"A smart boy like you should know when to be very careful, Jack. The Death Wranglers don't show mercy," Mussini said.

"No mercy," Runt whispered.

"But don't fear the forest, my children. You are always safe with me around," Mussini said.

Jabber stood and corralled the kids toward their tents. "Time for bed."

Safe like a fly in a spider's web, Jack thought as he made his way to the tent with the other boys. Jack slept in the tent with Boxer, Runt, and T-Ray. Jabber and Violet each slept in their own tents, and Mussini had his own tent, though the canvas walls did little to muffle the volcanic snores. After hearing the story, everyone was a bit jumpy. Boxer took the lantern and inspected the grounds.

"No Death Wranglers or animal tracks. No nothing," Boxer said as Runt pulled on his sleeve.

"Check my hammock for spiders, will ya?"

"All clear," Boxer said, after scanning Runt's hammock with the lantern.

"A kid could get scared here. Not me, but you could," Runt said to Jack, holding on to Boxer's arm. "Mussini and Boxer keep us safe."

T-Ray climbed up into the hammock above Jack. Runt leaped into his hammock and let one of his legs dangle over the edge.

"Let's tell Jack the rules of the top hammock," Boxer said.

"No!" Runt squealed.

Jack had the feeling the rules were made specifically for Runt.

"Rule number one: No farting in the top hammock," Boxer said. He had the dubious honor of sleeping in the hammock under Runt.

"It's too late. Too late!" Runt yelled as a cacophony of toots erupted from above. Boxer snatched his blanket up over his face and yelled, "Shields up!"

T-Ray and Jack followed Boxer's lead and pulled their blankets up over their noses to avoid the stench of Runt's farts.

"Rule number two: No monkey swinging," Boxer said, grabbing ahold of Runt's leg to still it after he'd gained momentum from swinging it.

"Rule number three: No peeing from the top hammock. Go outside to pee."

"Gross. Runt, tell me you didn't do it," Jack said, laughing.

"I thought I could make it out the flap without climbing down," Runt said.

"Earthquake!" Boxer yelled as he lifted his feet and bounced Runt around in a simulated earthquake.

"Rule number four," Runt yelled, clutching the edge of his hammock for dear life. "No kicking from the bottom hammock."

"Boxer, you should get hazard pay for sleeping under Runt," T-Ray said as he extinguished the lantern, casting the tent into shadows.

"It's not so bad," Boxer said.

Jack didn't sleep. He waited all night while one by one the others drifted off. He was familiar with the sound a person's breathing made when he fell asleep, probably from sleeping in the group home, with kids all lined up, sleeping in metal bunk beds with skinny mattresses and noisy springs. His mind raced as he planned his escape. The faster he got out of there, the better.

This wouldn't be Jack's first attempt at escape. The first time he ever ran away was when he was seven. After leaving the priest and his wife, he was sent to a new family. One day after lunch, he tied up a shirt and some clothes and stuffed his pockets full of sunflower seeds. It wasn't that the family was so terrible; he couldn't even remember them. The family just wasn't right for him. And so he walked down to the railroad tracks and followed them out of town, leaving a trail of chewed-on sunflower seed shells behind him.

It was just starting to get dark, the sun sinking into the dirty metal horizon of train cars, when a red light spun on top of a police car in the distance. Jack heard the dogs barking and knew they were coming for him. Two German shepherds, dragging a police officer behind them, sniffed him out. He was afraid, but not of the officers, or the dogs with their wet noses twitching in the air, sniffing him madly as they circled him. Jack was afraid that there was no place in the world where he could hide.

Sitting in the back of the police truck, the dogs locked up in their cage, Jack pulled a package of bologna from his bundle and tore off a wobbly pink circle. He ripped it into strips and slid the meat through the metal bars of the cage as the dogs devoured the lunch meat in chomps, licking his fingers with their warm tongues.

No bars could hold Houdini, no cell, no prison. Sometimes a cage was real metal, sometimes a cage was invisible. Mussini had him inside invisible bars, but it was still a prison.

Sleeping shadows loomed inside the dark tent. His right foot hung over the edge of his hammock and rested on the ground. The earth was cool under his bare foot. Sporadic bursts of snores and breathing filled the tent. Boxer was the loudest, not surprisingly. He looked like a kid who had been punched in the face a lot. Jack waited and then rolled slowly, letting his right arm fall to the ground; he slid from the hammock and onto his stomach. His hammock rocked above him. Boxer let out a loud snort, stopping Jack instantly. His pulse quickened, but he held steady until Boxer rolled over. Inching his way under his hammock, Jack pushed his duffel bag under the bottom edge of the tent and eased his body under the heavy canvas. The coolness of the early morning made him shiver.

He jumped to his feet and went quickly, not waiting to check that the rest of the troupe was still asleep.

Hesitation was deadly. The dawn had broken and it would be light soon. He had to hurry.

The smell of damp, burned-out campfire filled the air. Guilt swept over him. Except for Mussini and perhaps Jabber, they had been nice people. But this was not his place. Jack's plan was simple—retrace his steps down the road from where he came. And for the first time, he hoped he would get lucky and hit a wall.

He ran down the road till the air began to sting his lungs. The forest was a foreign landscape and could be filled with anything—lost souls like Mussini, wild animals, ghostly spirits and their keepers, the Death Wranglers. Jack tried to ignore Mussini's story, but the man's voice echoed in his head. This was not a good place to get lost. He rubbed the tattoo on his wrist and realized how helpful the mark of Mussini would be in getting out of the forest. He just didn't know how to make the magical compass work. He squinted down at his wrist and willed it to come to life, but nothing happened. Jack snorted. Magic wasn't as easy as it looked.

Strange sounds surrounded him. He heard a noise behind him, rustling in the trees, snapping twigs underfoot. He was probably just paranoid. A chain rattled. Demon or wild boar? Yeah, that's what it was, just an animal. He heard it again. Something was out there, following him. In a rush of panic, Jack broke through the trees and ran, pushing the branches aside, swimming through the deep darkness. Shadows raced through the trees alongside him. Jack jumped off the road and into the bushes to hide.

Running like a scared rat was futile. All he could do was try to defend himself by outsmarting the creature. He pulled his duffel around and reached inside for something to use as a weapon. Pulling a pair of handcuffs out of the bag, he held the two cuffs together, letting the steel rest on the outside of his fist like makeshift brass knuckles. He took a few deep breaths before taking off again, darting from one safe clump of trees to the next, glancing over his shoulder to see if the creature was following him.

Jack listened, his back pressed stone-still against a tree. Footsteps pounded the ground behind him. He burrowed down behind the tree and peered back. The beast was coming, parting the early mist with his hulking body. Jack's heart raced. A huge dark form strode through the underbrush right toward him. All Jack could make out in the low light were two huge horns spiraling out of the beast's enormous bull-shaped head. A Death Wrangler!

He had to do something. He only had a minute or two until the Death Wrangler reached him, and if he ran, the Death Wrangler would see him instantly. Hiding wasn't an option anymore. The massive bull didn't look like the type to go out for a leisurely morning stroll. He was on a mission, and that mission was to bring Jack back. Just like the German shepherds, he was hunting Jack down.

Jack had to think fast. He felt the handcuffs in his hands, and then he got an idea. If he was quick enough it just might work.

He waited for the hulking half-man, half-bull to get closer and closer. The ground shook. Jack waited one more second. Then, he sprang, closing the handcuffs around one massive wrist. The choking hand of the Death Wrangler wrapped around Jack's throat, lifting him off his feet. Jack thrust all of his weight to one side, sending the beast spinning off balance. They both fell against a tree, and Jack spun him around, forcing the Death Wrangler's back against the tree. He pulled his other hand around until both wrists touched, handcuffing the enormous beast to the tree.

He did it. Jack trapped the Death Wrangler. He slumped to the ground and heaved a sigh of relief.

Hoots of laughter filled the air. Not exactly what Jack was expecting from a mythological tyrant.

"Ha-ha! He got you, Boxer!" T-Ray came running out of the trees and grabbed the mask off of the large creature handcuffed to the tree, exposing an exasperated and sweaty boy. Jack hadn't captured a Death Wrangler at all. The creature stalking him was just Boxer in disguise. T-Ray held up an enormous papier-mâché head of a bull in his hands.

"What's going on?" Jack asked.

Jabber and Runt appeared from behind the trees.

"We knew that you would try and run away on your first night. Everyone does," Jabber said.

"Yes. We all tried to run on our first nights here. Now it's really fun when someone new comes. We followed you," T-Ray said.

"I thought you'd never go. You kept us up all night waiting," Runt said, yawning.

"What are you talking about, Runt? You were asleep the minute your head hit the hammock," Boxer said.

Runt scowled. "I was just *pretending* to be asleep."

"Your snoring was very convincing," T-Ray said.

"I don't snore. I just breathe heavy." Runt crossed his skinny arms over his chest.

Jack bent over and unlocked the handcuffs, reaching out his hand and helping Boxer to his feet. "Sorry about that, Boxer. I thought you were—well, you know."

"No hard feelings." Boxer rubbed his wrists.

"You're lucky it was just us and not one of the real Death Wranglers," Jabber said. "Think of this as a lesson. Next time we let them take you."

"What do you care if I get killed?"

"No skin off my back." Jabber shoved Jack aside, the tension between them growing.

"Come on, Jabber. Jack, you're part of our family now. We look out for each other." T-Ray handed Boxer the mask and linked his arm around Jack's.

"That, *and* I'm worth a lot more to Mussini alive," Jack said. He caught his foot on something, stumbled, and fell to the ground. Except instead of hitting leaves and dirt, Jack's hands and knees hit something much harder.

"Ouch! What is this?" Jack swept off the ground in front of him, revealing a huge wooden plank that looked like a door embedded in the forest floor. Inspecting the door more closely, he noticed ornate metal hinges and a huge oval handle. It was some kind of trapdoor.

"I've never seen anything like it," Runt said.

"It probably dropped off of someone's wagon and they left it here." Boxer kneeled down and inspected the metal latch.

"But the hinges are in the ground. And there's a frame to it. No, this isn't a random piece of junk that fell off a wagon. I think this is a real door." Jack looked up at Jabber. "You gonna tell us about this?"

Jabber dug his hands in his pockets and shrugged. "You're right. It's a door."

"Where does it go to?" T-Ray asked.

"Down, of course. It goes down."

"Down where? We're in the underworld, how much farther can we go, without getting a pitchfork in the butt?" Jack said.

"It's the labyrinth." A smirk spread across Jabber's face.

"The what?" Jack said. He was starting to notice that Jabber had an annoying habit of keeping them on a need-to-know basis.

"What's a labyrinth?" Runt asked.

"The labyrinth is an underground maze. It's the domain of the Death Wranglers. It's how they are everywhere and yet nowhere at the same time." Jabber motioned to the ground. "The Death Wranglers are always around. You just can't see them because they are beneath you. Probably right this very second." Jabber motioned to a thick metal stand with a charred head. "The trapdoors are marked by torches at night, so they can be seen in the dark."

Jack ran his fingers along the frame of the huge wooden door. "Let's open it."

"Absolutely not. Do I have to state the obvious? If you open the hatch, the beasts will figure out that we're here. They'll come after us."

Jack turned his back on Jabber, more determined than ever to get a look into the labyrinth, especially since Jabber didn't want him to. "Come on. Boxer, think you can get this hatch open?" Jack asked.

Boxer crossed his massive arms over his chest. "Sure, easy."

"Then let's see what's down there," Jack said.

The Labyrinth

Boxer wrapped his hands around the thick metal latch and heaved. The stiff metal groaned and Boxer grunted. Suddenly the hatch gave way, and the door lifted from the forest floor, revealing a secret passageway deep into the gut of the underworld. A gust of stale air flooded upward from the black pit. Jack kneeled close to the opening, his eyes adjusting to the darkness of the underground tunnel. The walls of the labyrinth were lined with stone that met a hard-packed dirt floor. Black metal rungs welded into the slick stone wall beckoned Jack downward. He glanced up at the others.

"So, who's interested in doing a little exploring?"

"Are you mad?" Jabber asked. "Now that you've had your look, it's time to shut the trapdoor and get back to camp."

"Come on. We can't open up the hatch and not go down and take a look around."

Jack's heart beat like a bird caught in the cage of his chest, fear restless inside him. The cold, dank air that drifted up from the hole in the ground caused a flurry of goose bumps to race up his arms. But if he was going to escape the underworld, then he needed to get as much intel on his obstacles as possible, and getting this close to the Death Wrangler camp was an opportunity he couldn't pass up. If Mussini made a deal with the Death Wranglers to pass through the gate at the North Wall, then so could he—now he just had to figure out what the deal was.

"You're crazy." Runt peered down into the dark abyss. "They'll rip you limb from limb and feast on your bones."

"I'm not moving in down there. I just want to see what it's like, take a look around, and get out. Easy."

"This is ridiculous! Did you three sleep through Mussini's story?" Jabber pointed down into the pit. "They live down there. They patrol down there. That is the hornet's nest. You don't want to go strolling around in the endless miles of tunnels. Do you have any idea what they are going to do to you if they catch you trespassing in their domain?"

"So we won't get caught. We just want to take a quick look around. And if there are miles of tunnels, then there are more places to hide. They won't even know we're down there."

"Look, you might have an early death wish, but they don't." Jabber poked Jack in the middle of the chest.

"We all die, so what's the big deal, right? I'm gonna die here anyway, so I might as well go out big!" Jack yelled. T-Ray stepped forward, his eyes peering down into the labyrinth. Jack sensed an opportunity.

"I bet Boxer and T-Ray will go. They're not chicken."

Boxer shoved his hands into his pockets and rocked back on his heels. "Yeah, I'll go. I'm not scared of the Death Wranglers."

"Me too. I'll go down." T-Ray's eyes darted around. "I mean, if Boxer's going down, then I'll do it."

"Fine." Jabber smirked. "Descend into the den of your greatest foe. I'll wait here and listen for your screams."

"I'll wait here, too," Runt said. "I'm not going to be a Death Wrangler appetizer."

Jack went first. He clasped the cold metal rungs and climbed down. Immediately his foot slipped and he banged his knee hard on one of the lower rungs. He winced. It was hard to act the tough hero when his knee was throbbing. He dodged Jabber's smug look and climbed deeper, the darkness of the pit enveloping him. His feet hit the dirt-packed floor, and when he looked ahead, torch-lit tunnels instantly absorbed the light like gaping, yawning mouths. Whichever way he looked, the tunnels offered the same threat.

The slick, seven-foot-tall stone walls were veined

with black, spidery mold. Pale gangly roots shoved their way through the cracks in the ceiling, reaching blindly like fingers. That's when Jack noticed that the cracks in the ceiling weren't cracks at all but gouges dug out by something sharp, like an ax or blade or *horns*. The heaviness of the earth pressed on his shoulders. A damp, musky smell filled the tunnel. The cold, thin air knifed through his lungs, and he coughed hard.

T-Ray jumped down, zipped his jacket, and pulled the hood up. An involuntary shudder jerked through him. Boxer landed next to him and gave him a nod. They seemed to have a silent agreement that made Jack wonder why they came down with him. Something was up, pushing them past their fear of the Death Wranglers and Mussini. But he could wait to find out until they were out of the monsters' cave.

"All right, smart guy, what do we do now?" Boxer asked.

"We pick a direction and go." Jack glanced down both sides of the tunnel. "I want to get a basic idea of what's down here."

"What are we looking for?" T-Ray asked. He fell into line behind Jack, with Boxer pulling up the rear.

"Anything that gives us clues about the Death Wranglers and how Mussini got on their good side."

"I don't think they have a good side. Mussini used his

magic to bribe them. He gave them something wondrous of unbelievable beauty." Boxer looked embarrassed for a second. "At least that's what I heard Jabber say one day when we were in town. The Death Wranglers are part human, and he figured out how to play to their egos."

"That's good to know." Jack turned to T-Ray and Boxer. "As I see it, we're a team. We're still alive. If we stick together, we can escape the Forest of the Dead and get home."

"What makes you think the Death Wranglers will talk to you? No offense, but you're no Mussini." T-Ray looked him up and down and shrugged.

Jack stood under a torch, rolled up his sleeve, and showed them his wrist. "Because I've got this." The fine-lined compass, etched into his skin, looked like an old-time navigational device in the flickering light. "And I'm going to use it to find my way out of here."

Boxer examined Jack's mark under the torchlight. "The mark of Mussini. News flash: We've all got one. And no one but Jabber can figure it out. It's worthless." Boxer rubbed the dull mark on the back of his wrist.

"It doesn't matter that it doesn't work. I figure if we run into any of the Death Wranglers, at least I can show them that I'm in league with Mussini, and maybe they'll make a deal with me to cross over the wall and get out of here."

Boxer's expression changed, and his uncertainty faded. "Either you're really brave or really crazy."

T-Ray rubbed his arms for warmth. "Let's get going. I'm freezing."

"Keep looking around. Come on." Jack waved them farther into the maze.

Torches flickered, giving off little in the way of heat. Jack pressed his ear to the wall and listened—nothing, no vibrations or sounds at all. Almost immediately they came to the first fork in the labyrinth, and they had to decide which way to go.

Jack stopped short. "I think we should go right, left, right, left. That way we can retrace our steps on the way back."

"Good idea. But I think we should mark the walls, too." Boxer pulled out a Swiss Army knife and carved a crude-looking arrow in the wall to show which direction they were going.

The dank corridors grew tighter the farther they crept along, narrowing with quick turns and then longer stretches. Jack dragged his hand along the cold stone, vibrations causing his hand to tremble. He glanced back, but both T-Ray and Boxer had already felt it and heard it. Something was up ahead. The tiny squeaks of rodents cried up from cracks and burrows in the stony walls, and their small shadows raced along the seam where the wall met the floor. Jack's shoes scraped against the stone floor as he walked down the corridors, but the sounds he followed were not the cries of minute creatures (like him), but the sounds of beasts.

Jack placed his hand on the wall and felt another shudder. "Something big is up ahead."

"Stay low," Boxer said.

"We should turn back." T-Ray felt the wall with his hand. "Takes a lot of Death Wranglers to make the ground move like that."

"We can't turn back now. Just a little farther."

Jack swallowed his panic about coming face-to-face with a Death Wrangler. He crouched down, taking the next turn in the tunnel. The tunnel opened up below them into a cavernous room, which must be the lair of the infamous guards. A crumbling wall provided cover for them as they peered over a high ledge down into the big pit. The gamey smell of wet dog and burned wood hit Jack's nose. The rough and tumbling voices of the Death Wranglers filled the cavern like water raging over sharp rocks. Jack peered down into the abyss.

The huge lair was divided into sections. Half of the lair was used for what looked like sleeping quarters, with bunk beds made of crude slabs of rock lining a wall. The other half of the lair was a working and training area with a fighting pit and a burning wall. That wall was scorched brick caked with soot and charred debris. Jack's stomach turned over as he realized that this was where the Death

Wranglers actually practiced hand-to-hand combat and igniting things.

The guards varied in size and shape, but most were over seven feet tall. They covered the human parts of their muscular bodies with thick leathery vests, wrist guards, and armored chest plates. But nothing could prepare Jack for what made the Death Wranglers so fearsome—their enormous bull-shaped heads covered in thick black fur, with two curved horns spiraling out of the top. A raucous crew, they yelled and slapped each other on the backs with their huge hands. The contrast of man and beast, human and animal was striking. These were monsters.

Two of the guards circled each other in the enormous fighting pit. One was noticeably smaller than the others, probably no taller than six feet: a runt by Death Wrangler standards. A cheering crowd surrounded the pit as the fight escalated. The larger Death Wrangler pummeled the smaller guard with blow after blow. The smaller guard tripped and bashed his head against the wall. A roar of laughter erupted from the crowd of guards who had gathered to watch. It was clear they were laughing at the loser. The pit was not a place for a fair fight.

The two fighters went round and round. The smaller guard took the brunt of the blows but, refusing to give up, he rose to his feet again and again. Blood soaked his shirt and splattered on the ground around him.

He took a wild swipe at the larger guard and threw

him off balance. The smaller guard in the ring capitalized on the larger guard's stumble and leaped upon his back in a bold attempt to take the larger guard down. Going low, the smaller guard took out the other's leg with a swipe of his sword and brought him down to one knee. An anguished howl filled the cavern as the guard clutched his wounded leg.

The smaller guard crawled out of the pit, victorious. He was covered in blood and soot, and the look in his eyes was not of joy, but of satisfaction. Jack knew that look; it was the look of a man long underestimated who finally proved his worth. And he proved it the hard way.

T-Ray pulled on the back of Jack's shirt. "I've seen enough. Let's get out of here before they decide to throw us down in that pit."

"Shh. Just a few more minutes." Jack couldn't take his eyes off the Death Wranglers. He inched forward and leaned against the ledge to get a better look. A cascade of broken rock tumbled over the edge and rained down on the Death Wranglers below them. Jack ducked, and the three boys froze.

The action stopped. An eerie silence filled the cavern. Jack peered through a crack in the ledge and saw a Death Wrangler pointing to their location and mouthing instructions to another Death Wrangler, who immediately took off in their direction. He was coming for them.

Boxer grabbed the back of Jack's shirt and yanked

him through the narrow archway. Once in the tunnel, they raced back through the quick turns of the labyrinth. Jack was thankful to see the arrows that Boxer had carved in the walls to lead them out, but then again, the Death Wranglers would see the arrows, too, and know which way they went. But he didn't care. All he cared about was getting out and as far away from them as possible.

Rumbling echoed all around him like a stampede of bulls. The walls shook, sending a shower of dirt down on top of their heads. Relief flooded through him when he saw the pale dawn light from the hatch pouring down into the dark labyrinth.

Jack grabbed the rung and climbed up as fast as he could. He burst through the hatch and back up into the light and air, T-Ray and Boxer at his heels. "Run! We've got to get out of here. Death Wranglers are right behind us. They're coming." Jack gasped.

"I told you!" Jabber grabbed Jack by the shirt and pulled him close to his cold face. "It's too late to run now. Get ahold of yourself and do exactly as I say."

T-Ray grabbed Jack's sleeve. "Let's go!"

But Jabber, barking orders, drowned him out. "Climb up the trees. You can't outrun them! You have to hide! Go up!"

"No way! They'll tear down the trees. Or they'll wait till we have to climb down," Jack said. "We'll be easy pickings."

Jabber got in his face again. "They won't be able to see you. The Death Wrangler can only see straight ahead or side to side. He can't move his head up. Our only chance is to go up and hide in the trees above them."

Runt needed no convincing and scurried up one of the trees to perch in the crook of the branch. He was half hidden in the heavy mist that perpetually hung in the sky of the forest. "Come on! He's telling the truth!"

"Fine." Jack hooked his fingers together to give T-Ray a boost up the closest tree, and then Jabber did the same for him. Once Jack had made it up the tree, he turned and looked down. Jabber jumped up and grabbed on to the tree next to Jack.

Boxer grabbed a tree and tried pathetically to climb, but he was too big and cumbersome, and his arms and legs tore at the bark and snapped the thin tree limbs. His face was white as a sheet, his muscular arms cut from the rough bark. He shook his head at Jack. "I can't make it!" Boxer yelled. He looked around frantically.

"Boxer!" Jack's voice was thready with panic. "Hurry, they're coming. Just try. You can do it."

Sweat streaking down his face, his eyes wide with the panic of a wild animal trapped, he helplessly groped at the tree. Jack's heart caught like a stone in his throat. The rumbling of the Death Wranglers grew louder. He had no idea how to help.

Jabber slid down the tree he had expertly scaled only

seconds before to help Boxer. "You'll have to hide, and I'll distract it. It's your only chance." Jabber shot Jack a vicious glance like it was all Jack's fault, which it kind of was. Boxer curled up in between the deep grooves of the tree roots while Jabber frantically covered him with leaves. But by the time Boxer was covered, it was too late for Jabber. He was trapped out in the open.

The battered horns appeared first, rising up out of the trapdoor. And then the enormous creature with the body of a man and the head of a bull climbed out of the pit. The beast circled Jabber, snorted and growled, but he never looked up into the trees. The beast was huge compared to Jabber. There was no way Jabber could put up a fight. The Death Wrangler stared into Jabber's face, his black eyes pitiless. Jabber stood his ground, not moving a muscle, never once flinching or recoiling from the beast. Finally, the Death Wrangler spoke with a deep, gruff voice.

"You invaded our territory, charge of Mussini."

"Yes, I did. But it was for a good reason."

"For your sake, it better be."

Jabber walked over behind the tree and picked up the mask of the Death Wrangler that Boxer had worn to scare Jack. Jabber held up the likeness to the beast and bowed, going down on one knee, presenting the mask as an offering. "I offer you this gift in thanks."

Jack didn't think that a huge papier-mâché likeness

of the Death Wrangler's head was that great a gift, but Jabber treated the crude craft project like a sculpture that had been dipped in bronze.

The beast snorted and walked around Jabber, wary of the prize. "Is this a trick?"

"No trick." Jabber set the mask at the Death Wrangler's feet. "An offering of thanks for letting us pass through the wall two nights ago."

"It is good to bring us gifts." The Death Wrangler picked up the mask and held it gently out in front of his huge body. "I will take this back to the others. But beware, charge of Mussini, you are not free to enter the labyrinth ever again. Gift or no gift, we will punish you severely."

"Yes, sir. I will remember." Jabber bowed his head until the Death Wrangler climbed back down into the pit and closed the hatch behind him. No one moved until the rumbling beneath the earth stilled.

Runt slid down his tree. "You're a hero, Jabber."

Boxer crawled out of the pile of leaves. "You saved me. He never knew I was here."

"No problem." Jabber brushed his palms together cheerfully, as if the entire incident was nothing.

"Weren't you scared? One swipe and the Death Wrangler could have wiped you out." Runt made wild swinging motions with his arms.

Jack listened to them chat from up in the tree, and

then finally climbed down, ashamed that he had been weak and cowardly—frozen in the treetops while Boxer struggled on the ground. Jabber was the strong one, facing the Death Wrangler, saving them all.

He offered Jabber his hand. "That was really smart. I owe you. I should have listened when you said not to go into the labyrinth," Jack said, struggling to admit his mistake out loud.

"You don't owe me. It wasn't *you* I was saving." Jabber brushed the dirt off of his top hat and secured it back on his head without shaking Jack's hand. "Now let's go home."

When they got back to camp, it was fully light and Violet was stirring a big bubbling pot of oatmeal over the campfire. She looked up as Jack passed by.

"I suppose you want your breakfast now that you're back."

"Sure. Did you kill that oatmeal all by yourself?" he tried to joke, but he was too tired; his arms and legs felt like limp rubber bands.

Violet's eyes went wide. She reached out and touched a scratch on Jack's cheek that he didn't even know he had. "What happened? Boxer didn't hurt you, did he?"

"No, it was my fault. I screwed up and put us in danger. And what's worse, I knew I was doing it and did it anyway."

"This place is dangerous. It's not like back there. Your old home."

Runt ran up and squeezed between Jack and Violet. "Violet, I'm going back to bed. Wake me for lunch, please." Runt went into the tent, and Jack tried to follow before Jabber stopped him.

"I'll take this." Jabber took Jack's duffel bag. "Mussini wants to have a word with you, and I wouldn't keep him waiting."

Jabber walked Jack to the Amazing Mussini's tent. Through the flap Jack could see the inside of the tent was much more luxurious than their humble hammocks. Persian carpets covered the ground, and jewel-toned lanterns cast a colorful glow. Silky pillows littered a round futon on the floor. It looked like the *Arabian Nights* had exploded all over the place.

Jabber pushed Jack inside the tent and nodded to a stool for Jack to sit on. Mussini didn't face him, but whirled a thick bristle brush in a bowl, working up a lather of shaving foam.

"I summoned you here to discuss your act in the show."

"You're not angry at me for trying to escape?"

"Your escape was anticipated, Jack. I don't waste my time on unnecessary emotions. When I'm angry with you, you will know it, and I won't send a bunch of kids in masks to get you back. I'll send the real Death Wranglers, and they're twice the size of Boxer."

"Yes, sir." Jack reddened. Mussini had seen right through him. "Listen—can I just go home? I miss Mildred." It was a futile attempt, but Jack had to ask. He sighed and sunk down into a cushion, too sweaty and exhausted to think of a clever argument.

"Never mind about the other side. We are your family now. This is your home." With his face half-covered in shaving cream, Mussini stared at himself in a mirror.

"I don't think he's convinced, Mussini," Jabber said. "Seems recklessness is in his blood."

Mussini dragged a razor down each of his rough cheeks and wiped what was left of the foam from his face. Then he lifted a thin oilcloth blanket from his dresser, exposing a collection of long, sharp throwing knives. "Lovely, aren't they? My first act onstage was throwing knives at a pretty girl who shook like a scared lamb. I was very good back then, never even nicked her delicate skin. Knives relax me." His hands wavered over the deadly instruments like a surgeon selecting a scalpel. Snatching one up, without a second's hesitation, Mussini spun the blade in the air, and it pierced the wooden support beam of the tent above Jack's head as if spearing an invisible apple. Jack flinched and eyed the wobbling blade handle, mere millimeters from his scalp.

"Illusion is half skill, half lie. These beauties demand real talent." Mussini picked up another knife and inspected the blade, pointing it at Jack. Then he suddenly rushed toward him, his face so close Jack got a good whiff of shaving cream and a good look at Mussini's eyes. "You have no idea what it's like to be dead. I can never go back to the real world as the man I was and breathe fresh air into my lungs." Mussini pulled away, circling the tent. "Circumstances change. Magic was my life back then, but here, in the Land of the Dead, I have made it my destiny."

Mussini removed his outer shirt and stood in front of Jack in a white undershirt. He leaned one of his biceps toward Jack so that he could get a good look at the huge tattoos that covered both arms. Each tattoo was of a woman. One was a wicked redhead with a stunning face and devilish grin, and the other was a pale, angelic woman with a cascade of blond hair around her shoulders. Jack swallowed, mesmerized by Mussini and the beautiful women inked into his skin forever.

"I am in the middle of two beautiful women. One is my heaven; one is my hell. I can never leave the forest, Jack. All I have is the show. Nothing will stop it. Do I have your word you won't try and escape again?"

"I'm not making any promises. Especially ones I can't keep." Jack stood his ground, wanting to see just how much chain Mussini was going to give him before yanking him back. Foolish, perhaps, especially standing face-to-face with a man whose relaxing hobby was throwing knives at people, but Jack knew that to show a sign of weakness was worse than a sign of insolence. And he was sick of being afraid.

Mussini grabbed the knife out of the splintered wood above Jack's head and set it back on the dresser. Turning around, he pulled the neck of his shirt down. Jack expected to see another tattoo on Mussini's chest, but what he saw caused his stomach to drop to his shoes. He reeled away from the man, stumbled backward over the stool, and fell onto the carpet. It was grotesque and wondrous at the same time. Beneath his shirt, a huge patch of skin over Mussini's chest was clear, almost translucent, like a sheet of plastic wrap. Under the thin surface of clear skin, his bloody heart was still beating, thumping in his body; pumping blood through a dead man. It couldn't be real.

"What are you?" Jack gasped.

"A magician!" Mussini glowered at Jack. He adjusted his shirt and grinned.

"But you're dead," Jack said.

"Technically, yes, I am dead, but my heart refuses to die. A man is nothing without heart, Jack. Illusion is everything, even if it isn't real."

Jack stumbled to his feet. Now he knew why Mussini wasn't afraid of anything. He had already conquered death. Jabber pulled the handcuffs out of Jack's bag and set them on the table in front of the Amazing Mussini.

"What do we have here?" Mussini swung one of the handcuffs around on his finger.

Jack tried to grab the cuffs from Mussini. "Hey, those are mine."

"He's good with them, quick, too," Jabber said. "You should have seen him trap Boxer. I thought maybe he could use them in his act."

"Our escapist. Our handcuff magician." Mussini grinned at Jack. "It's brilliant!"

Mussini turned to Jabber. "Help him. We'll put him on early to test him out. See how he does. Oh, this is interesting. I might have actually gotten my trouble's worth for this scrap."

Jack followed Jabber out of the tent. "What was that all about?"

"We get into the next town tomorrow, and if I were you, I would start worrying about my act."

Jack stuffed his handcuffs back into his duffel bag. "I don't have an act."

"You're either a magician or you're deadweight," Jabber said.

"I guess if those are my choices, I'd rather be a magician than dead."

"We'll help you and get you anything you need. Trust me—it's only utterly terrifying the first dozen or so times. Then it gets *slightly* terrifying."

"What does?" Jack asked.

Jabber smiled. "Performing for the dead."

Minor Illusions

After leaving Mussini's tent, Jack wandered over to the campfire, which was now just a mound of smoldering coals. A good stoke and some kindling would set the fire ablaze again, or the coals, if left alone, would cool off and die down to ash. That's how Jack felt, like he could go either way. Being threatened only made Jack more determined to get out, but after seeing Mussini for the monster he truly was, Jack knew he couldn't do it alone. He needed allies. He rested his back up against a tree and stared down into the glowing coals. His shoulders relaxed against the bark. Exhaustion overwhelmed him. His head bobbed. His eyes fluttered closed.

A deep guttural moan echoed from the distant woods. The Death Wranglers! Startled, Jack jumped to his feet, but when he stared down at himself, he was wearing Jabber's black clothes and top hat. Mussini and Jabber tromped through the woods toward him, dragging a long chain between them. Jack couldn't move, but could only watch them advance. Mussini wrapped the heavy links of chain around and around, cocooning Jack in the heavy metal.

"Stop it! Let me go!" Jack screamed, but Mussini ignored his pleas and continued winding the chains from his feet to his neck. Off in the distance, the wooden doors of dozens of hatches to the labyrinth opened up at once. The huge, armored bodies of Death Wranglers poured out of the underworld with swords in hand. Cries of battle filled the air as they ran toward him faster than he thought beasts that big capable.

"Let's see how brave you are now." Jabber shoved Jack, encased in his metal-chain cocoon, to the ground and covered him in a pile of dry leaves. The ground rumbled and shook under the heavy boots of the army headed right for him.

"Fine, bring it on." Jack squeezed his eyes shut but within seconds felt hands grabbing the chains and shaking him. But when he opened his eyes, it was Professor Hawthorne. "You came for me!" Jack exclaimed. "Hurry, Professor, the Death Wranglers are coming."

The professor's clothes were rumpled, his hair a wild mess. He yanked Jack up to a sitting position and looked *into his eyes, but he didn't loosen the chains. "Listen to me. Stay out of the labyrinth, my boy. Don't go underground. There is another way. Be cunning. Use Mussini's magic against him."*

"Help me, Professor. You can't leave me here."

"I'm sorry, my boy. I can't save you. They're coming." The professor's image wavered. He drifted backward and melted into the forest. Jack thumped over into a pile of leaves, the chains weighing him down. His head hit the ground that trembled with the force of the approaching Death Wranglers.

"Let me go! Let me go!" Jack yelled, and suddenly the shaking stopped. He was awake, lying on the ground, surrounded by strangely masked faces.

A sharp-beaked bird cocked its head to the side. "You fell asleep."

"Must have had a bad dream." A short gray mouse wearing a black jacket inched closer to him. A huge bear-masked kid wearing a T-shirt lifted him to his feet and dusted him off.

"Boxer, is that you?" Jack asked.

Boxer pulled off the bear mask. "Are you OK? You were calling out and shaking on the ground."

Jack ran his hands through his sweat-drenched hair. "I'm fine."

"Don't worry. The nightmares go away eventually." Runt lifted his mouse mask up off his face and gave Jack a light punch on the arm. "The Halloween tour will take your mind off of it."

"What's the Halloween tour?" Jack asked, hoping that might explain the masks they were wearing.

"Our show just started our Halloween tour. We travel from town to town all leading up to the finale on October thirty-first," Boxer explained.

"Halloween's the best night! It's the Night of the Dead," Runt said. "When the living and the dead can hang out. No rules, just scary fun. I can't wait. There will be magic and costumes and candy and music."

"And mayhem and ghosts and goblins," Violet said.

"Time to practice your act. Come on." Boxer slung Runt over his shoulder and headed toward a clearing in the trees. Runt leaned up and yelled, "Don't worry, Jack. You still have time to get your act together before Halloween."

Halloween was weeks away, and Jack didn't want to think about being stuck in the forest that long. He watched as the others went about their routines, preparing the sets and costumes for the show. The campsite looked like a carnival garage sale. The lids of trunks hung wide open, their contents strewn around the forest floor. Yards of crushed velvet stretched out, and colorful costumes, bicycle wheels, and musical instruments littered the leafy ground. A group of upended crates with a board on top formed a worktable, which was covered with tubs of water and white paste. Gigantic forms, which looked like the skeletons of metal creatures with skinny metal bones, covered the makeshift table.

Jack looked at Violet. "What's with the masks?"

"You put it on your face and you become something else," Violet said, raising an eyebrow in his direction.

"I know what masks are, but what are you making them for?" Jack toyed with a thin strip of metal. On closer inspection, the finished masks were remarkably lifelike and decorated with brilliant colors and fabrics, fur and feathers. Wild animal masks and exotic long-beaked bird masks littered the table next to mythical beasts and glittery fairies.

"The masks are for the audience. It makes the dead feel like part of the show," T-Ray said from his seat near the makeshift table. "Plus, it's more fun to wear a mask. It's a relief not to have to be yourself all the time."

Jack motioned to a box of paper that T-Ray held in his lap. "What are those?"

"They're part of the show."

Jack dug his hand into the box and picked out one of the paper birds. The box was filled with frogs and dragonflies, butterflies and bears, all made of paper that looked like it had been torn out of a school notebook.

"You made these?"

"Yes, and I've gotten pretty good. When I first got here, all I could make were paper airplanes. But I practiced really hard, and now I can make anything out of paper."

Jack tried to imagine how long it would take to learn how to make the beautiful paper creatures. "How'd you get here? Mussini trick you, too?" Jack asked.

T-Ray pulled a worn-out Spider-Man comic book out of his back pocket. "It was all for him."

Jack smiled. "What did Spidey ever do to you?"

"There was this comic book store near the apartment I lived in with my mom that I went to all the time. It used to be a magic shop before it went out of business, and the guy who owned it decided to sell comics instead. One day I noticed some old boxes in the storeroom, and I snuck back to see if the guy had some old comics that might be worth a lot of money."

"Did you find any good ones?"

"No, but there were lots of leftover magic tricks and stuff. That's when I found this really cool jewelry box with an *M* carved on the lid. My mom's name is Meesha, and I thought she might like it. The owner of the shop wasn't using any of that junk in the back. He probably wouldn't have even missed it. So I took the box home and opened it. Turned out the *M* stood for Mussini. He came for me that night. I've been here ever since."

"That stinks." Jack shook his head. "The professor used a trunk to trap me."

"I miss my mom. Do you really think—"

Jabber kicked through the leaves, cutting T-Ray off. "Jack, Mussini said I should help you out. Show you the ropes."

Digging into his duffel, Jack pulled out three pairs of regulation handcuffs, the kind that cops use, nothing fancy or vintage, and set them on the table. Not what anyone would call an illustrious collection.

Jabber picked up one of Jack's handcuffs and then tossed it back on the table, unimpressed. "This is all you've got?"

"Yep. That's it."

"Maybe we can get some more," T-Ray said, slipping his fist into one of the cuffs. Jack closed the cuff around his wrist and T-Ray's eyes widened. "Hey."

"We're going to have to. The act has got to be good. The dead have very discerning tastes," Jabber said. "What do you really want? Mussini can get you anything."

Jack pulled the Houdini picture out of his pocket. "What about these?" He pointed to the length of handcuffs that encircled Houdini's wrist. There were seven vintage handcuffs total, beginning with the Russian manacle and ending with the Berliner. Jack didn't expect that Jabber could really get them. Maybe he could dig up a Darby-style cuff somewhere. Maybe even one of the dead was still wearing it, locked around his guilty wrists. He suspected that a few of the criminal kind were among the dead in the forest.

Jabber and T-Ray stared down at the photograph as T-Ray still struggled to get the handcuff off of his wrist. "Those look impossible to get out of," T-Ray said. "That's a good act if you can do it."

"A little ambitious, don't you think?" Jabber asked.

"You asked me what I wanted. Can you get the handcuffs or not?"

"There's nothing Mussini and I can't get. I suppose you want the keys, too."

"Of course I'll need the keys. It's not like I'm going to wave a magic wand to get out of them. The act is all one big trick, like Mussini said: half skill, half lie."

"You should start with just a few. Maybe just one or two, and one of those easy ones that you brought." Jabber motioned to Jack's handcuffs. "We don't want you falling on your face the first time onstage."

T-Ray held up his manacled wrist. "Someone get it off of me."

"Will you need anything else for your act?" Jabber asked.

"I'll need a black box with a hole in the top and a curtain on one side." Jack unlocked the handcuff attached to T-Ray's wrist.

"How big should the box be?" Jabber asked.

"Big enough for me to fit inside."

"You mean like a coffin." Jabber smiled devilishly.

"Real funny, Jabber."

As night fell, they packed up the wagon. Only one tent was left up for the boys to sleep in, while Violet slept in the wagon. Up ahead, Mussini, dressed in his long black traveling coat and black boots, slipped the gold mask of a hawk over his face. Half man, half predator, Jack thought as he watched Mussini sweep out into the night.

"Where's he going?" Jack asked.

"He's going to check out the next town. We'll catch up with him in the morning. You better get some sleep. Tomorrow starts early, and the real fun begins."

It was early morning when Jack rolled over to the sound of the wagon being closed up, and it felt like he had just fallen asleep. Still groggy, Jack leaned up and rubbed the sleep from his eyes. The camp had been broken down, the chill of morning hung in the air. Violet handed Jack a biscuit wrapped in a handkerchief before she disappeared into the back of the wagon. Stuffing the biscuit into his mouth, Jack ran his hands through a bucket of water that had been left on the ground for him to wash up.

"Better hurry. We're leaving in few minutes."

Jack washed his face and changed his clothes. He tossed his duffel bag into the back of the wagon and stared around at the misty campsite. It was as empty as if they were never there at all. Climbing up, Jack sat next to Jabber as he jolted the reins and the horses pulled the wagon to a slow crawl. He rubbed his arms to warm up a little and looked over his shoulder as the carriage rolled along, Mussini ahead of them, the wall behind them, and the Death Wranglers beneath.

Freak Show

The best freaks are born that way.
They wake up from the womb and all eyes are on them.
An obvious oddity to be kept under glass,
held down by a thin, sharp pin.

The circus is full of them,
displayed in cages and on pedestals.
They are the real moneymakers, ten-cent draws.

The crowds shove and stare, witnessing
a human reminder that life is so much weirder and wilder
than ordinary mortals can imagine.

Harry joins the circus,
performing in the curio halls and dime museums,
alongside acrobats, greyhounds and clowns,
dog boys and wild men.

He makes friends with his fellow performers.
Count Orloff with his thin glass skin
that looks like a stained-glass window

to view his heart beating in his chest, his body a church,
a temple of chemical miracles.

He will write to them in years to come,
remembering their small kinship in the freak show.

Under the big top the crowds pours in.
Look! Look! Come and see:
The world is filled with living wonders.

12

Mister Amazing

The wagon ambled toward the town like a prehistoric mammoth. The wheels groaned as the painted beast lurched along the beat-up road. Ahead, the town sprouted up in the trees like a wild bunch of mushrooms. The buildings seemed to have come directly from different times in history, a patchwork of eras pieced together. Medieval thatched huts gave way to stone cottages and brick-and-mortar taverns. No two buildings were the same. Jack marveled at the surroundings, and how even in the Land of the Dead, people gathered together and held on to a sense of normalcy.

As the wagon ambled along, Jack watched the dead. They seemed just like ordinary people, until he looked a little closer. Then he could see the telltale sign of death in their hazy bluish skin, as if they were dusted with a thin coat of ash. It was kind of like they were disintegrating right before his eyes, the way stone statues melt from the force of wind and rain. The residents of the town all dressed in clothes from various times, as if they had been plucked from different slots on a time line. The dead stopped and gathered in tight knots, whispering and gawking as the wagon went by.

Mussini, wearing his golden hawk mask, appeared as a flash of gold moving through the crowd. Without a word, Jabber snapped the reins. The crowd parted as the golden hawk advanced, clearing a path for Mussini. A few people cast their eyes down or gave a nod or a slight bow to the hawk. Jack felt a tingle of pride at the respect Mussini was shown, although it might have been respect out of fear. Goose bumps multiplied on Jack's arms. The air crept up behind him and rubbed his shoulders, and he jerked his head around to make sure no one was there. Jabber must have sensed his nerves.

"Don't worry. We're almost to the theater. You'll get used to the dead. Soon you might even like it here."

"'Like' is a strong word."

Finally, the wagon came to a sudden jerky halt at the bottom of a crude wooden platform. A wheel must have broken, Jack thought, because this couldn't possibly be the place. The stage was a dismal barren slab of wood set at the bottom of a clearing. Rows of butt-numbing wooden benches stretched out from the stage until the worn and dented hillside took over. It was not exactly the ideal locale for a show, and not even a good place for a picnic. Boxer threw back the curtain, jumped out of the wagon, and started to unpack their gear.

"We have arrived," Jabber said with a grin. Smiling, he looked almost alive.

"This is it? There isn't anything here, just a wooden stage and benches," Jack said, not budging from his spot on the wagon.

"Were you expecting the life of a thespian to be glamorous?" Jabber asked.

"Not fancy or anything. Just not so . . . pathetic."

"It's a little sparse, perhaps, but full of potential."

"Potential disaster."

"All it needs is a little spit and polish."

Jack jumped down and followed Jabber, who was clearly delirious if he thought this was the place to put on a show. At the very least, Jack expected the theater to be indoors.

"Was a roof too much to hope for?" Jack asked.

"It's called alfresco, doofus," Runt said as he sprang from the back of the wagon and leaped around the stage like a spring-loaded toad.

"Is that Italian for 'we can't afford a roof'?"

Jabber adjusted his hat. "Just wait and see. We might surprise you."

Setting up the theater was a sweaty, blister-raising, labor-intensive challenge. Bolts of deep-red canvas were unrolled and pitched high above the stage on tall poles. Pulling and heaving, they raised the fabric like hoisting the sails of a ship on spindly masts. Yards of velvet, draped over the top, created a curtain. Runt lined the lip of the stage with elaborate paper lanterns and dropped a candle down into each one.

After hours of work, Jack rested his back against the leafy hillside. He wiped sweat from his forehead. As the sky darkened, the luminaries cast an eerie glow on the theater that they had transformed from an ugly slab of wood into an enchanting, man-made illusion.

The next day, Jabber brought Jack a box and some vintage handcuffs with the keys as requested. He tossed the heavy steel onto the ground at Jack's feet: two Darbies and a Russian manacle. Cool. Jack lined them up on the ground, inspecting each one in turn. The metal was blackened and worn, smooth in his hands. Rusted old joints, probably stiff. He hoped the locks still worked. Slipping the key into each lock, it felt like he was loosening the shackles of a tin man. But they worked. The keys fit.

The Darby was the easier of the two handcuffs to maneuver due to the link of chain that hung between the two cuffs. The Russian manacle was a different story; two great loops were connected with a large lock that hung like a clock face. It was heavier, and there was no play between the two thick metal bars that held his wrists. But, as Houdini would say, it wouldn't be a challenge if it were easy. For the rest of the day, Jack practiced with the handcuffs and planned out his act.

Then he was ready for his dress rehearsal. Jabber sat in the gallery and watched as Jack stood on the stage and practiced his tricks.

"It's not what you can do, but what you make the audience *believe* you can do. It's called showmanship," Jabber yelled up to him.

"I know what it is."

The soul of Houdini, now *that* was the soul of a showman. Jack admired that about him. But unlike Houdini, Jack would rather face a firing squad than a room full of people staring at him, especially if they were dead. He wasn't a center-of-attention kind of guy. Jabber was making him nervous, so Jack wandered off alone to practice with his new cuffs.

The problem was that Jack wasn't sure he could do it. He always imagined himself in the midlands of success, the number three or four guy down—the bronze medal winner. He always wondered about those people who really believed in their guts that they were number one, the top dog, the king. Were they born knowing, or did they just decide one day? Mussini was like that, and Houdini believed obsessively in his own great destiny. Jack wanted to believe he had a destiny. Maybe performing for the dead would force him to find out.

Darkness on opening night brought a clamor of activity backstage. Jack paced back and forth, rehearsing his act in his head. He peeked out from behind the curtain. An emotional soup of nerves, excitement, and dread stirred up in him as he watched. Young and old, the dead found their seats and eagerly slipped on their masks, ready for the show to begin.

Dressed in a suit and bowtie, Runt strode onto the stage with his chest pushed out. He roared into the megaphone, a lion in a boy's body. *Ready or not.* Jack wiped his sweaty palms on his pants. The red velvet curtains swung back in a jerking motion as T-Ray pulled on the rope and suddenly all eyes, behind the glittering masks, were on Jack. He opened his mouth, but nothing came out. His voice caught in his throat, and he coughed.

"Ladies and gentlemen!" Runt bellowed into his megaphone and glanced at Jack. "I present: the Kid!"

T-Ray carried out a painted board that read, simply: *The Kid.* Great. It might as well have read: *Goat* or *Pig* or *Loser.* No one made a peep. Jack's stomach growled loudly. A dead guy sitting a few feet away laughed. They all waited. Jack feared that at any second he would throw up on the entire front row.

"Um, good evening," Jack stammered.

"We'll tell you how good an evening it is when you're done!" an audience member yelled up at him.

"My assistant here is going to shackle my wrists with these handcuffs."

Jack held up the vintage handcuffs and two of his own. At that moment, he wished he wasn't using his handcuffs at all, so he could focus on one challenge. The crowd settled a bit. Then some guy in the back yelled, "Check his pockets to make sure he doesn't have keys!"

"Yeah, check his jacket and his shoes!" someone else yelled.

"The crowd's a feisty one tonight," Jabber whispered as he placed a pair of handcuffs on Jack's wrists.

"Don't put them on too tight," Jack whispered.

"I know." Jabber tightened the cuffs. "You look a little green."

"I'm fine. Now pat me down and pull my pockets inside out."

With dramatic flair, Jabber showed the crowd that Jack had nothing up his sleeves or nothing concealed in his pockets. Jack had the keys hidden right under his shirt at his collarbone, so if anyone from the audience insisted on patting him down, they wouldn't feel the keys, yet he could reach them with his mouth if he had to.

"And now I will enter the box." Jack nodded toward the box, but when he raised his hands, the metal twisted around his wrists—the string of cuffs was heavier than he thought, the weight pulling him forward. As Jack stared into the sea of masks, his stomach churned. Jabber pulled the curtain back, Jack stepped inside the empty black box, and Jabber closed the curtain behind him.

Immediately, Jack snatched the key from his collarbone and went to work on the handcuffs. His heart raced. He felt like he was back inside the cart on the night he first arrived—a captive of his own trick. He panicked and went out of order. He was going to undo his cuffs first and then the vintage cuffs in order of difficulty, but he was too nervous and screwed it up. He got one of the Darbies off quickly and tossed it out of the curtain and onto the stage. Laughter exploded from the crowd—not a good sign. His act wasn't supposed to be funny, but watching a box was only interesting for about a minute, tops. The dead shuffled in their seats, whispering and coughing. The box was suffocating, and his collar was too tight. His sweaty fingers slipped on the metal. It was taking him too long to get the cuffs off. Jack sensed the crowd's restlessness, now plummeting into a state of boredom, hallmarked by raucous laughter sprinkled with chatter, catcalls, assorted snorts, boos, and other lowbrow grunts.

Runt peeked under the curtain, and then shimmied inside the box next to Jack. "Just so you know—you're bombing big-time."

"Thanks for telling me, because the deafening boos

didn't tip me off." Jack tried to focus on the lock and not his impending fiasco on stage. "It's my first time. The crowd can't be *that* bad."

"They're throwing stuff, if that's any sign. Pretty ingenious that you put yourself into a box, so you didn't get hit by the garbage."

"The dead are throwing garbage?"

"Mostly rotten vegetables. I barely missed getting beheaded by a rotten cabbage. Don't let it get you down. We all bombed our first time." Runt patted his shoulder. "It's much more fun to watch you bomb instead of it being me."

"I'm glad my failure makes you feel good about yourself." Jack tried twisting the key in the lock, but had to use his teeth to turn it.

Runt held his forearm over his face. "I'm headed out. Cover me."

Long moments later, the last cuff was off. It was almost over. Jabber poked his head inside the box.

"You better do something and quick. I've never seen the dead like this before. I heard whispering of a lynching."

"A lynching just because they don't like my act?"

"Tough break, kid."

"You're going to let them lynch me?"

"Showbiz is a heartless calling. I'm not about to risk *my* neck."

"But your neck is already dead. It won't matter if they lynch you."

"Jack, I still have feelings." Jabber touched his neck. "You better come up with something. What would your friend Houdini do?"

"We aren't actually friends. I just like him."

"Why?" Jabber asked.

"For one, he made escape seem easy."

"Ah, but it's not, is it?" Jabber nodded.

"No. It's hard. If they only knew how hard it was, they wouldn't be so smug." And then Jack got an idea.

"If you survive, chap, we'll all be hiding backstage waiting." Jabber ducked out of the box.

The jeers and boos escalated, if that was even possible. Grudgingly, Jack threw back the curtain and bounded out of the safety of the box. The stage resembled a salad—a dead, rotten salad. Heads of lettuce and cabbage were scattered among rotten potatoes, crushed pumpkins, and squashed tomatoes. Runt was right; it was a good thing he had been in the box. The dead were ruthless.

"Be quiet!" Jack yelled. "Be quiet and listen! Listen to me!"

Jack held up the great Russian manacle that only seconds before lay discarded on the stage.

"Does anyone know what this is?"

A hushed silence fell over the crowd, and again all eyes were on him.

"Come on. Anyone?"

Jack walked down into the crowd. "You, beautiful lady. Can you guess?" The woman shied away from Jack, shaking her head and giggling behind her sparkling mask. Jack turned to a man a row back. "What about you, sir. You look like a worldly, intelligent man. Know what this is?"

But before the man could answer, a voice yelled from the throng, "A handcuff!" A few choked laughs followed, but the crowd kept their eyes on Jack, who jumped to the edge of the stage and held the manacle up like a prize.

"None of you seem familiar with it, and that shouldn't surprise me, because if you were familiar, and I mean really familiar with this, *the Russian manacle,* you wouldn't be here watching the show. You would most certainly be roasting in hell with some of the most ferocious and heartless criminals who ever dared march across the steppes of Russia." Jack paused for effect and held the cuffs up. "It's kind of shaped like a heart, isn't it? It replaces the one the vile murderers were born without. The manacle was saved for only the vilest, most heartless of beasts. It's considered impossible to escape, or so you should hope, unless the wearer loses a hand or two. And you laughed at me. Maybe I earned this cuff. Did you ever think of that?"

Jack jumped down onto a small bit of space on the bench in the front row. The dead gasped. But Jack just tossed the cuffs to Jabber, who, with a nod from Jack, threw him one of the Darby-style handcuffs.

"But wait, look at this one." Jack held one cuff in each fist, and he pulled on them, rattling the chain in between. "This, my new friends, is the Darby. Scotland Yard slapped it on the wrists of their most treacherous murderers. They would have put these same manacles on the butcher Jack the Ripper. That is, if they had ever caught him. Maybe he's here now, tonight, watching the show and waiting. I challenge bloody Jack the Ripper to escape these cuffs I have tonight. But I don't think he's got the guts to try them on, do you?"

The dead were enraptured. They shook their heads in disbelief.

"Do any of you have the guts to try them on? Come on! Anyone want to try on my pretty bracelets? Any ladies? Any gentlemen? You can keep them, if you can get out of them. Take them home as a present."

The dead laughed at the joke. Jack took his bow and walked off the stage.

"Now that was more like it!" Jabber said, patting him on the back.

Jack kept walking, then turned back to Jabber and said, "They never were going to lynch me, were they? You made that bit up?"

"Yes, I did. And look what it brought out in you. The fighter! Just needed the right incentive."

"Fear of lynching is a great motivator."

Jack shook his head and watched the other acts from the side of the stage. He couldn't be too mad at Jabber—he was just glad to be off. Jabber went next. A Renaissance kid, he could act, sing, play almost any instrument, ride a unicycle, and juggle. He and Violet did a funny skit where Jabber pretended to be a wolf dressed up like Violet's grandmother, Little Red Riding Hood style. He chased her around the stage, and then she pretended to throw a bucket of water on him. The dead gasped.

"The dead hate water," T-Ray said while he and Jack watched the act from the wings.

"Why?" Jack asked.

"They just do. I guess even the dead are afraid of something."

Over and over, Violet pretended to throw the water and the dead gasped and laughed. Finally, she spun around and threw the water out of the bucket onto the audience, and they screamed until they realized it was just glittery confetti and not really water at all. Applause filled the theater.

Next, Violet sang a haunting song while Jabber played the violin. The spotlight glowed on her skin, and her voice rose up like a sad angel's. Jack was captivated by her sweet, lonely voice, but the dead were restless. They chatted among themselves, not listening to the song.

Boxer went on next. His act was simplicity itself: the Strongest Kid Alive! He broke things, bent things, and tossed them around. The dead ate it up. Boxer lifted a bench, which the dead were sitting on, high above his head. He grunted and strained against the weight of six people. The audience cheered.

"They aren't that heavy. After they die, they get lighter, like shells," T-Ray whispered. "But they don't know that."

The finale was next. The thrill of the crowd was infectious, and their energy and excitement spread over Jack, rippling through the air like an invisible ocean rising and crashing at his feet. T-Ray ran through the aisles depositing his paper creations, pulling handfuls of them out of a basket and dropping them to the ground. He wove his way in between the dead, dropping in their laps paper butterflies and goats, dragonflies and frogs, bears and hawks.

A clap of thunder erupted from above, and the Amazing Mussini stepped onto the stage. The Amazing Mussini was the only one in the theater not wearing a mask, and the contrast between him and everyone else was striking. He was instantly set apart, so superhuman and alive, as if he wanted the crowd to know immediately that his powers were not a trick.

Exaggerated, bold, and confident, every expression on Mussini's face played to the crowd. He wiggled his fingers. He raised his arms and flapped them like a bird, to hoots and howls of laughter. Jack couldn't figure out the game. He danced around the stage like a madman, spinning, leaping, and squawking into the sky like an exotic bird. T-Ray banged on a snare drum, building in intensity. Jack could feel the rhythm of it in his chest. The anticipation in the theater rose to a pinnacle, until suddenly, something stirred, and there was a gasp followed by a small cry.

Jack stared into the crowd, his eyes caught by movement in the audience. The drum sputtered and stopped. The paper creatures stirred up from the floor, but they didn't float like paper airplanes tossed aimlessly to the ground. They rose up as if by will. They flew, stretching new wings. They crawled to life. Jack gasped. They were real. The butterflies drifted between the audience members. Zinging dragonflies and swooping hawks filled the air with sheer glassine wings and crimson feathers. A tiger lazily ambled down the aisle. A bear cub bounded down off of the stage.

It was truly amazing. Mussini gave the dead the one thing they craved more than anything: He gave life to the lifeless. Gasps were followed by laughter and applause. The dead jumped to their feet and begged for more. They pulled off their masks to get closer to these beautiful creatures, rubbing their cold cheeks against soft warm fur. The stage lights twinkled on the thrumming air as beating hearts sparked to life.

Jack reached out his hand as a butterfly floated by, and the creature landed for a brief second on his outstretched finger. No wonder the dead had hated his act; all he gave them was cold, hard steel. They'd had enough of that. Mussini gave them the best gift of all—a taste of life, a stunning spectacle of wings and fur, of beating hearts.

And like the greatest of showmen, after a few minutes, Mussini took it all away. The animals soon fell to the ground, returning once again to their paper shells. He made the audience want to see the act again to get them coming back, show after show! That was the beauty of the trick and the test of a true showman. Jack jumped to his feet and clapped as loudly as the dead.

The Handcuff King

Harry needs an angle,
some slant of magic to set him apart
from the sleight-of-hand artists, the brother acts,
the mystics and conjurers.
He needs to escape the ordinary act.

Danger is a good lure.
Criminals and the law that lays them down
have a lot in common.
Experts in the steel laces,
they study the twisted metal labyrinth.

Harry can see inside with his X-ray mind,
his perfect memory for the lock face,
as if she were a long-lost love, a mistress of cold metal,
manacles, shackles, chains, and cells,
but she will not hold him in her long thin arms for long.

He never leaves anything to chance,
replaying every horrific scenario.
Humiliation is a terrible way to die.
The Challenge is littered with pitfalls:
broken locks and jammed insides.

He makes sure the cuffs open and close,
like doors and windows.

Cuffs snaking up his wrists burn and twist.
The hushed audience sways back and forth,
he holds their fragile attention with his charm,
caught in his allure.

His wrists strung up with cuff after cuff,
a boy king adorned with golden rings.
But Houdini has a thousand keys
to release his locked-up kingdom.

13

Dead Ringer

Jack couldn't sleep. The rest of the troupe had gone back to their tents behind the stage, but the thrill of the show coursed through his body like a current of electricity, and he stood at the edge of the stage to relive the moment one more time. The dead were gone. They were probably sound asleep by now, tucked in their beds. As he stared out at the empty rows of seats, Jack wondered if the dead dreamed, and if so, what they dreamed about.

At one of his foster homes, Jack lived next door to a really old guy, and when Jack was bored he used to sneak over and stare at him sitting out on his back porch, watching the plants grow. Sometimes he and the man just sat, watching centipedes walk one tiny leg at a time across the cement patio like small, armored tanks. Bugs had a disgusting allure, especially caterpillars covered in spiky hair—their odd faces looked like masks slipped over their soft bodies.

Sometimes the old man fell asleep, his arms twitching in the chair. When he woke up, he told Jack that he dreamed himself young again, playing the guitar perfectly. His bent fingers and joints, twisted with arthritis, moved smooth and quick when he was asleep. He dreamed of the song spilling out over his fingers, the snap and play of the chords, the music breathing new life into his old body. Maybe that was what the dead dreamed of—hearing the song of their lives one more time, holding the music in their outstretched fingers. Maybe that was why Mussini's heart was still beating, because the show was his music.

Jack spotted T-Ray wandering through the theater aisles, picking up the paper animals and insects and putting them into a basket. He jumped down off the stage and joined him. Some of the folded paper creatures had gotten torn during the show and needed repair. T-Ray used some clear Scotch tape to mend a wing or a beak. Others were past repair, and T-Ray unfolded them and smoothed out the paper. "I'll have to make another lion," T-Ray said. "The big cats don't last long. I always have to make more of them after two or three shows."

Curiosity nagged at Jack. He wanted to know how Mussini did it. The animals were so real, but the magical feat was impossible. "How's the trick work?" Jack asked, but T-Ray just rolled his eyes.

"No way, man. No how." T-Ray shook his head.

"Come on. I want to be more like Mussini, learn how he does magic," Jack said.

"What do you take me for, a third grader?"

"You've got to know something." Jack propped his foot up on one of the benches. "I'm just gathering facts—information is power, T-Ray. The more I know about Mussini and how he does his magic, the better prepared I'll be to help us escape."

"You want leverage." T-Ray pushed a handful of paper animals down into the basket. "Can't you just enjoy the trick? It's always a disappointment once you find out how the trick is done."

"I won't be disappointed, trust me."

"I just fold the animals like he taught me," T-Ray said, resisting the temptation to spill his guts about what he knew about Mussini. He held up one of the paper animals to show Jack. "Look—the hawk, one of my favorites. He could just fly away from here, but not us. We're here to stay." T-Ray pulled his jacket up around his neck and shuddered.

"Don't tell me it's just folded-up pieces of paper." Jack held the paper tiger and rubbed his finger along the paper's edge. He winced and then examined his fresh paper cut as if the big cat had bitten him. "Its teeth sure weren't made of paper."

T-Ray sighed. "Mussini's been really good to me. I don't want to set off his temper." He set the basket down and rubbed his arms to ward off the cold.

"Mussini will never know, 'cause I'll never tell him." Jack gave the tiger back. Getting T-Ray to talk was like trying to get a hook out of a fish he had already caught. "Don't you want to get out of here and see your mom again?"

T-Ray grabbed Jack's wrist. "Don't talk about my mom!" Almost immediately the anger left him and he sighed, but he still held Jack's wrist tight. "Promise if he catches you that you won't tell him that I told you?"

"I promise. I swear," Jack pleaded, prying T-Ray's cold grip from his wrist.

Kicking the basket out of his way, T-Ray collapsed down on a bench. "Mussini keeps all his secrets in his tent. All his tricks are written down in a notebook that he has stashed in a trunk. That's what Jabber told me, anyway."

Great. Another trunk. The last trunk he broke into landed him in the forest. Jack could only imagine where he would end up if he went digging in Mussini's box of tricks.

"Have you ever looked inside the notebook to see how he does it?"

"Are you crazy? Mussini is always around." T-Ray glanced around the empty theater. "Even when he's not, he is. Like the Death Wranglers."

"Come on. You're not a little curious? You really don't want to know how he does it? How he brings the creatures to life?" Jack reached down and grabbed a handful of paper animals from the discarded basket and let them tumble from his fingers. "They weren't just paper animals anymore. They were living, breathing tigers and bears."

"Well sure, but if I knew, the trick would be ruined then. And I want it to last."

T-Ray had a point, because once Jack knew how a trick was done, it wasn't fun anymore. That was the downside of being a magician. The illusion was over. But he couldn't help it. Jack had to get that book. Not only could he learn the secret of the trick, but also he could see if there was anything in the book to use against Mussini.

"Hey, I bet that book is valuable." A realization filled him. "Really valuable."

"It's priceless. It's Mussini's most valuable possession." Shock washed over T-Ray's face. "No way! What are you going to do?"

"Nothing right *now*. I'm just thinking out loud. But if I could get my hands on that book, it might be the leverage we need to get out of here."

Both T-Ray and Jack jumped as Mussini's thunderous

voice erupted backstage. They rushed across the stage and slipped behind the heavy velvet curtain. Mussini stomped around, waving his arms wildly as he huffed and puffed. Tears streamed down Violet's face. He grabbed her by the hair. She yelped like a kitten being held up by the scruff. Like most adults Jack had encountered over his life span, Mussini's actions were purely self-serving. He was nice when nice got him what he wanted, and he was cruel when cruelty got him what he wanted, too. At times, Jack wondered where the butt-kicking patron saint of pushed-around kids was when he needed him, because he sure wasn't here. Jack clenched his fists. He couldn't stand watching Mussini yell at Violet.

"Stop it!" Jack blurted out. "Stop it! You're hurting her."

Mussini whirled around, tossing Violet to the ground. "Shut your mouth or I'll sack you." The huge man snorted and took a step toward Jack, then thought better of it, turned around, and stormed off. Jack and T-Ray rushed over to Violet.

"What's he talking about?" T-Ray said.

Violet stood up shakily and brushed the tears away from her face.

"Did he hurt you?" Jack said.

"He's angry at me again, T-Ray." Her violet-colored eyes glistened with tears.

T-Ray gave Violet a sympathetic look. "Because of the song."

Jack stared at the two of them, baffled. They obviously knew something he didn't.

"What was wrong with the song you sang? I thought it was nice—not that I'm an expert or anything."

"It was too depressing, too dull and boring, according to Mister Amazing," Violet said, crossing her arms.

"The dead want an upbeat act," T-Ray whispered to Jack.

"But the act with Jabber was great. Everyone was laughing." Jack couldn't figure it out. "One of the best of the night."

"It's not enough," Violet said. "It's never enough."

"Maybe we can help you. There has to be something we can do," Jack said.

"There is something!" The great hulking figure of Mussini pushed through the curtains, making them all jump. T-Ray fell over a trunk and onto the floor.

"What! What do you want me to do?" Violet recoiled from the man, wrapping her arms around herself.

Mussini sneered at Violet, as if he took the slight personally. "Get out! That's what you can do! You're fired."

"What?" Violet said, her eyes going wide. Her voice cracked. "But I haven't got anywhere to go."

Mussini threw the red cape that Violet wore for the wolf act at her. "Go work for someone else."

"No! She can't go." T-Ray scrambled to his feet and held on to Violet's skirt.

"If that's what you want, then I'll go." Violet faced T-Ray. "It's all right," she whispered, then turned and ran from the theater.

Everything had happened so fast that at first, Jack just stood there. Most of the time he stayed out of other people's arguments, but he couldn't let her go out into the streets all by herself.

Jack darted out of the theater and ran after Violet. She was quick. The streets were dark, lit by faint gas lanterns, giving the whole scene a haunting glow. He followed the shadow of her, the scarlet cape with the hood pulled over her head. He wandered behind her as she ran through the narrow streets, some paved with packed-down earth, and others paved with uneven stone. Violet slowed down. Jack matched her pace, catching his breath. Suddenly, she took off again. She must have seen him. Violet ran like someone was chasing her, but without direction. Jack had been moving through the dark streets of his life like that for a long time. It wasn't hard for him to keep up with her.

The smell of roasted meat wafted through the air. Jack's stomach growled, and he was relieved to see Violet duck inside a dingy tavern. Posted in the dirty window was a sign with *Help wanted* scribbled on it. He was about to walk into the shop when someone grabbed him from behind and pulled him down an alley. His feet were kicked out from under him as a storm of hands grabbed at his clothes and pulled him deeper into the dark crevices of brick, far from the meager streetlamps. He felt like he had been shoved into a meat locker and bounced between cold, hard bodies. The smell of wet earth was thick and cloying. Jack kicked and pulled out of his captors' hands. When he looked at the group of boys that surrounded him, he was sure of one thing—they were all dead.

A pale, gangly kid pushed his way forward. "Where've you been, Skimmer?"

"Skimmer? What's a skimmer?" Jack asked as he inched his way away from the group.

"Not a what, a who. And he's you. Why you been hiding?" The kid stuck his blue-tinged face so close that Jack felt a waft of cold air brush against him.

"You got the wrong guy. I'm not Skimmer." Jack glanced down the alley, looking for an escape route, but the group moved as if anticipating his need to run.

A kid wearing an old-fashioned newsboy cap hooked his thumbs under his suspenders and came forward. "I don't think that's him. He smells funny. Like grass."

The pale boy snorted and narrowed his eyes. "He sure looks like Skimmer." He sniffed and rubbed his chin. "Hey, wait a minute," he said as if slowly realizing the obvious. "You're not dead!"

Voices erupted among the group. Cold hands reached out and pushed him, closing in on him. Jack's back rubbed up against a brick wall.

"We should end it for him. Put him out of his misery," the newsboy said.

"I'm just fine," Jack said quickly. "I'm not in any misery."

"You will be. Didn't anyone tell you? We don't like your kind." A kid wearing a baseball jersey swung a well-worn bat near his head.

"Look, you guys got the wrong kid. I'm supposed to meet a friend, so just let me go and I'll be out of your way."

"The best way to get rid of your kind is to make you one of us," the pale boy said.

"Yeah, dead like us. Then you'll be normal. And not freakish." The newsboy snapped his suspenders.

Jack stood tall. "The dead liked me fine at the show last night. And Mussini likes me fine. I work for him, so unless you want to take my place, I'll be going."

The pale kid rolled up his sleeves, revealing stick-thin arms covered in cuts and scrapes, scars and old wounds. He smiled thinly. "I'm not afraid of Mussini. And Skimmer owes me, so since you're the best I got, you owe me."

"Owe you what?" Jack knew from experience his best bet to get out of this alley was to keep the kid talking, because if he was talking, he wasn't hitting.

"My share of the skim!" He snatched Jack up by the shirt, wide-eyed and manic. His clammy knuckles pressed into his neck. "And I'm getting it from you if I have to break every bone in your warm body."

THE CARNIVAL of LOST SOULS

"If you tell me what a skim is, maybe I can get it for you." Jack gritted his teeth as icy fists twisted into his skin.

The kid paused, seemingly thinking it over. Finally, he released his grasp and took a step back, giving Jack some room. "Skimmer's a skimmer. He cruises a crowd and skims stuff right out of their pockets and person. He was working our street, so he owes us a cut of the take."

"Skimmer's a thief?" Jack asked.

The baseball jersey kid poked Jack with his baseball bat. "You got it, Liver! Ha, get it? He's alive, so I called him Liver!"

"Liver! That's your new name. And since it's such a good name, we won't kill you right away, 'cause then it wouldn't be funny anymore," the pale kid said.

A whistle shot down the alley, pulling everyone's attention away. "It's Skimmer!"

"Skimmer's back!"

For a few seconds the kids completely ignored him as a shadowy figure wearing a dark jacket approached. Jack wanted to run, but he couldn't move. The closer Skimmer got, the more Jack felt stuck. He was looking at his own face, only paler, with dark blue shadows under his eyes and down his neck. Skimmer's expression shifted quickly—eyes darting, mind racing. He walked right up to Jack and held out his hand to shake, and Jack saw that each finger had a fat, gold ring on it. He gripped

Jack's hand too hard and Jack bit his lip. The other boys cheered as Skimmer held his hands up and wiggled his jeweled fingers.

"Is this what you boys were looking for?"

Skimmer pulled the rings off of his fingers one by one and passed out the stolen gifts. Bracelets and long gold chains spilled from up his sleeves. He showered the boys with gaudy golden loot.

Jack couldn't stop staring. Looking at Skimmer wasn't quite like staring into a mirror, but like looking at another version of himself—a copy. The closer he looked at Skimmer, the more he noticed all the little things that made them different. He was a little taller and not as thin as Skimmer. His hands weren't as rough. But the worst part was the look in Skimmer's eyes. It was dark and bitter. Prowling the streets of the underworld, stealing trinkets off the dead, was a life that left Skimmer looking drained, like a husk of a kid. And when Jack looked around, he realized all the kids looked that way.

"You looking to join the gang?" Skimmer asked.

"No. I was just minding my own business when these guys grabbed me."

"Maybe it's fate then. Or good luck. Are you a lucky kid?"

Jack thought about it for a nanosecond. "No, but I do OK."

"We could use someone like you. We could be a

team, seeing as you could be my long-lost brother. We could plunder these streets good. Join us."

"Can't. I work for Mussini. But I'll keep you in mind."

"So, what if we want you to stay? What then?" The pale kid's pockets overflowed with gold chains.

"Let him go." Skimmer held up his hand. "He'll come around."

"Thanks, but I doubt it."

"You haven't been here that long. You'll see."

Jack didn't stick around to argue. He took off down the alley, rounded the corner, and ducked into the tavern that Violet had gone into earlier.

He dove under the windowsill so he could hide and still get a good look at the street as the boys ran by. He was in the clear for now.

Firelight wavered behind an iron grate, and flickering candles lined the bar, giving the shadowy room a sense of uneasy activity. The dead took on a new aspect to him now. Patrons roared with laughter, sloshing their drinks on the tables. The bottoms of Jack's shoes stuck to the floorboards as he crept across the room.

Violet was talking to the bartender, whose arms were so hairy it looked like he was wearing long sleeves. He blew his nose into a rag, handed Violet a piece of paper, and went back to serving drinks. Hand-washing was a formality—the Forest of the Dead didn't really need a health code. Jack slid down into the seat next to Violet at a rickety table. She barely looked up at him.

"You're a fast runner," he said. "Especially for someone wearing a long skirt."

Violet tried to smile, but it wasn't a convincing one. They ordered a meaty stew and crusty bread. Jack shoveled the food into his mouth. Violet pushed her spoon through the stew, not taking more than a few bites.

"It won't be so bad working here." She glanced up at Jack. A group of rowdy dead guys in the corner tossed chewed-on corncobs and chicken bones onto the floor while they guzzled down mug after mug of murky ale. "Though some of the patrons have deplorable table manners."

"Talk about a dead-end job." Jack couldn't imagine Violet working in a dump like this. Since his recent run-in with the dead gang, he realized how dangerous the dead were, and being alone made her a vulnerable target.

"It was sweet of you to come. But you shouldn't be here. Mussini will fire you, and then you'll be no better off than me."

"I'm not going to just leave you here. It's not safe." Jack glanced out the window.

"That's very noble, but I don't need rescuing. But you could help me fill out this application." Violet brushed some bread crumbs off of the highly stained paper. "Obviously I'm not the first to apply for the job," Violet said, attempting to find a place on the page where a name hadn't been written in and scratched out.

"At least they recycle." Jack could only imagine what had happened to the previous applicants.

"Let's see. Name—Violet. Skills—hmm. Well, I can sing terribly boring songs and dance a little and oh, yes, recite dreadfully long monologues by heart."

"I wouldn't put that down." Jack glanced around the room. "I don't think you want to entertain in a place like this."

"Oh, right. Too many ruffians. Well, I can serve drinks and cook a little."

"Why are you still here?" Jack asked. "You're dead, you could just move on and leave the forest forever, right?"

"I'm not ready," she snapped. "I did a bad thing, a very bad thing that I can't move past."

"How bad could it have been? You're a nice girl."

"I'm from an earlier time. There were expectations of girls. My parents arranged a marriage for me, in exchange for our family's financial security."

"They sold you to a guy for money?" Jack simplified.

"It was for the deed to our land, for the property and horses, so my parents and family would be taken care of. I was the prettiest girl for miles and miles. I had suitors lined up, and all I had to do was stay. But

I was too selfish. I wanted true love and adventure. So I ran away with a vaudeville charlatan who promised me a life filled with fame and fortune. And then he sold me to Mussini. My fate was to be a treasure sold to the highest bidder, and I abandoned my family. I can't forgive myself, my selfish ways. At least here I can try to take care of my new family, the boys. Though now I've lost them, too."

Jack's heart ached for Violet. It wasn't her fault, then or now. He had to think of a way to help her stay with the gang. And then something occurred to Jack. Why hadn't he thought of it earlier? It was perfect. He smiled at her. She raised an eyebrow into a highly annoyed arc.

"Why are you so happy all of a sudden, while I'm in misery?"

Jack leaned over the table. "Because I just thought of a perfect plan to save you from this awful place."

"Oh, really? Are you going to give me a job, Jack the Kid?"

"That depends. How good is your memory?"

"It's sharp as a tack. Why?"

"What about your ability to keep secrets?"

"Well, you can't tell by looking at me, but I am filled with secrets, locked up tightly in my heart. Even the most scandalous secret is safe with me." Violet twisted her hand as if locking her lips and throwing away the key. "Do you have a scandal to share?"

"You're a natural onstage. I don't know why I didn't think of it before."

"What are you talking about?" Violet drummed her fingers on the table.

"You could be my assistant. How could Mussini say no to that? Every magician needs a beautiful assistant." Jack blushed. "I mean a *smart* and *talented* assistant. Not just pretty." Jack felt himself sinking into a hole; he thought it better to shut his mouth before he got any deeper.

Jack chose his friends wisely—though, in truth, unless he counted Mildred, he didn't have any friends. The professor had almost been a friend, but he betrayed Jack. And though he tried to go through life as an optimistic, glass-half-full kind of guy, deep down, he always braced for the worst. He expected Violet to say no, to roll her eyes and walk away. But that's not what happened, not even close. She looked at him as her eyes welled with tears, but she didn't cry. They were tears of relief.

"Well, you do owe me for breaking my comb. I suppose this makes us even now," she said, and like many before her, she crossed her name off of the application. As they left the tavern, the only thing on Jack's mind was convincing Mussini to keep Violet.

Early the next morning, the whole gang gathered outside of Mussini's tent. Violet wrung her handkerchief and breathed in short gasps that made her sound like a wheezing cat.

"Calm down. You're making me nervous," Jack said.

It was decided that Jabber would go in first to let Mussini know that Jack wanted to talk to him about his act. T-Ray's and Runt's wide, glassy eyes stared at him, but Jack didn't pay attention to their fear. What could Mussini do to him? Jabber threw the tent flap back and stood out of the way as Mussini walked out of his tent.

"What's this about your act?" Mussini said to Jack, then he saw Violet. "What's she doing here?"

Jack stood up straight and hooked his thumbs in his belt loops. "She's with me. That's what I wanted to talk to you about."

Mussini clamped down on his pipe. "This ought to be good. I'm listening."

"I'm expanding my act, and I need an assistant. Violet has agreed to fill the job. Every real magician needs an assistant."

"What's wrong with Jabber?" Mussini asked through his teeth.

"Everyone knows the audience likes girl assistants. Girls are trustworthy."

Mussini glared at Jack, mulling over what the boy had said. He held up one of his beefy fingers. "One chance. That's all I'll give you. If your act doesn't improve, I'll get rid of both of you. That's the deal." Mussini stretched out his hand and they shook on it, and Jack winced with pain from Mussini's vise grip.

"I'll take it."

Mussini grumbled and put his fingers in his mouth, forcing out a high-pitched whistle.

"Pack it up! Move it, you lazy lizards. Tonight we roll. The tour moves on."

A collective sigh of relief filled the air as the group hustled to pack up the tents and load the gear back into the wagon.

"That was brave," T-Ray said. "He could have fired you, too, Jack."

"I couldn't let him throw her away like that." Jack loosened the ropes and their tent fell to the ground.

"I don't know what we would do if we lost our Violet." Runt zipped around, folding up hammocks. "The act better be good so she stays."

Within a few hours the scene was empty, the stage returned to a barren slab of wood, the gear packed up tight. Everyone boarded the wagon, Jabber snapped the reins, and the tour rolled on.

14

The Criminal Kind

The next day, after they made camp, Jack paced outside of Jabber's tent. He wanted to get Violet a new hair comb after breaking hers during the pig hunt and was hoping Jabber would take him into a town with decent shops. Jack hated to ask for help, and having to ask Jabber only made it worse. Jack didn't trust him. Jabber always seemed so smug, and Jack was sure Jabber didn't like him. Jack stopped and cleared his throat. He heard movement from inside the tent, and Jabber threw back the flap and stared at him as if he were a mosquito.

"What?"

"Um, so you've been here a long time, and I haven't, and that's cool, so I was wondering—you know I broke Violet's comb, and I want to make it up to her, go to town and get a new one. I thought since you know the territory, you could help me out."

"Help *you* out? You've been here a week and you have already managed to break Violet's most treasured possession and endanger Boxer's life. And now you want me to help you out?"

Jack sighed. "Do it for Violet, then, not me."

"Fine," Jabber reluctantly agreed. "Let's get going." He flicked his sleeve back and whispered. His voice easily set the tattoo on his wrist in motion. He followed the dance of lines and directions projected on his skin and in the air. Jabber was comfortable using both magic and illusions on and off the stage. Jack wondered if there was other real magic Jabber knew.

They rode on horseback through the tangle of trees around the camp. Jack used to like forests, but the Forest of the Dead left him feeling numb, caught in the cool current and the endless rows of trees. He knew the longer he stayed, the harder it would be to escape. Deep rumblings of rushing water came from a distance and approached on the calm air—a river.

Jack and his aching backside were thankful when they finally dismounted and guided their horses along the obsidian water that seeped up into the ground around the shoreline, heavy as ink.

"This is the Black River. It's the river the dead will take to their final resting place," Jabber said.

The horses dipped their soft snouts into the water as the boys rested for a few minutes. Jack wrinkled up his nose and scooped his hand into the Black River. When he pulled his cupped hand up, the water in his palm was crystal clear, not black like he expected the tar-stained river to be. He let the water drain from between his fingers.

"It's not the water that makes it dark, it's what's at the bottom, deep under the surface," Jabber said, as if reading Jack's mind.

Jack examined the tattoo on his wrist and tried to command it to life with his will, but nothing happened. He squinted at his wrist so hard a vein in his forehead pulsed.

Jabber snorted. "You're trying too hard. Magic is subtle. You can't force it."

"Why would you help me figure it out?"

"Maybe I don't want you to stay. Have you ever thought of that?" Jabber picked up a rock and skipped it across the black surface of the river. "That compass is powerful, but it's only the tip of the iceberg as far as the kind of magic Mussini knows. It's no big deal."

Jack thought it was a big deal, but obviously Jabber had set his sights higher. Jack tried to relax. He breathed deeply and closed his eyes. But still nothing happened. "What am I doing wrong?"

"Try visualizing what you want to happen. See the compass coming to life. Breathe life into the magical device with your will. You are as much a part of it working as the compass is. Don't get so stressed out when you fail."

"OK. I'll try again." Jack pictured the compass in his mind's eye and saw it working, directing him through the forest. He saw the arrows jump to life and spin around on his arm. His wrist tingled. The compass's arrow wobbled, and the inky black river undulated lazily across his arm. He might not be as fast as Jabber, but he smiled in spite of himself. At least now the device seemed to work, and that was progress.

Jabber laughed. "Finally. I thought you would never figure it out."

Jack didn't want to argue. He slumped to the ground next to the river. The slow, dark pool lapped against the shoreline, leading away to an unknown end.

"What's it like to be dead?" Jack asked, the image of Skimmer flashing in his head. It was like staring at the ghost of his future. Every second he stayed in the underworld, Jack felt himself slipping closer to the same desperate role—a lost kid, skimming the crowds for gold and glory.

"Some days it's terrible. The scenery is always the same," Jabber said. "Nothing ever changes on the outside. It's in here." He tapped his temple. "I can move on if I want to, but the truth is, I haven't accepted my past, and my future scares me."

"If Mussini doesn't own you anymore, then why are you still here?"

"One day the show will be mine. So don't get any ideas about trying to muscle in on my spot." Jabber turned away. "Plus, I have a debt to pay, a very big debt."

"Don't worry. I don't want to take your spot in the show." This explained why Jabber disliked him. "So what do you owe a debt for? Did you do something bad, like steal something?"

"Have you ever had to wait for something?"

"I wait for homes all the time. I stay at a group home sometimes with a lot of other kids until I get sent to another home."

"Well, being in the forest is a holding place, a place of reflection, where a person must face aspects of their life that they are unwilling to see. For some reason the dead here can't move on yet. We have things to think about, or lessons still to learn, or a debt to pay. That's why so many of the dead are untrustworthy or frightening. The kinder souls are able to move on more quickly. Plus, they have a paradise to look forward to, but some of us are on the fence—we're not sure where the river will take us—and we prefer the forest."

"But Violet is kind, and she stays. She feels guilty about her family. But it wasn't her fault."

"A person has to face what they have done or left undone in their previous life. Taking care of us helps her."

"So, the dead get to live here in the forest as long as they want?"

"As long as we work and are part of the society, then we are allowed to stay and we don't have to face the river. Plus, Mussini makes it worth staying. He's the father I never had. And the show makes us all feel alive. It's the most important thing I've got, and I *won't* lose it."

"I get it."

"Just remember, no debt goes unpaid."

"Mildred calls that facing the consequences." Jack wondered what Jabber had done that was so bad. The more Jabber resisted telling him, the more he had a feeling it was something terrible.

"Your ninja angel is very wise. Come on. We don't want to linger here too long." Jabber flipped up his collar and pulled his horse along. "It's not too much farther."

Up ahead, at a bend in the river, Jack saw a hodgepodge of old wooden buildings propped on high pilings. All the houses were connected to one another, either by wall or bridge. Some just leaned their old, tired walls against the building standing next door, and like gracious neighbors, the buildings held each other up. Smoke trailed out of rickety chimneys. Laughter and music floated down the river. Jack stopped and listened to the happy sounds.

"What is it?" Jack asked, walking up alongside Jabber.

"The River People."

"River People? I thought the dead didn't like water."

"Normally they don't, but when the dead realize that their time in the forest is ending, they are instinctively drawn here to the river. When the final boat comes for them, they take it gladly."

Jabber motioned to the water's edge. Rows of boats crowded the shoreline, resting against the docks like men sleeping on their backs, one against the other in their wooden beds. Jack followed Jabber up onto an old wooden pier. A maze of docks wove in between the rickety buildings like a dilapidated Venice with inky, reed-choked canals. The buildings balanced above the watery depths, and it was impossible to tell which came first, the city or the river.

Jabber quickly snaked between the buildings along the dock, and Jack tried to keep up while marveling at his surroundings. Laundry dangled from lines that hung from window to window. A boy walked along a wooden board that stretched across a thin arm of the river. He balanced fearlessly as if he were completely unaware of the dark water beneath him. Jabber stopped and adjusted his hat.

"This way," he said. Jack admired the way Jabber expertly navigated the tangle of docks. He couldn't tell which way he was going. To Jack, all the docks looked alike. They stopped at a food stand that was serving up sizzling-hot battered fish right out of the oil. Jabber placed his order and then turned to Jack.

"You want to follow this dock here around the bend and take a right. Then keep going until it smells like bread. Take a left, then keep going until you almost think you are lost and you see a sausage shop. Take a right. If you see an exceptionally round man with a tiny dog on his shoulder, stop, turn around, and run the other way. Whatever you do, don't engage him in conversation. Then follow the dock until you hear a horrible banging like a hammer to the forge. The shop will be right in front of you."

"Sounds easy enough." Jack rolled his eyes. If he couldn't find the place, at least he might end up getting a sausage sandwich.

Jabber took a grease-stained paper from the vendor. Jack eyed the crispy fish longingly.

"Run on now. We'll meet back here when you're done," Jabber said, crunching down on a mouthful of fish.

Jack made his way through the city past the scent of bread and the sizzle of sausages, and the bang of the hammer, until he found his way to a shop with windows filled with all sorts of metal: jewelry, cutlery, knives, swords, even a suit of armor and shields. Inside, a girl with stringy brown hair and huge brown eyes stood behind the counter. She jumped when Jack opened the door. The glass cases were filled with gold and silver bangles and bracelets. Jack stared down at some silver rings and ropy gold necklaces.

"Do you have any hair combs?" he asked the girl, who was nibbling on her fingernails. She pointed nervously to a glass cabinet in the front of the store. Jack wondered why she was so jittery.

"Can I see that one?" Jack pointed to a pretty silver comb with a cluster of silver stars. He wanted to get Violet a metal comb so there was no chance it would accidentally break, but there were so many choices. Jack kept looking until he saw one that would look perfect in her dark hair.

"They come in a set." The girl pulled the two combs out and handed them to Jack. He held them up, letting the metal catch and reflect the light.

"I'll take them. Oh, um. How do I pay?" Jack winced. He had completely forgotten about the minor detail of money.

"New in the Forest of the Dead, are you? It's easy. You just have to prove employment in the forest or neighboring towns and then Shepard, my boss, barters a service from *your* boss. Like a trade."

"Cool. I work for the Amazing Mussini."

The girl made a little yelp sound, and her brown eyes went wide.

"Do you know him?"

Her head bobbed up and down, and she scurried behind the counter to wrap up the combs. A loud clank echoed from the back room. The girl jumped again as her tiny fingers nimbly wrapped the combs and tied a bow around the package. Nice touch, Jack thought, but he couldn't help wondering what made the girl so jumpy, especially when he mentioned Mussini. But then, just knowing Mussini was enough to make anyone a little nervous.

"Squirrel! Squirrel! Hurry up and give me a hand!" a man yelled from the back room, followed by more loud clanking. Jack figured there must be a workshop in the back.

"Is that your name? Squirrel?" Jack asked.

"Yes, it's a nickname."

"It's cute." Jack smiled. It definitely suited her.

The distinct hammering of metal chiming against metal echoed from the back room. Jack glanced over to a velvety green curtain, stained with splotches of oil, that separated the front and back of the shop. Another chorus of banging made the curtain tremble. A louder clank of a tool hitting the floor was followed by a litany of curses that made Jack and Squirrel smile.

"Squirrel! Bring me a Band-Aid!" a voice bellowed from the back.

The girl darted behind the curtain. Patience was not one of Jack's virtues, so he inched his way over and peeked behind the curtain. The back room was dark except for the glow emanating from the soot-coated belly of a stove. A man wearing a welder's mask was pounding away at a piece of metal. A shower of sparks leaped up every time the hammer slammed down.

Squirrel scurried into the room and spilled a box of Band-Aids all over the workbench. Her eyes practically bugged out of her head when she saw Jack had wandered into the back room. She waved him away, and Jack nodded. He didn't want to get caught where he didn't belong, especially with a guy brandishing a hammer, but when he turned around, he saw a sight that stopped him dead in his tracks. Behind him, on the wall of the back room, was the most splendid sight. The wall was lined with shelves of every style, manner, and make of handcuffs that Jack had ever seen or read about. Even some he'd never heard of or imagined. A few of the cuffs were blackened or caked with rust, while some were shiny and bright, like freshly minted coins. It was a menagerie of manacles, the end of the rainbow— handcuff heaven.

A deep throat-clearing startled Jack into turning around again. The welder's mask had been removed, revealing the man behind it. His face was wiry and weathered, his skin gaunt, and his bones close to the surface of his bluish skin. White hair sprung up all over his head, contrasting with his crystal blue eyes, giving him a frosty appearance. In fact, the man's entire presence made Jack shiver, despite the heat that radiated from the stove. A wire-thin smile spread across the man's face.

The three of them stood and stared, and it was Squirrel who broke the silence.

"He works for Mussini," was all she said, and the smile wavered in the tanned folds of skin on the man's face. His jaw clenched as if he were holding something back, like a bark or a bite. Jack swallowed hard.

"He does, does he?" the man said, forcing a grimace. "Any friend of Mussini is a friend of old Shepard."

"We're not actually friends. More like master and servant."

"Of course. Come on into my office, and we can have a chat."

Shepard motioned for Jack to come over to his workbench, and Jack wasn't about to say no. He eased his way behind the tool-strewn worktable and sat up on a stool next to the man.

"Sorry we don't have any tea and biscuits."

"I'm not hungry, but thanks." Jack glanced down at the workbench and caught sight of Shepard's feet.

The laces had been pulled out of Shepard's worn black leather shoes. But what really caught Jack's attention was above that. The skin was terribly raw. Black and purplish bruises encircled his bony ankles. They looked like they had been beaten on with a hammer. One thing that could cause those bruises was a heavy iron shackle with a short chain. The look of disgust on Jack's face must have been apparent.

"Are you looking at what the executioner did to me? They had me chained up for weeks." The man rubbed his ankles. "It's impossible to find a polite hangman anymore. They just string you up and push you to your death. Mine didn't even say good-bye."

"Yeah, no manners," Jack said, cringing inside. Magicians weren't the primary occupants of handcuffs— criminals were. And Shepard reeked of bad deeds.

"I had it coming, so I can't hold a grudge." His ice-colored eyes shined.

Jack's gaze drifted away from Shepard, over to the table that was piled with tarnished black keys of every shape and size. The man noticed Jack's interest.

"There's more where they came from." Shepard dug around in a box and let a pile of antique keys fall from his fingers like gold coins from a treasure chest. He looked around for the girl. "Squirrel, bring my coat!" he yelled, and chuckled at Jack. "Wait till you see what I've got."

Squirrel hurried into the back room, laboring under the weight of a long black leather coat draped over her skinny arms. Shepard took it from her and slipped it on. He paraded around the room like a convict just sprung from a lifelong sentence. Jack started wondering if Shepard was *all there* as the old man ran his hands down the front of his lapels.

"Don't I look nice? Like an upstanding citizen," Shepard said with a formal air.

"Yeah, you look real good," Jack said.

"See, nothing here." Shepard opened one side of his coat and revealed the bare leather interior. "And nothing on this side either." Again he showed Jack inside his coat. "But wait, with a twist of this hand . . ."

Jack strained to see what he was doing, following Shepard's every move, watching him turn a button on the inside of his coat. He smirked coyly at Jack.

"Looky, looky what Santa brought."

This time when Shepard opened his coat, the inside was lined with hundreds of keys of all shapes and sizes. Jack beamed, as did the old man. One golden key in particular sparkled up through the sea of tarnished and blackened metal.

"What's that key unlock?" Jack asked, pointing to the gold one.

"That unlocks a very special pair of handcuffs. Custom-made for a fellow. Wait. I'll show you."

Shepard pulled a gold pair of handcuffs down from a shelf. They were a beautiful twist of metal that looped around the wrists of the captor. Jack wanted to touch them, but he didn't dare. They looked like pure gold. Shepard lowered his face to Jack's.

"I don't know what the guy plans for these cuffs, but whoever gets trapped in them will never escape. The lock is impossible to cheat. It has a lock within the lock. And I swear on my cold grave these cuffs know what the wearer is thinking. They are made with very sensitive metal. It's like they have feelings: a tiny lonely soul. No one gets out of them without the key. No one. I call them the devil's handcuffs, because you would have to be as tricky as him to get out of them."

Jack marveled at the shiny handcuffs and without thinking said, "I bet Houdini could get out of them."

"Well, I don't know any Houdini, but I do know a secret I learned about handcuffs while I studied the trade of making them."

"What's that?"

"Everything in the world has a weakness, especially locks. They're like puzzles. Watch them." Shepard held up the handcuff like a crown resting in his grubby hands.

Jack traced the woven vines of the golden cuffs with his eyes, searching for a clue to their secret, and then the metal moved all by itself. Jack blinked rapidly, watching the impossible, and stumbled backward. Shepard let out a low chuckle.

"It's alive. A living maze, a twisting prison of gold. A piece of art, really. I always wanted to be an artist. Attention to detail—that's what makes an artist great." Shepard was captivated with his devilish handiwork.

"You said the lock has a weakness. What is it?"

"That's a secret."

Jack couldn't take his eyes off of the handcuffs, but he had to focus. Shepard might have some real information that could help him escape the forest. Criminal types knew things, especially the fastest way out of a jam. Swallowing hard, Jack asked, "Do you know anyone who has escaped the forest?"

"Maybe, but it's a dangerous way."

"So it's possible." In his excitement, Jack grabbed Shepard's arm. Finally, he was getting a break. The haggard-looking man eyed Jack.

"The wall surrounds us all the time. Only a handful have even seen it, and those who have crossed it never come back. All but one man, and he trades in the living— stealing small, precious souls. But you already know him."

"Mussini." Jack whispered the name as if the man could hear him. He could practically feel his wrist tattoo pulse. Mussini's mark gave him the map of the underworld. But why? Because he knew that even with a map, Jack was trapped.

"If you go to the wall, be prepared to make a deal with the Death Wranglers."

"Yeah. I figured that. Thanks anyway. I better get going."

"Not so fast. If the deal goes south, just remember there is always another way."

"Another way out?"

"Keep looking, that's all I'm saying. The Forest of the Dead has rules. The dead don't always fill you in to all the mysterious ways. The answer might be right in front of you."

"Right, see you around," Jack said. He already knew that his best chance was to make a deal with the Death Wranglers, and now Shepard was just speaking riddles.

"You ever leave Mussini, you give me a call. I could always use a good apprentice. You'd do well here."

"Thanks, but I'm not done trying to be alive."

"That's what I told the executioner," Shepard said.

Squirrel placed Jack's package on the worktable in front of him. It reminded Jack that Jabber was probably tired of waiting for him. Jack ducked out of the shop and disappeared into the tangled docks of the River City. He made his way back to the meeting spot. Jabber grabbed him and pulled Jack back down to the river.

"Come on. We've got to get back. Mussini will be missing us."

"Sorry. I met the weirdest guy."

Jabber ignored him. "We're going to keep this visit a secret," Jabber said, hurrying Jack along.

"Why?"

"Mussini doesn't like anything that's not his idea. Got it? So keep it quiet."

"But I told Shepard I worked for Mussini to barter for the combs." Jack showed Jabber the package.

"I'll take care of it. And another thing," Jabber added. "Don't trust the dead."

"Yeah, you said that before."

"Just remember it."

Jack had been around long enough to know what Jabber meant, that no one should be trusted on face value. After all, some really nice people did bad things. Jack sort of liked Shepard, but he knew deep down that he was a sinister man, capable of anything. At heart, Shepard was a criminal kind, dead or alive.

Water Escapes

Houdini stands on the bow as the boat rocks on the sea.
With chains wrapped around his body,
he goes into the water.
No one checks the locks.
That's the key.

Death is always close to him, patiently waiting:
A mythical woman drifting in the water,
wrapped in chains of braided hair,
reaching up from the sandy bottom of the sea.
She sings a siren song to pull men down
into their watery graves.

Death rests her hands on the water's surface,
waiting for a mistake,
calling down into the sea for Harry Houdini.

We want the waters to part. We want him to rise up
out of the deep like a fish that flies with unfettered wings.

And then he breaks through the thin surface,
free from his chains.

Impossible, some will say.

The sea is a diversion.
It's right back where he started.

Water is the perfect illusion.
He doesn't lock the locks.
He hides in the ditch of the waves,
in the brutal siren's sea,
with only death the wiser.

She calls for him.
She sings a magical song.
But he cannot hear her through all of our applause.

15

The Violet Letter

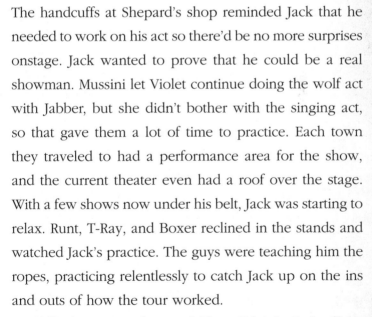

The handcuffs at Shepard's shop reminded Jack that he needed to work on his act so there'd be no more surprises onstage. Jack wanted to prove that he could be a real showman. Mussini let Violet continue doing the wolf act with Jabber, but she didn't bother with the singing act, so that gave them a lot of time to practice. Each town they traveled to had a performance area for the show, and the current theater even had a roof over the stage. With a few shows now under his belt, Jack was starting to relax. Runt, T-Ray, and Boxer reclined in the stands and watched Jack's practice. The guys were teaching him the ropes, practicing relentlessly to catch Jack up on the ins and outs of how the tour worked.

Talk about a tough crowd. They didn't let Jack off the

hook for any tiny mistake—no stumbling over his words when he made the speech about all the ghastly criminals who'd worn the handcuffs, and definitely *no* fumbling with the handcuffs.

"Cool as a cucumber," T-Ray said.

"And no sweating onstage, either. The dead can smell sweat a mile a way."

"And they can smell fear like a pack of wild dogs." T-Ray threw his head back and snorted. "A pack of wild, dead dogs."

"No they can't," Jack said, throwing an acorn at T-Ray. For the first time, he felt like people wanted him to succeed, and he wanted to make them proud. Or, at the very least, not embarrass them.

The large black ghost house was the biggest obstacle for Jack onstage. That was what Houdini called his black box. A long time ago, fake séance conjurers used similar tricks to dupe clients to thinking ghosts were real. One side of the box, where Jack entered, was made of a black velvety fabric. A hole was cut in the top of the box for Jack's head, so that the audience could see he was still inside, with the rest of his body concealed behind the curtain. In a way, it was a relief to be inside the box while trying to get the handcuffs off; while his body was hidden, Jack could use every means possible to get out of the handcuffs without the audience being any the wiser.

Jack concealed keys all over his body. T-Ray let him

use his Scotch tape to hide keys under his pants legs and in his armpit—he even made pockets out of flesh-colored fabric and taped them to his thigh or inside bicep. He also used the seam of his pants and the backside of his leather belt to hide keys. Using his clothes and body to their fullest potential to hide the keys was crucial because once onstage, he was subjected to the inspection and cynical eyes of the dead.

The challenge part of the act seemed simple enough. Anyone could bring in a pair of working handcuffs, and Jack would escape from them. Mussini loved getting the dead involved in the show. Jack had the feeling that Mussini didn't care if he got humiliated onstage or not. In fact, it wouldn't surprise Jack if Mussini secretly *wanted* him to fail, to flounder in front of the dead, unable to free himself.

To avoid that humiliation, Jack took precautions to ensure the show went smoothly. Boxer inspected any cuffs brought up by the audience and made sure that they worked. He was also the "heavy" in case any wise guys tried to bring up damaged cuffs. Boxer, Violet, and Jack developed a secret way of communicating while onstage, sort of like the way a third-base coach gave signals in baseball, just not so obvious. They had to be subtle: A raised eyebrow meant suspicious, and a half smile meant a good choice. A wrinkled nose meant something stunk about someone.

As his assistant, Violet was onstage the entire time, so it was important for her to get used to handling the handcuffs and remembering which keys went to which cuffs. Violet's memory was practically photographic. Soon she knew each key and each lock by heart. The box was dark, so they needed to know which key went in which lock by touch alone. They practiced reaching into a bag, holding the keys in their hands, and guessing which lock they opened. Violet also made her own costume with glittery gossamer wings sprouting from her back and a small black mask that rested just across her eyes. She looked like a cross between a fairy and a bandit.

Jack had waited a few days to give Violet her combs, not wanting them to seem like a bribe for helping him. He handed her the brown paper package with the nice bow on top.

"What's this?" she asked, and her face narrowed in mock suspicion.

"Just a present."

Her face brightened. "I love presents." She ripped the paper off like she hadn't received a present in a hundred years. "Oh, they're so perfect. Stars! There aren't any stars here, just clouds. I love them."

Violet's face lit up the same way the gang of dead kids' faces lit up when Skimmer showered them with gaudy rings. Then he remembered Jabber handing over the papier-mâché mask to the Death Wrangler. In the world of the dead, beauty was more important than wealth or influence. Jack realized that whatever he traded to the Death Wranglers didn't have to cost much, but it had to be beautiful—something special.

Jack leaned against the tree and stared out into the street, watching the dead walk by. Through the crowd he thought he saw Mussini, with his scruffy beard, wild hair, and long black coat, milling through the crowds of people. Yep, Mister Amazing all right, out for a Sunday stroll.

"Hey, where's Mussini going?"

"To town. He likes to drum up excitement about the show himself." Violet twisted up her hair and shoved the combs in over and over until she got them just right. "Promotion is a big deal in show business."

"So he'll probably be gone a while?" Jack asked.

"He's usually gone for at least a couple of hours."

Just the lucky break Jack needed if he was going to break into Mussini's tent and *borrow* his book of magic tricks. The book was the only thing he could think of worth enough to trade the Death Wranglers for passage out of the underworld. With the magical tricks inside, the Death Wranglers could create as many beautiful illusions as they wanted. T-Ray told him that Mussini kept the secrets to his tricks inside his tent in a locked box. All Jack had to do was to sneak inside the tent and find the box. Easy.

"Hey, I'll catch up with you later. I'm going to practice with some of the handcuffs that I left in my tent."

"You practice too much. Have some fun."

"Right. A regular old party with the dead." Jack waved to Violet as he headed back toward the tents.

After making sure the coast was clear, Jack ducked inside Mussini's tent. He was surprised to find the interior completely different than the last time he'd been inside. All the exotic fabric was gone, leaving the tent barren and empty. Every step Jack took reverberated on the floorboards. Mussini's golden hawk masks lined row after row of shelves, and a battered collection of knives and pipes sat on his dressing table next to his bed. Jack paused, soaking in the thrill of being in Mussini's tent, spying on the master magician. His fingers hovered over the knives, but he pulled his attention away and focused on his task. A desk and a worn-out leather armchair were the only other furniture in the tent.

Jack found the trunk under Mussini's bed (definitely not the most original hiding place). He dragged it out and ran his finger over the lock. He shrugged and tried to lift the lid. Jack almost laughed when it opened immediately without a key. Either Mussini was incredibly confident or ridiculously crazy not to lock up his valuables, and from what Jack could tell, Mussini was anything but crazy. He probably didn't think any of the kids were smart enough to perform his magic tricks or nuts enough to steal from him.

Jack heaved open the lid and there it was—Mussini's

magic book. Lifting the book out of the box and setting it on his lap, Jack opened the cover and flipped through the wondrous pages filled with magic tricks and their secrets. It included all the shows and all the magic Mussini had performed from the time when he was not much older than Jack to the present. He had been a magician his entire life; the book was his legacy. Jack's attention raced across the pages, his gaze dancing over the spectacular tricks—treasures of Mussini's amazing imagination. He admired the meticulous detail of the tricks, like an architect constructing a house made of magic. This book showed commitment and the kind of dedication only a few possessed. It reminded him of Houdini.

Absorbed in the tricks, Jack's head jerked when he heard a rustling noise outside of the tent. Someone was coming. He slammed the trunk closed and threw himself under the bed, pulling the trunk in behind him. Crammed under, he clutched the book to his chest and held himself perfectly still. Thick-soled boots tromped across the floor.

"What's wrong with you lately? Where's your head?" The tone of Mussini's voice was somewhere between concerned and annoyed.

"I've had things on my mind," Jabber said, defensive.

Jack slowed his panicked breathing. One of the tent supports pinched against his side. He winced and tried not to lean against the wood for fear of bringing the whole tent down on top of them. Jack turned his head enough to glimpse Mussini's black boots positioned in front of the dresser.

"Out with it then. No use keeping it bottled up."

"You promised that I would inherit the show." Jabber's voice was harsh. "I've been here the longest and I know the ways of the underworld better than anyone."

"If I recall correctly, I said that *if and when* I decide to move on and leave the forest, the best performer would inherit the show."

"I'm the best performer. I always have been. Jack doesn't come close to matching me with showmanship. He's an amateur." Jabber sat down on the bed, which pressed the thin mattress against Jack's face. He gasped. Beads of sweat broke out across his neck. The pressure and heat were suffocating.

"Is that a hint of jealousy I hear in your voice?" Mussini asked, amused.

"Jealous of that kid? Not in a million years. What you hear is my faith in your word dwindling."

"Jack's got spunk. He's fresh, and the dead like that."

"The dead won't have anything to like if he escapes. He's tried once and he'll try again. You can't trust him."

"I have a plan to make his escape meaningless."

"What are you going to do? *Kill him?*" Jabber snorted.

Mussini scoffed. "Don't be so dramatic. Death is natural. We know that better than anyone. It's going to happen sooner or later. But in Jack's case, it might just happen sooner."

"But it's not his time to die. You can't do that. Not even for the act." Jabber rose from the bed, relieving the weight from Jack's body, but the weight on his mind stayed firm.

Mussini planned to kill him to keep him in the forest forever.

"You're not going soft on me, are you? A second ago you were ready to get rid of him yourself. I just want a little insurance on my investment. I hate to do it. The dead love to watch the living perform, but he has enough star power to keep their attention, so being dead might not matter."

"But if he's dead and such a *star,* then you'll probably make him a permanent member of the show."

"Right." Mussini laughed. "It's still my call and my show."

"That doesn't change things with our arrangement. I want your word that I will inherit the show, not Jack."

"You know I can't give you that. So you have a little competition. Let the best man win. Plus, it will still be a long time before I leave. You two will have plenty of time to fight it out. Now come on. Time to drum up some excitement." Mussini's boots scraped across the floor, the flap fluttered back, and they were gone.

The tent was quiet. Jack let out the breath he was holding. A wave of claustrophobia overwhelmed him. He pushed the trunk from under the bed, crawled out, and shoved everything back in place before rushing out into the cool air. With Mussini's magic book concealed under his shirt, Jack stumbled back to his own tent and dove into his hammock before anyone could see the hard outline the book made through the cloth. He slipped the book out and hid it under his blanket.

"What's up with you?" Runt asked. "You're sweating like a pig."

"I'm fine." Jack edged off his hammock and sat on the floor.

"What'd you do now?" Boxer asked.

"Yeah, you've got 'guilty' written all over your face," T-Ray said.

The victory of taking Mussini's magic book was marred with the news that Mussini planned on killing Jack, but he didn't want to dwell on that. "I just got our ticket out of this place."

"Brother, not this again. Escape, escape, escape. Is that all you think about?" Runt asked, perched on the edge of his hammock.

"Yes! We need to get a plan. I wasn't ready the first time, but this time, I'm not going to screw up," Jack said, his voice frantic.

"What did you get?" T-Ray asked. He shivered despite a blanket wrapped around his shoulders.

"I got us something to trade to the Death Wranglers to secure our safe passage through the gate and out of the forest."

"No way!" Runt yelled. "What is it?"

"I'm not saying just yet. I need to know if the three of you are prepared to leave with me and make a plan to get out together."

The three of them exchanged glances. T-Ray answered, "We'll go. But we need an airtight escape plan. We don't want any Death Wranglers sneaking up on us like last time. Sorry, Jack. It's not that we don't trust you. We just need to be sure this is going to work."

"Knock, knock," Violet called from outside of the tent, and the boys stared at each other not making a sound. "I have a basket filled with sandwiches that I will use as bribery to enter the tent," Violet said, peering in through a crack in the canvas.

Runt flung himself off of his hammock and flipped up the tent flap. Violet walked in with a basket filled with snacks. "Oh, Violet, you're a dream. Bribe accepted." Runt ravenously burrowed into the basket and pulled out a sandwich.

Violet passed out the food. "What are you boys up to? You didn't come to dinner."

"Nothing," Jack said.

"Yeah, nothing." T-Ray took a sandwich out of Violet's hand and her eyes widened. He jerked his hand away.

"Oh, no. T-Ray, why didn't you say something?" Violet asked.

"Say something about what?" Runt asked.

"Nothing." T-Ray picked at the bread of his sandwich. "It doesn't matter. It's going to be too late soon anyway."

"Too late for what?" Jack asked.

"Nothing, man. Just leave it."

"What are you two talking about? It's not too late."

"Tell them," Violet said.

"About two weeks ago, I started getting cold all the time. I just couldn't warm up. I didn't think anything of it at first. But my skin was always clammy and then one day it stopped bothering me so much. That's when I knew it was happening."

"Don't say it." Boxer paced the floor.

"He has to face it," Violet said. "And if he won't say it, I will."

"Violet's right, Boxer. You tell them, please," T-Ray said, tossing his uneaten sandwich to the ground.

"T-Ray's dying."

Jack's stomach sank. This couldn't be happening. Not right in front of his face. He didn't even see it coming. No wonder T-Ray had been so moody—he was desperate.

Jack hardened his resolve. "That just means we need to get this plan under way even faster. Violet, how much time does T-Ray have?"

Violet inspected T-Ray's hands, fingernails, and eyes. "Probably a couple of weeks, at most."

"OK, then. You guys heard her. That gives us two weeks at most to get out of here. Now we just need a plan to slip out of camp, unnoticed, and get to the gate. I've got the map and directions covered." Jack motioned to his wrist.

"Will you help us, Violet?" Boxer asked. "We can use all the help we can get."

"Absolutely," Violet said.

"It'll work," Jack said.

"I don't mean to complain, but so far the plan is that we need a plan," T-Ray said. "We haven't gotten very far."

"I'm great with strategy and signals," Violet said.

"I think we should go at night, after the show lets out. And we need to wear masks so that we blend in with the crowd," Jack said.

"We'll need food for the journey," Runt said, devouring a hunk of chocolate cake that he pulled from Violet's basket.

"We'll need some light camping supplies in case we get stuck out in the forest overnight. I can take care of that," Boxer said, rubbing his hands together.

"But what about Mussini? He watches the entire show

from beginning to end. He doesn't miss a thing. How will we escape without him noticing?" T-Ray asked.

"You'll need a distraction," Violet said. "I can be very distracting when I want to be. Jabber could help."

"I don't know about Jabber. He might tell." Runt leaned against Violet like a satisfied pup. His belly protruded and there was a ring of chocolate around his mouth that Violet wiped from his face.

Jack kneeled down on the ground and wiped an area in the dirt clean with his hand. Then he picked up a stick and drew a diagram of the stage, the audience, and the backstage area. "Mussini is the closing act, so he'll be onstage." Jack pointed to the stage and drew an *M*. "Jabber is out front, manning the door and making sure nothing goes wrong with the audience and the animals." Jack marked *JB* where Jabber was always stationed during the final act.

"That's it, then. We need to make some trouble to distract Jabber and Mussini," Violet said. "Then the rest of you can sneak backstage and make your getaway."

"No, it's too dangerous. I don't want you to get punished by Mussini for helping us. He'll fire you for sure," Jack said. "We have to come up with a distraction that Mussini won't trace back to you."

"That's up to me, isn't it?" Violet put her hand on Jack's arm. "Let me help my family."

T-Ray spoke up. "I could make a distraction. We

always have a set number of animals for the finale. What if I made more of them? Then Mussini would have to try and control them all. He would be up to his armpits in animals."

"Like a flock of pooping pigeons!" Runt laughed.

"Or a bunch of squealing weasels," Violet added.

Laughter with a flicker of hope echoed through the tent. The plan just might work after all. Boxer clapped T-Ray on the back. "That's a great idea. We'll nail Mussini with his own trick."

"Where are we going when we leave the camp?" T-Ray asked Jack.

"We need to go to the wall. Then I'll deal with the Death Wranglers."

"All I want to know is: When are we going?" Runt asked.

"I'll have to sneak the animals into the basket when he's not looking, so it has to be a day that Mussini doesn't inspect the trick first," T-Ray said.

"How will we know if the escape plan is a go if we're all spread out?" Boxer asked. "T-Ray won't know until the show starts."

"A signal!" Violet said, her eyes growing wide. "But what?"

"A hand signal," T-Ray said, making a winged shadow bird appear on the tent flap as Boxer shined the lamp on his hands.

"No, that's too obvious." Jack leaned back against one of the trunks and tried to think of a distraction that could be seen from the entire theater but not be obvious and raise suspicion.

"What about a necklace," Violet said, touching her throat. "I could wear a necklace or put my hair up."

"We need something big and visible. A necklace is too small."

"I know! It's brilliant." Jack said, sitting up as the idea hit him. "A letter. You can wear a letter pinned onto the front of your costume. Like in the story."

"What story?" Runt said.

"*The Scarlet Letter.* Where that girl Hester has to wear a letter attached to her, you know, her front." There was no way Jack was going to say *bosom* in front of a girl.

"Why would she do that?"

"How should I know? I didn't actually read the book. I just heard about it."

"I like to wait till books come out as movies," Boxer said.

"Sounds perfect. I can sew it on. What letter?" Violet asked.

"*V,*" Jack said. "For Violet and for Victory."

"It's settled. We wait for the Violet Letter, and then we escape!" T-Ray said.

They finalized the plans and divided up the jobs. T-Ray was in charge of the animal distraction. Boxer would handle the supplies, and Violet was the signal. Jack was in charge of logistics once they left camp, and Runt was in charge of keeping his mouth shut. An uneasy silence fell over the tent, and they all looked at one another, unable to believe that they were really going.

"It will all be worth it," Jack said. "No need to be nervous."

"I'm not nervous," T-Ray said. "The worst that happens is that Mussini catches us, and then we're dead meat. But I'm dead either way." He paused. "I just want to make it back to see my mom again."

"You'll see her," Jack said. T-Ray had a lot to live for. More than Jack, maybe.

"I hope you've got something good to trade with the Death Wranglers?" Boxer asked.

"Oh, it's good. Trust me," Jack said, giving T-Ray a knowing glance. "It's gonna work like magic."

16

The Challenge

"Jack, you're on."

The stage lights dropped, shrouding the theater in darkness. Jack stepped onto the stage as the curtain rose. A wild sea of masked faces stared back at him. For the first time, the audience applauded when Jack was announced, and the cheers thrilled him. He started the act with some easy handcuff tricks, quick escapes, locking and unlocking the cuffs from behind his back.

The challenge act was next—the most nerve-racking part of the show. A knot twisted in Jack's stomach. Restlessly, he locked and unlocked a pair of handcuffs while he waited. Violet raised her pale arms up into the air, and a hush fell over the audience. Boxer stood next to Violet at the edge of the stage with his massive biceps crossed, ready to give the eagle eye to any handcuffs that the dead might bring up. This was mostly for show, since the dead rarely had their own handcuffs. To keep the show moving and to add some excitement, Jabber organized the plant, which was a pair of Jack's cuffs that one of the dead pretended he brought to the show.

The audience member, a skinny, rat-masked man, scurried up to the stage with a shiny pair of handcuffs and tossed them to Boxer. Jack recognized the cuffs right away. They were Bean Cobbs. Wait. Jack grabbed the handcuffs. Something was wrong. These weren't his handcuffs. All the plants were supposed to be his handcuffs, the ones he practiced with millions of times, so there would be no mistakes. Was this Jabber's idea of a joke? Or was he trying to set him up . . .

Jack eyed the audience, searching for Jabber in the crowd, but the bright stage lights flashed him in the face like the headlights of oncoming traffic. He squinted and shielded his eyes. A bead of sweat appeared on his brow. He couldn't get out of these cuffs. He didn't have the key and couldn't pick the lock in time. Time to get creative. Jack nudged Violet's hands to put the cuffs on the largest part of his arm (that way he could slip them clean off his smaller wrists and wouldn't have to pick the lock). This was a time when he wished that he had thick, muscular forearms like Houdini. Quickly, Jack entered his box and pulled the handcuffs over his wrists. The

THE CARNIVAL of LOST SOULS

right cuff slipped off easily, but the left cuff was tight. It was mind over matter, or in Jack's case, metal over wrist bone. It hurt, scraping a chunk of skin from his wrist as he wrestled the handcuff off. He tossed the unexpected cuffs out with more relief than triumph. But his challenge wasn't over.

Another volunteer raised a pale white hand into the air. A commotion ricocheted among the crowd like a pulse of electricity, snapping the audience suddenly to attention. After the stress of the strange cuffs, Jack had a bad feeling about where the act was headed.

White hair appeared above the heads of the audience. Wearing a dark leather coat, the volunteer made his way to the stage. That's when Jack recognized his weathered face and the dark blue bruises on his skin. Jabber was right. Don't trust the dead.

A haunting trail of whispers propelled the man up to the stage.

"Shepard," they all said.

This wasn't part of the plan, at least not *Jack's* plan. With his limitless supply of custom handcuffs, Shepard was Jack's walking nightmare. The whole thing reeked of Mussini. Jack glanced over the audience; Mussini's hawk mask glittered in the candlelight. He raised his arms and began a hard clap. This was what Mussini lived for— the surprise, the unexpected twist. Either that or he was getting back at Jack for helping Violet stay in the show.

How could Jack have been so stupid? A blind man could have seen this one coming. Jack had handcuff déjà vu. His memory flashed to Shepard's wall of handcuffs.

The devil's handcuffs—they had been made just for him and ordered by Mussini. He should have known only someone as heartless and brilliant as Mussini could come up with such a stunning and tortuous pair of handcuffs. Shepard reached into his coat and pulled out the golden intertwined locking cuffs and held them high above his head for everyone to see.

"The devil's handcuffs, that's what I call them." Shepard spun them around for the dead to admire.

Boxer glanced at Jack and shrugged his shoulders. There was no way Jack could turn down the challenge, and Mussini knew it. Tonight, Jack was being given a taste of how Mussini operated. If Jack beat the cuffs, the crowd would celebrate his victory; if Jack failed, the crowd would be in awe of Shepard's evil cuffs. Both ways, Mussini's show won.

The crowd buzzed with excitement, greedily gawking at the devil's cuffs. Jack nodded to Boxer, who took the handcuffs from Shepard and inspected them. His mind raced. He needed to come up with a way out of this mess and *fast*. Jack turned and addressed the audience.

"I'll accept this challenge, but only if Mr. Shepard can first prove to me that the handcuffs work. He must open and close them right now."

"You have my word, that should be enough," Shepard said, dripping mock sincerity, which caused the audience to reel with laughter, suspecting what Shepard's word was worth. No more than the word of any of the dead, Jack thought bitterly.

"No offense, sir, but I'd like to see you unlock the cuffs with my own eyes."

"Very well. I'll prove it to you." Shepard pulled the golden key from his pocket. It sparkled as a spotlight caught it. *Nice touch*, Jack thought. Shepard was milking this for all it was worth. He opened and closed the lock to the devil's handcuffs, making it look easy, like a baby could break out of them. Jack watched as Shepard returned the key to his left-hand breast pocket. Now he had no choice but to accept the challenge and take his chances.

Violet held up the handcuffs, and T-Ray snared the drum in the background. She closed them deliberately around Jack's wrists, not too tightly, though it hardly mattered. Instantly the cuffs tightened of their own accord, strangling his wrists as if they had a score to settle. Violet pulled back the curtain to the box, Jack entered, and the music began to play. Jack took one last look at Shepard and the audience, and ducked his head inside the box so that he could concentrate. Crammed inside the box, Jack struggled with the handcuffs; none of his keys worked on the lock, and he couldn't figure out the internal formula of the lock system. Shepard was right about the lock, for it twisted and turned inside as if somehow anticipating every move Jack made to pry it open. It was obvious the cuffs were smarter than he was.

Lock-picking was like navigating a maze. Jack closed his eyes, pictured the cool metal surface of the lock inside his mind, and the box disappeared. He was in the woods at night, and all the sounds around him were wild and alive. He entered a labyrinth with metal walls. He tried to follow the formula of the grooves, each twist and turn, the empty spaces in between, but every time he thought he had the lock figured out, it moved, snakelike, refusing to be undone. He didn't know what to do.

Jack remembered what Shepard told him in the shop—that every lock had a vulnerability, like a secret door built in by the locksmith. If there was a weakness to the devil's handcuffs, it wasn't in the design. Then it hit him. The weakness was not the handcuffs—the weakness was the man who made them. Shepard was the key.

Jack had been inside the box for many minutes before he whispered for Violet. She poked her head in the box, bringing a cool breeze with her.

"Violet, I can't get them open." Jack held out his wrists, battered and cut from the vicious metal handcuffs.

"What do you want me to do?" Violet's brow wrinkled. "Should I get Boxer? Maybe he can break them open?"

"No, no. You have to get the key." Panic raised Jack's

voice. He was drenched in sweat and his legs were starting to cramp from standing in the small space.

Violet's eyes flashed. "The key?" she asked. She didn't like how the trick had turned.

"Yes, get it from Shepard. It's in his left-hand breast pocket." Jack shifted his weight, trying to get more comfortable in the tight space. That made the box sway, causing gasps from the audience. Violet steadied the box and waved to the crowd before turning back to Jack.

"How do you expect me to get inside of a man's pocket? You do realize that Shepard is *wearing* the coat with the key, right?"

"Use your girl powers," Jack blurted out as the cuffs twisted tightly around his wrists.

Violet pulled back in the small space. "My what?"

"Just smile at him. Chat him up, be *really* nice and then pick his pocket."

"Jack, are you suggesting I steal it? Which, I must say, is not an entirely unacceptable option, but . . ."

"Please, Violet, you're my only hope." Jack sighed.

"I'll try, but I'm not going to do anything disgusting to get that key, so if he tries any funny business, I'm going to get Boxer to wring his skinny neck."

"It wouldn't be Shepard's first time."

Jack tried to relax while Violet disappeared from the box and into the crowd. He hated making Violet steal, but he was reaching his limit—the wringing metal cuffs and the suffocating walls of the box. The challenge closed in on him. He couldn't let Mussini beat him, and in the dark of the box, his options were slim.

The image of Skimmer and the shower of stolen rings that he gave his gang floated through his mind. It didn't matter that the gold was fake; the gifts were still so valuable to the other boys. Skimmer was their hero. Using a sleight of hand, he made the impossible happen. Was that so wrong?

Stealing isn't a noble pursuit, at least that was what the little voice inside Jack's head, which sounded a lot like Mildred, said. But it wasn't as bad as some things, like hurting another person, he reasoned. At McDovall Academy there was this kid, Brian Ryan, who was super-skinny and hated everyone. The only thing he liked to do was shove kids into the brick wall behind the school. Brian was surprisingly strong for such a string bean. It became the infamous brick-wall burn, because any exposed skin got scraped against the brick. One poor guy got scraped on the tip of his nose, and Brian called him Rudolph for the whole six months that he was at McDovall. Brian ended up in juvie, and Jack wasn't a bit sorry for him.

Jack wasn't exactly squeaky clean when it came to obeying the law, so he could understand how Skimmer slipped up. He stole from the school cafeteria once, though it wasn't entirely his fault; his penny-pinching foster father only gave him exactly sixty-five cents for lunch, which was the exact price of a reduced cost lunch in the cafeteria. It was bad enough that Jack was forced into the humiliation of the poor kid's lunch, but then to have to count out change was mortifying. And the cheapskate gave him nickels and dimes, not even quarters. The guy probably fished the loose change out from the sofa cushions.

Anyway, Jack had already bought his lunch before noticing the cupcakes. Good cupcakes, not cheap hydrogenated oil–filled cupcakes that could withstand the next ice age, but homemade chocolate cupcakes. He had to have one, and he was sick and tired of counting out change like a street urchin. Houdini only used his sleight of hand once to steal food, potatoes from a vendor on the freezing streets, but then he was starving. Jack slipped the cupcake up his jacket sleeve when the lunch lady wasn't looking and ate it in a beat-up stall in the boy's bathroom. In that delicious moment, he didn't care if it was wrong to steal.

Mildred would say he was becoming desensitized, and that the line between right and wrong was blurred because of his circumstances. Maybe that's where Jack was right then, squeezed in the tight space between a cupcake and a brick wall. Jack poked his head out of the top of the box, and the dead laughed and slung a few choice insults: Loser! Give up! Stupid kid! His forehead was covered in beads of sweat. From the audience's perspective, it looked as if his head was sitting on a table. T-Ray had rejoined Jabber on the stage, and they tossed bowling pins back and forth, juggling them high into the air to entertain the crowd, while they anxiously waited for the Kid to escape the handcuffs.

After what seemed like forever, Violet hurried backstage and whispered instructions to Boxer, who looked at her strangely and shrugged. Boxer walked out onto the stage and addressed the crowd. The audience waited eagerly, barely breathing. Boxer cleared his throat.

"Perhaps the Kid needs a kiss for luck, from his beautiful assistant."

The crowd cheered. Violet strolled out onto the stage. She brushed Jack's hair back from his forehead and bent down face-to-face. The cool tip of her nose brushed against his cheek. Their lips touched, and she pressed her lips tightly to his. Her tongue pushed open his lips. Jack's eyes widened. He felt the key as she slipped it inside his mouth with her tongue and then quickly pulled her lips away. The taste of metal made his mouth water.

Within moments, Jack thrust his hand through the hole in the top of the box—holding up his golden trophy. He was free from the devil's handcuffs. The crowd roared with applause. Jack threw back the curtain of the ghost house and emerged victorious onto the stage to take his bow. The dead leaped to their feet. For all they knew, the great and dangerous Shepard had been fairly beaten. Jack had done the impossible. Mussini glared at Jack and then rose to his feet and applauded just as loudly as the rest of them. He had been beaten, too, but his star was born that night, and he knew Jack's popularity was worth the minor loss.

After the show, Jack cornered Jabber backstage. "You knew that Mussini talked to Shepard and ordered a pair of the devil's handcuffs to be made for me. You knew that he would be here tonight. Why didn't you tell me?"

"I knew. It was my job to know. I work for Mussini. But Mussini didn't know that I took you to the River City. I thought that if you met Shepard, he might tell you something that could help you. I hoped he might give you a clue to how the handcuffs worked."

Jack's nerves were frayed after the tough show. "Why should I believe you?" His temper boiled over. "One minute you hate me, the next you try and help me. I don't get you." Jack shoved Jabber into a stack of crates.

"I told you not to trust the dead." Annoyance was thick in Jabber's voice. "This isn't all about you. And for the record, I am neither your friend nor your enemy."

"What are you then? Answer me—what *are* you?"

"I'm dead! This is my world, not yours." Jabber stormed off.

Runt bobbed backstage and wrestled the golden handcuffs from Jack's clenched fists. "That was one of the best acts yet! Don't know how you're gonna top that."

"Maybe I won't have to," Jack said. "It's about time we got out of here. Once and for all."

After Jack's run-in with the devil's handcuffs, it was clear that devils were all around him.

The Art of Misdirection

A torturous week and two new towns came and went before a chance to escape finally arrived. Jack and Boxer stood backstage waiting, anxious to get the plan under way. All week long, Mussini had been minutely inspecting the finale; no matter how hard they planned everything else, the escape hinged on the trick with T-Ray's paper animals. Mussini's sudden obsession with inspecting his final trick was *not* part of the plan.

Jack and Boxer watched from the wings as Mussini pulled each paper animal out of T-Ray's basket, inspecting and counting each one like a mother hen. Mussini glared. T-Ray quivered like a leaf.

"You'd think T-Ray would be used to it by now," Boxer said. "But Mussini never inspects his tricks this much."

Jack watched on pins and needles. "He's the point man. That's a lot of pressure. If T-Ray screws this up, we're all dead meat."

"I bet Mussini knows," Boxer said, cracking his knuckles. "I *know* he knows. Why else inspect the trick every night for a week?"

"'Cause he's turning into a paranoid wreck like you." Jack put his hand on Boxer's arm. "We just need to stay cool and wait. We've got him right where we want him."

Boxer pointed at Mussini. "You mean going through T-Ray's shirt pocket?"

All Jack and Boxer could do was watch, listen, and hope T-Ray didn't snap under the pressure. To cope with the stress of living in the Forest of the Dead, he had made himself a pet, a skinny electric-green garden snake, out of paper. Its name was Linguini. When Mussini stuck his big fat hand in T-Ray's pocket and pulled out the tiny paper snake, pinched between his fingers, it looked like T-Ray was about to have a nervous breakdown.

"What do we have here?" Mussini asked, holding the snake up into the light.

T-Ray's eyes bulged; he gulped. "Please, sir. It's just my pet, Linguini."

"Linguini, eh? It looks like a paper snake to me."

"That's his name," T-Ray said. "He's a snake, not pasta. That would be pathetic if I carried around a strand of spaghetti as a pet. I just like to hold him during the show when he comes to life. Calms my nerves, that's all."

Mussini rolled his eyes. "I have a strict policy about creating more animals than I need."

T-Ray stared up all doe-eyed at him and Mussini's glare softened. To Jack's surprise, he held out his hand. T-Ray gingerly took the snake out of Mussini's fingers and slipped it back into his pocket. "But Linguini winds around my wrist during the show and then goes back to paper when it's over. He's no trouble, really."

Mussini rubbed his mustache and pointed his finger in T-Ray's face. "Just this once, then. No more. Or I'll put a nest of baby rattlesnakes in your hammock while you're sleeping, got it?"

"Yes, sir," T-Ray said, and smiled brightly. Little did Mussini know that stuffed in T-Ray's other pockets were a flock of pooping pigeons, a band of squealing weasels, a half-dozen goats, two dozen fruit bats, and a miniature pony. Sometimes rules weren't meant to be broken—they were meant to be shattered with a baseball bat. Jack and the gang were getting out of the Forest of the Dead with a finale to rival anything Mussini had ever encountered. Just *who* was amazing now?

But it would all be ruined if Mussini stopped to pat T-Ray down. If Jack knew one thing, it was that he needed a distraction.

The concept of misdirection wasn't too hard to grasp—it was all about attention.

Attention was *focused* on one thing to *distract* from something else. Jack simply had to focus Mussini away from the basket and from T-Ray. He glanced over his shoulder to Boxer, and the two boys advanced. Boxer brushed Jack with his shoulder, and then Jack bumped into him and so on, until they resembled pinballs slamming into each other.

"Hey, watch it, buddy!" Boxer yelled at Jack, shoving him into T-Ray's basket, sending it flying to the ground.

Jack turned around and pushed Boxer. "You watch it, you big dork. And I'm *not* your buddy."

"Don't push me! I'll squash you like a bug." Boxer cocked his arm like he was about to hit Jack. Mussini grabbed Jack and pulled the two fighting boys apart.

"Cool off, you two!" Mussini barked. "What are you two messing around for? The show starts any minute."

Jack sneered at Boxer. That second, Boxer spun around and elbowed Jack square in the nose, causing a glorious fountain of blood to spray all over Runt, Mussini, and T-Ray. Jack wailed in pain and clutched at his face. "You jerk! Ouch, ouch!" Jack hocked a loogie onto the floor between moans of agony.

"Gross!" Runt yelled. "That's disgusting. There's

blood on my costume." Runt frowned and wiped at the splattering across his vest.

"It's broken. I bet his nose is broken." T-Ray shielded the basket with his hand and tried to avert his eyes.

"I guess you won't be coasting by on your good looks anymore, eh, kid?" Mussini said as he inspected Jack's bloody nose.

"I feel queasy," Runt said, pulling off his bloody vest and clutching his stomach. "I can't stand the sight of blood."

Mussini handed Runt a handkerchief. "Wipe off your face."

"I think I'm gonna barf." Runt swayed unsteadily and started dry heaving like a cat about to hack up a hairball.

"Suck it up, kid. You're on." Mussini pushed Runt onto the stage and glared at the rest of them. "Clean up and get ready. No mistakes out there tonight, or heads will roll . . . literally."

After stumbling onto the stage, Runt proceeded to barf into his megaphone, but being the true professional that he was, he tossed it aside, cleared his throat, and bellowed out the introductions at the top of his lungs.

Over the years in foster care, Jack had learned that blood and agony were two of the best distractions. A cleverly placed blood pack and a little screaming, and no one would be looking as T-Ray dropped the paper animals into the basket. A *bloody* perfect misdirection.

As the night progressed, each act was a triumph as loud, confident voices carried across the stage. Jack's voice boomed the loudest during his act. Perhaps it was the knowledge of his impending freedom—he felt loose and easy on the stage that night, as if all his secrets had been told, and he had nothing left to hide. Violet glided onto the stage during the act. The violet letter was pinned to her blouse like a beacon—a shimmering violet V sewn to her fairy bandit costume. Jack's stomach did a somersault as he quickly escaped three sets of planted cuffs. They were going to make it.

Finally, the moment had come—*the finale.*

The finale began as it normally did, with T-Ray dropping the animals all around and Mussini doing his little dance on the stage, followed by the animals springing to life. Except *this* time the animals just kept springing and springing and springing, until the theater was a zoo. Overhead, birds fluttered and squawked, shedding feathers like confetti down on the masked heads of the audience. The aisles were crammed with small herds of sheep and goats. A group of hairy, long-armed monkeys swung from the curtain. A lion roared and hungrily eyed an agile gazelle leaping over a bench—right over the heads of the audience. Jack hoped the animals didn't start eating one another.

T-Ray was the first to leave, weaving through the heavy curtains backstage. Violet kissed him on the cheek and pulled up his coat collar. Boxer hurried up behind her, and she jumped a little when he touched her back; he had been so quiet. The look of anticipation spread across his flushed cheeks with a grin. They were *so* close to leaving. Jack was next. He left the handcuffs in the wooden box Mussini had lent him. It was similar to the dirt-filled box the professor had in his office, only smaller. Jack didn't like it. The magical box connected the magician and the curious boy; it reminded Jack why the professor picked him in the first place, because he loved magic, but Jack didn't want to be *anything* like Mussini.

Jack felt a thrill rising in him, and his heart beat madly in his chest. Leaving felt like he was lighting the end of a fuse and watching it catch the gritty trail; at the end there was a pile of dynamite—Mussini. Jack hurried backstage, trying not to walk too loudly on the old, wooden planks. He was so close to getting out of Mussini's grasp. Once outside of the camp area, they would make a run for the woods, getting lost in the forest of trees just long enough to escape.

Everything was going perfectly. Jack rushed up on his friends. Boxer and T-Ray both had their jackets and masks on. T-Ray gave Jack a nod when he pushed through the trunks backstage. They were ready to go. Jack squeezed Violet's hand, the coolness making him shudder. He was so excited that he almost forgot that she was staying behind. She looked at him as if she knew what he was thinking.

"I don't want to say good-bye. So go, all of you, just go," Violet said.

"Wait. Where's Runt?" T-Ray asked, pushing his fox mask up on his forehead.

Violet glanced around the backstage area. "He's so forgetful."

"How could he forget this?" Jack asked. "We can only wait a few seconds, and then we have to leave or he'll blow it for all of us."

"Oh, please, Jack. Please wait for him. I'll never forgive myself if poor Runt gets stranded here," Violet pleaded with him.

Jack couldn't say no to her. "OK, we wait for Runt, but he better hurry up."

"I'll go look for him out front. Maybe one of the dead held him up." Violet rushed past the boys and back out to the front of the theater.

"Hurry, Violet!" Jack called after her.

T-Ray stroked the tiny head of the neon green snake, Linguini, who was curled around his wrist, while Boxer and Jack peered through the curtains. The theater was in chaos. Pigeon fights erupted over the heads of the spectators, showering the audience in feathers. Goats nibbled on clothes as they paraded through the aisles.

Weasels raced underfoot, and women let out high-pitched screams as they leaped up to avoid the scurrying beasts.

"See anything?" Jack asked, gritting his teeth. "That kid better not ruin this."

"Nope. No Runt. But the animals are going wild."

"What'll we do, Jack?" T-Ray asked. "We're losing time."

"I know. I know. But I promised Violet."

They all stared at one another as Mussini's booming laughter grew closer and closer. Boxer dropped the curtain. They had to go now, before it was too late. T-Ray gasped. The bright green serpentine body of Linguini slid from T-Ray's wrist and fell to the stage floor.

"Linguini!" T-Ray yelled. He snatched up his pet, now just a paper shell of a snake. "He's dead."

Jack knew instantly what that meant. "The show's over!" Jack yelled. "We gotta go." He pushed T-Ray toward the forest, but it was already too late. The dark silhouette of the Amazing Mussini appeared on the other side of the curtain. Suddenly it swung open, and Mussini strode backstage.

"What do we have here? Looks like lambs to the slaughter."

The boys froze. Mussini's stare was like a tractor beam, locking them in place. He propped his massive boot up on one of the trunks while he lit his pipe. Thick gray smoke trailed into the air. Mussini waved out the match and exhaled the smoke right into Jack's face.

"My little lambs. Did you really think you could escape me?"

"Nothing's going on here. We're all just cleaning up after the show," Boxer said, trying to cover.

"Lying's not your game, kid. Don't insult me." Mussini's dark gaze pierced Jack right down to the bone. "Did you really think *you* could defeat *me*?"

"I took my chances," Jack said.

"The bloody nose was a nice touch. Very theatrical."

Mussini took three huge steps and pulled three earth-caked sacks out from behind some trunks, dropping them onto the ground at their feet. Mussini had found their stuff and dug it up. He'd known about the plan the whole time and was just toying with them. They were just a big joke to him. Jack clenched his jaw. Since the magic book had been in Jack's sack, Mussini must have taken it back, and now he had nothing to trade the Death Wranglers.

"Your little menagerie was no match for me."

Jack pushed past the others to face Mussini. "Where's Jabber? Did he tell you we were leaving? He's a coward if he did!" Jack yelled. Someone must have given them up. It was the only way Mussini could know so much.

"Ah, the ringleader. I should commend you. It was an ambitious plan, using my own trick to try and escape. Commendable. But not ambitious *enough*. And no, it wasn't Jabber who gave you up." Mussini's black eyes gleamed and he bit down on his pipe.

"Who? Who gave us up then?" But Jack barely got the words out before he saw Violet push back the curtain with a disappointed look. Then he knew full well who had done it. Jack's stomach sank. Runt cowered by her side.

"Runt." Jack's anger drained, replaced by bewilderment. "How could you do it? How could you tell Mussini?"

"Because I don't want to go, that's why. I don't want to go back to the real world. I hate it there. I like it here with Violet and Mussini, and you, too, Jack. I'm never hungry or cold or lonely here. I start the show. I'm special. And I'm never going back to that other place." Tears streamed down the boy's cheeks, and he buried his face in Violet's skirt.

Mussini placed his hand on Jack's shoulder. "Don't you see? We're a family. I love all my children. I couldn't bear to lose any of you."

Jack couldn't tell if it was sarcasm or truth coming out of Mussini's mouth. Did he really love them? Mussini put his massive arm around Violet's shoulder. Sorrow filled her face.

Everything had been planned so perfectly, but it had never occurred to Jack that Runt had no one to go back to, no one waiting for him on the other side. The poor kid. Who could blame him? Jack knew all too well about the forgotten children of the real world—he was one of them. Maybe he was an idiot for wanting to go back.

What did he have to go back to, anyway? More foster homes, more bad schools, more trouble.

Still, there was Mildred. Had she even realized he was gone? If so, she was probably worried sick, and she got hives when she worried. And then there was the professor, who had gotten him into this whole mess. Were they looking for him? Were they trying to bring him back?

Jack knew as he stared at the Amazing Mussini that whatever fire fueled him, he was getting out of there and back to the real world. He wasn't about to give up, not even now.

18

The Straight and Narrow

Breaking down, packing gear, and setting up became a familiar routine each time they left one town and moved to another. "No roots" seemed to be the motto of life on tour. Each town offered new opportunities and a fresh start. After two botched escape attempts, failure was becoming second nature to Jack. So it was time to change tactics. The last thing he needed, while figuring out his next escape plan, was Jabber and Mussini breathing down his neck, so he needed to make them believe that they had defeated him and that he was resigned to staying in the forest. Jack rarely toed the line, but he wasn't about to let his pride ruin his chances of getting out this time. He did what he had to do to survive—if that meant performing well in the show, so be it.

In order to keep Mussini happy, Jack had to come up with bigger and better performances to satisfy the insatiable appetite of the dead. The audience craved new and dangerous tricks, and even though his handcuff tricks were good, they weren't going to pack in the crowds for long. Jack needed a real showstopper. When he finished his chores with the horses, he made his way back to the latest camp. Jack had a new idea for a trick, and he needed Boxer's help if he was going to pull it off.

That night, Jack stood in the center of the stage with his back to the audience as the lights gradually illuminated the theater. A low rumble emanated from the crowd, curious mumblings from behind many masks. Violet drifted onto the stage. Black eye makeup streamed down her face as if she had been bawling her eyes out. She twisted a damp handkerchief in her fist and stared out into the audience, frantically looking for someone.

"Has anyone seen the Kid?"

The audience stared at her in bewilderment.

"Please, please, won't anyone help me find him?" Violet begged as tears carved thin black trails down her powdery cheeks. Her skin looked extra pale against her mournful black dress starched stiff as a board. Finally, a member of the audience lifted his mask and yelled up to her.

"Do you mean *him*?" The man pointed to the spot

where Jack stood. "The Kid is standing right there, miss. Can't you see him?"

"Tell him to turn around and show us his face," shouted another brave audience member.

Violet spun in tiny frantic circles like a scared rabbit unable to find a hole to hide in. She looked up at the audience, staring dramatically over their heads to the back of the theater.

"That's not the Kid—not anymore. Not after what happened to him."

That was Jack's cue. He shifted sluggishly from side to side; his head bobbed, and his chin rested on his chest. Lost in his own tortured thoughts, he ambled around the stage, and then turned to face the crowd. A collective gasp filled the theater.

"What happened to him?" the audience member asked.

"Who did this to him?"

Jack's eyes were bloodshot and rimmed with dark circles. His face was paler than a ghost's, and his hair was a matted nest on his head. Groans rose from his chest. He stumbled on the stage and fell to his knees.

"This boy you see before you isn't the Kid. True, he *looks* like the Kid and seems so much like him in manner and grace. At first, even I thought it was him when he stumbled into camp. But the real Kid must have gotten lost in the woods at night." Violet twisted her hankie.

The audience groaned. "Oh no, poor boy."

"Not the woods at night."

"The dead of night," Violet continued, stroking Jack's hair as he kneeled on the stage in a mad stupor. "We all know what lives in the woods at night. The horrible creatures that lurk in the darkness."

"He was such a nice kid, a good kid," someone said from the first row.

"Creatures so lost and aching they search for souls, and they hunt the lost boys who wander into the woods. Last night they found the Kid, and they plucked out his soul, and look what they left us with," Violet said to the distressed audience.

"He's gone mad."

"The Amazing Mussini took pity on him. He will let him stay in our camp and live here in this very theater," Violet said.

"Mussini is a great man! A great and gracious man!"

"But wait!" Violet held up her hanky to silence the crowd. "There was a condition to Mussini's kindness, as there always is."

"What? What was the condition?" an audience member yelled. The audience was on the edge of their seats, breathless with anticipation. Behind their glitter and fur-covered masks, they looked like a pack of make-believe animals, eager for the story of which they were a part. Jack looked at them with unfocused eyes. The act was going even better than he'd planned. Violet winked at him and raised her arm.

"The condition is that he can never take off the jacket!"

"The jacket!" the crowded yelled. A spotlight focused on Jack. The crowd gasped. For the entire time Jack was on the stage, stumbling in near-darkness, he had been wrapped up tightly in his straitjacket. His arms were securely twisted around his own body, the buckles done up the back. Violet eased her way toward Jack, tentatively pulling on the jacket to show the crowd how tight the binding was. Of course, being the great assistant that she was, Violet had left Jack just enough wiggle room to work with.

"Oh, I assure you, he cannot get out. Mussini locked him up himself. It is the finest straitjacket available—no one has ever escaped from it. Not even one of the dead."

The crowd nodded with assurance. Violet paused dramatically and then continued, "But whatever you do, do *not* let him out of the jacket. I can only imagine what he might do if he were to escape! For whatever it was he saw last night in the forest, it has certainly driven him mad."

"We won't let him out."

"The poor boy's gone mad with fear!"

A frightful laugh rattled Jack's body. Violet stumbled away from him. Jack rose to his feet and stumbled around the stage yelling, "You can't hold me! Nothing can hold me!" Jack violently wrenched his arms side to side, trying to free himself from the straitjacket. This was the hardest part for Jack. He had to get enough slack to get his arms free. He didn't need to act this part, because it was a real struggle. Violet raced around the stage.

"Help! Someone help! Please stop him before he hurts himself!"

That was Boxer's cue to pull the rope. Jack fell to the floor and wiggled around in the jacket as if trapped in a tight cocoon. There was a rope fastened around his ankles and when Boxer yanked on it from behind the stage, the rope hoisted Jack up into the air so that he dangled perilously high above the stage.

"No one go near him!" Violet yelled. "It's for his own good."

Jack had gotten enough slack while wiggling around on the floor, and with the help of gravity from hanging upside down, he was able to get his arm up and over his head. Jack gasped, finally able to catch his breath. The blood rushed to his head. He swayed from side to side and had to rest for a second to get his bearings. Jack wondered, as he stared down at the stage, what it had been like for Houdini when he had dangled above the hard cement of New York City. The crowd had swarmed below him, undulating like a black river of suits. Did they look like insects, craning their necks to see the great Houdini dangled forty-five feet above them from a steel girder, only the tender loops of rope to hold him up?

Boxer anchored the rope so it didn't sway too far from side to side. Luckily the theater was in the woods, and they were able to use a branch of the oak tree to throw the rope over and hoist Jack up. (It also helped having a really strong friend.) Raising Jack's weight was not hard for Boxer at all, so they didn't need help from Jabber, who sat in the audience and instigated the excitement and mutterings of the crowd. Each member of the audience stared up to get a glimpse of Jack. Even Mussini was standing on his feet.

Jack was nearly free. With his arms already free, all he had to do was slide them under the jacket and unbuckle the strap between his legs and then pull it over his head, and then the jacket would crash to the floor to the gasps of the crowd.

And then something strange happened.

A beetle flew into Jack's face. Then one fell into his hair, and then another, jerking Jack's attention up the rope. A barrage of insects raced to the edge of the branch and down the rope. Swarms of ants and spiders crawled toward Jack: a confetti of bugs plummeted to the stage below. Jack wiggled and jerked his legs. He swatted at the bugs and swung back and forth on the rope. Where were they coming from? Before he could steady himself, a burning smell filled the stage and bits of ghostly ash fell from above. Jack swallowed. This was not part of the plan.

Screams filled the theater, followed by a crack and a pop, and then suddenly the tree that held the rope was engulfed in flames. Fire and smoke filled the night air. The audience rose to its feet. Jack had only seconds to unfasten the buckle. First he did the one between his legs, and then he pulled and yanked until he reached under the jacket and shimmed it over his head. Finally, Jack wrenched the jacket from his body and threw it to the ground. But his ankles were still tied to the rope hanging from the tree. He pulled himself up and madly tugged at the knot that Boxer had tied to his feet.

"Lower the rope! Lower the rope!" the crowd chanted as smoke filled the theater. But the rope was already burning. Boxer ran out onto the stage just as the twine closest to the branch ignited and burned to charred shreds. Jack fell headfirst toward the stage. He closed his eyes before Boxer's massive arms caught him. It was a perfect catch—they couldn't have planned it better. The audience erupted in applause.

Mussini rose from his seat and snapped his fingers. The fire disappeared in a cloud of smoke. Boxer set Jack down on his feet. Both of them were shaking and covered in sweat.

Trying to keep the show moving, Violet ran up to them and put her arms around Jack. "Take your bow," she whispered into his ear.

Jack stumbled out to the edge of the stage. The audience jumped to their feet. Cheers and applause filled the theater. Masks flew through the air. Jack was a star. But no matter how perfectly he planned a trick, Jack would never be able to control one thing: the Mussini factor. The tree igniting into flames was pure sabotage, and it was *just* Mussini's style.

Jack exited the stage after his third bow and collapsed onto a pile of burlap sacks. Violet hurried backstage and brought him a glass of water, just in time for Runt to grab the glass out of her hands and splash the water in Jack's face.

"He's fine. He's fine, people. Jack's a professional," Runt said, as the water ran down Jack's face and shirt.

Boxer and T-Ray crowded backstage with the others. "That was amazing!" T-Ray yelled.

"That wasn't in the plan. You had me worried for a second." Boxer helped Jack to his feet.

He steadied himself against Boxer's arm as the stage seemed to sway beneath him. "I'm just glad you caught me."

As if attracted to the noise and energy of the night, the Amazing Mussini pushed through the curtains, clapping his massive hands.

"Bravo! Bravo! I couldn't have planned this night better if I tried."

Everyone went silent and turned to watch what would transpire between Jack and Mussini. Jack's shoulders slumped, and with a calm voice he said, "But you did plan this. All of it. You could have killed me." But Jack knew that was the plan—to kill him.

"That was the point. I had to see for myself what you're made of. The handcuff tricks could have been luck. And make no mistake—you are lucky. I needed to know if you have the drive, the guts to live when all around you is dead."

Jack's eyes burned with anger. "Sorry I screwed up your plans by living."

"I'm still proud of you—alive or dead. Tonight you are a *star*. They loved you. How does it feel to be *really* loved?" Mussini gestured to the stage, where they could still hear cheers for the Kid. "That was my gift to you tonight. So hate me if you have to." He smiled. "You'll come around."

Mussini was always a step ahead of him. Pushing him, shoving him harder and harder. Nothing was ever good enough. Jack stormed out of the theater. He didn't want to look at Mussini for one more second. *Proud of him.* Was he nuts? Was he proud that Jack didn't get his brains bashed in, falling from the burning rope? The fact that the crowd loved the act was little consolation.

With nowhere else to go, Jack wandered back to the campfire. He needed to blow off some steam. No one was around to bother him, so he kicked at the smoldering log in the campfire, and a volcano of sparks erupted into the air. The sparks lit up the dark figure standing near the back of the wagon. At first Jack thought it was Jabber, but Jabber was still at the show. Jack took a few steps toward him. The figure moved.

"The show's over. You can't be around here," Jack said, walking faster over to the figure, his anger at Mussini bolstering his confidence. The person turned and fled, heading toward the town. Instantly Jack reacted and raced after the figure and out into the dark streets. He could use a little cat-and-mouse game. The stranger was quick, his body zipping around corners, but Jack matched him stride for stride, keeping him in his sight. After being chased plenty of times in his life, for once, it felt good to be the one doing the chasing.

Straitjacket

He could die like that,
swaying above the ground, chained to a steel girder.
But the crowd wants to see a struggle,
to feel the jacket tightening with their eyes,
the long sleeves of the coat wrapping him
in a claustrophobic embrace.

Houdini struggles like a madman,
splitting the seams of panic,
endless hours devoted to a dream
that, even standing on their toes, most will never reach.

There is no trick, no tools to the straitjacket escape,
just the battle with canvas, leather, straps, and buckles.
Joints give and take, muscles pull.
He wrestles with the insane impossible,
the struggle is not enough.

He enters a small door inside his mind,
a maze unwinds before him,
a memory of escape that he follows
like a linked thread that is so heavy it pulls him down
toward the black river of suits shifting beneath him,

men and women craning their necks
to see if he will untangle this trick
or if he will fall like a feather
out of some myth like an awestruck boy
and die on the ocean of cement
or break free, shedding the jacket like a skin,
he grows larger and flies.

Rivals and Allies

Jack darted through the streets of the town, sticking to the intruder's trail. He shoved his way past the dead pedestrians who lingered in the streets after the show. There were no stars out, no moon to lighten the midnight sky—only pale gaslights illuminating the dark stone-slick streets. The cold night air clung to his throat, but he kept his eyes locked on the quick figure.

Was the person one of Mussini's spies sent to figure out Jack's tricks? But if he worked for Mussini, why sneak around the campsite, why not walk around in the open? A flicker of hope flared up in him—could it possibly be someone who could help him get out of the forest? The farther they ran, the narrower the streets became. Jack shifted around a corner, trapping the person down a dead-end alley. The figure skidded to a halt and froze with his back to him.

"Turn around! Who are you?" Jack shouted.

The collar from the person's coat shielded his face. Jack's pulse raced. Could it possibly be a hero, coming to help him, rescuing him from the Land of the Dead? He wished with his whole heart that it was. He wanted his very own Houdini. His dry lips whispered *please*, but no one heard him, not even the man at the end of the alley. Jack stepped toward him. A gaslight flickered. He tried to think of anyone who cared enough to help him. He called out, "Professor?" The sound of his voice was smaller than he intended. Something on the figure caught the light—a glimmer, a golden spark. Jack spotted a gold ring on the person's finger. His stomach dropped, his heart sinking like a rock to the bottom of the black river. The guy he saw was *no* Houdini, and not the professor, either.

"You!" Jack spun around and stormed back out the alley. The figure chased him and grabbed his shoulder, pulling him back into the shadows. The coat slid from his shoulders, revealing a confident smirk that Jack could've recognized from looking in the mirror. It was the thief, Skimmer.

"Who's the professor?"

"No one." Jack shoved his fists into his pockets, disappointed.

"Told you I'd be seeing you again."

"Is business so bad that you have to come and spy on me?"

"I have a proposition for you."

"Why did you run away from the camp?"

"I want to keep a low profile. I don't want Mussini catching wind of our deal."

"No thanks. I'm not making any deals." Jack turned away, but Skimmer's wiry fingers clenched his arm. Jack pulled out of his grasp and spun around.

"Don't walk away. Give me a chance."

"A chance for what?"

"Hear me out," Skimmer said, clearing his throat. "As I see it, we make a perfect team for thieving. You're my alibi. I'd do all the work, all you would have to do is sit out in the open in a respectable establishment for everyone to see, while I'm relieving the dead of some materialistic burden." Skimmer shined his ring on his sleeve.

"Looked like you were doing fine on your own."

"The Death Wranglers came looking for the thief, and I had to give up a lot of merchandise to avoid punishment."

"They do that? I thought they just kept everyone from crossing the wall," Jack said.

"They keep the dead in, the living out, and they make sure things stay reasonably fair in the towns—if you have enough to bribe them." Skimmer rocked back on his heels. "But with you and me working together, they would never catch me."

Jack rolled his eyes. "Is that what you were doing at the theater tonight? Stealing from the crowd after the show?"

"I'm an opportunist. It's the first commandment of thievery—never let a good crowd go to waste. It was easy. The show must have been a good one, because everyone was all glassy-eyed and smiling. And the masks make sneaking around almost too easy. It was a great night. "

"Look, I'm not going to work your scam with you, because I'm getting out of here."

"Well, I hate to state the obvious, but Mussini tried to cook your goose tonight. The way those trees went up in flames was not natural. The Amazing Mussini is one of the most powerful guys in the forest. He has centuries of bad deeds under his belt."

"Mussini likes to keep us on our toes for the good of the show." Jack glanced away from Skimmer. He scratched his neck. He could still feel the tiny, frantic legs of the insects crawling all over him. "I knew the tree was going to catch on fire. I thought it made the trick exciting," Jack said, blustering. "It was all part of the act."

Jack averted his eyes. Skimmer was right, and he knew it. Mussini's trick had *almost* cost him dearly.

Skimmer snorted. "You can't kid a kidder. I know Mussini personally, and I know what he is capable of. You're the star of his show, but fame is fleeting. The dead have a very short attention span. Soon the Amazing Mussini will need another trick to satisfy the crowds, and who knows what he'll do to you."

Skimmer had a point. The dead bored easily, always needing more and more excitement and danger to feel alive. Jack knew it was only a matter of time before Mussini pushed him too far.

"Come on," Skimmer said, motioning toward a tavern. "We can't talk out in the street. Someone could be listening."

Jack followed Skimmer inside a gloomy tavern and sat at a low-lit booth in the corner. A waitress followed them over, and they ordered a round of root beer. Then Skimmer leaned over the table and addressed him in a hushed conspiratorial tone. "Who's the head kid at Mussini's show? The one in the hat?"

"Jabber. Why?"

"Because he followed you here. I spotted him a couple blocks back."

Jack jerked around in his seat.

"Too late now. He's coming over. You've got a lot to learn." Skimmer smirked.

Jabber moved so quickly and silently over to their table that Jack hadn't even noticed him. "Everything all right, Jack? We missed you back at camp."

"Everything's fine," Jack said, even though he didn't mean it.

Why did Jabber have to follow him? He ruined everything. Sure, Jabber had never outright lied to him. But Jack still didn't trust him—he was too honest, and the things he said were too hard to hear.

"Who's your new friend?" Jabber asked, narrowing his eyes at Skimmer, who with a swipe of his hand cleared the peanuts off of the table. Jabber had clapped his hand on Jack's shoulder and was trying to guide him out of the chair, but Jack wasn't budging.

Skimmer cracked a peanut shell between his teeth. "Shove off. Can't you see we're talking business here?"

Jabber crossed his arms over his chest and glared at Skimmer from under his hat. "Jack works for Mussini, and any business he does goes through him," he said.

Jack did a double take at Jabber's comments. "I might work for Mussini, but he doesn't own me. I'll talk to whoever I want to." He could be honest, too, and Jabber needed to leave them alone.

"No need to get hostile. You two don't mind if I join you?" Jabber pulled up a chair and sat down. "What kind of business are we talking? Maybe I'd like to get in on the action."

"Right." Jack smirked. "The only action you want in on is how to get rid of me permanently." Jack couldn't forget Mussini and Jabber plotting to kill him.

"Ah, that." Jabber looked concerned. "So you know."

"I know Mussini wants to kill me. I'm sure you're thrilled."

"You might not believe me, but I don't want you dead. If you're dead, then you are a part of the show forever. And this is my show, or it will be, and I don't need you."

Jack huffed.

"I came to warn you," Jabber said.

"I could have used a warning about the bugs or the fire."

"I knew it wasn't planned!" Skimmer exclaimed.

"What else is there to warn me about besides death?" Jack asked.

"Mussini has a trick planned for you. He's having it brought in tonight. The very best trick he could find." Jabber crushed a peanut shell between his thumb and forefinger.

Jack knew that the trick would be the most dangerous one Mussini could get his hands on, maybe even one of Houdini's tricks. And then he instantly knew what it was. "No, not that. That's impossible!"

"Mussini deals in impossible. He wants you to do the famed Chinese Water Torture Cell, and he expects you to be an utter failure."

"I won't do it. I can't. I'll just have to leave before the trick, and I'm guessing since you're telling me all this that you have an idea of how I can escape."

"You could escape to a life of crime." Skimmer smiled,

leaning across the table. "Why work with Mussini, when you can join my gang and live a life of criminal leisure? Forget about Mussini and his torture."

Jabber flicked a peanut at Skimmer. "No chance of that if he stays in the forest. Mussini will never forget about Jack. He'll track him down. So he can't stay. He must escape."

Jack couldn't believe what he was hearing. When he considered his options, they were dismal at best. What was clear was that he needed Jabber's help. He didn't have the energy to hold a grudge anymore, and deep down he was relieved to have some help, even if it was for Jabber's ulterior motives.

Skimmer cracked a peanut shell between his front teeth. "How do you expect to get Jack out of the forest and, more importantly, past the Death Wranglers? You can't just whisk him away," Skimmer said.

"Do you know what Mussini traded for safe passage?" Jack asked, but even as he said it, his hopes sank. The only thing he had to trade to the Death Wranglers was Mussini's book, and he wasn't getting that back anytime soon. "I was going to give them Mussini's magic book before Runt betrayed us and Mussini took his book back." Jack stared down into his glass.

"Mussini would never trade them the whole book. Are you mad? That book is priceless. You want to trade as little as possible. Mussini performed one trick, giving the Death Wranglers a beautiful gift."

"I won't ever be able to match Mussini in magic. What are we going to do?"

"There is another way to get through the North Wall without dealing with the Death Wranglers." Jabber paused for dramatic effect.

"Well, are you going to tell me?"

Jabber leaned across the table and spoke directly to Jack. "We're talking about the one night that the living and the dead mingle. The one night that the dead are free to leave the forest and roam the land of the living. When the barrier between our two worlds is as thin as a ghost." He drew out the word *ghost*, and a tingle ran up Jack's spine.

"So when is that?" Jack hoped Jabber was being melodramatic. Even though he was living in the Land of the Dead, he tried not to remind himself everyone around him was dead.

"Halloween." Jabber smiled. "It is the one night that you would be free of your obligations to Mussini. The one night the dead can cross the wall and the living can escape!"

"At the end of the tour?" Jack asked. "I thought Runt was kidding about that. Are you sure it's not just part of Mussini's plan for a good show?"

"No, it's real," Skimmer said. "It's a really stupid plan, though."

"Why doesn't anyone in camp talk about this?" Jack asked.

"Because it only really benefits the living," Jabber said.

"So, if the gate is open on Halloween, why don't you guys escape and leave the forest?"

Jabber and Skimmer smirked like Jack was the most clueless kid alive. "In case you haven't noticed, we're dead. On the other side we turn to ghosts." Skimmer shuddered. "There isn't much I'm scared of, I don't even mind water that much, but being a ghost is awful. Plus, going back just brings up memories of a life that's over. It's sad, really. But though some try, most don't bother with that side anymore. I don't know how Mussini and Jabber can stand crossing the wall."

"As a magician, Mussini knows how to stabilize our forms." Jabber rocked back in his chair. "It's a temporary state, similar to the animal magic he does."

"Well, if you're so smart, tell Jack why it is impossible, even if he wanted to leave on Halloween, and if he tries he will probably end up dead," Skimmer said.

"Tell me."

Jabber's eyes narrowed. He lowered his voice and Jack leaned in to listen. "Just because you will be free from Mussini's contract doesn't mean he won't try to keep you here. The forest will be crawling with Death Wranglers paid off by Mussini, traps will be set everywhere, and if you are caught you will be hanged and your lifeless body tossed into the Black River, where it will sink to the bottom, and your spirit will stay here in servitude to Mussini forever. I will try and help, but you must escape Mussini on your own. The gate at the North Wall will be unlocked, and if you make it that far, you are free to leave."

"The gate will be unlocked and we can just walk out? No deal-making with the Death Wranglers?" Jack considered it.

"If you make it that far," Skimmer said. "It's a huge risk."

Jack leaned back in his seat and thought about T-Ray and Boxer and knew it was their only chance—their last chance. "If it's the only way, then I say we go."

"Excellent. Maybe it's time Mussini gets tricked for once," Jabber said.

Jack knew that Jabber had personal reasons for standing up to Mussini, tricking him by getting rid of Jack, and proving that he was a worthy heir to the show. Everyone had an angle. But as long as that meant he would help, Jack didn't care about Jabber's motivation.

"But you still need a trick for the show. Mussini is expecting a huge finale. Halloween demands it."

Jack stared at Jabber. "I *still* have to do the trick? Can't we just leave before the show starts and avoid the torture cell all together?"

"Mussini's suspicious of you. He knows you are going to try and escape. You *have* to do the trick."

"How will I do that?" Jack asked. "You keep forgetting that I'm not actually a real magician."

Jabber drank down the last swallow in his glass. "Magician or not, you must risk your life for the good of the show."

"Or you could forget about the show and work with me," Skimmer said, grinning. "Partners. Seventy/thirty split on the merchandise till you learn the ropes. Leave Mussini and the show behind."

"I can't leave T-Ray and Boxer."

"I hope you're terrified," Skimmer said. "If I were alive, I know I would be."

"I'll do it. I'm not afraid." But Jack *was* afraid. "It's the only chance we have."

"It's just a little torture. Nothing to be afraid of," Jabber said, then turned to Skimmer. "And I've got a job for you, too."

"I don't work for Mussini." Skimmer shifted his weight away from Jabber.

"Think of it as a freelance opportunity." Jabber stood to leave. "I'm not taking no for an answer."

"If you're not taking no, then this job of yours better pay."

Jack stood. "I get the feeling everyone pays in the forest."

20

The Chinese Water Torture Cell

The enormous glass tank stood center stage. An attention getter. A spotlight hog. Genius in its simplicity—a glass rectangle that looked like a telephone booth. It also resembled a glass coffin standing on its end, but Jack tried not to think about it as his own personal death trap as he walked around it. Once inside the glass chamber, he would be like a fish caught in a hard glass net. Jack shook the image off. *Focus!* No time to freak out now. If he wanted to stay alive, he needed to do a lot less worrying and a lot more practicing.

Jabber had positioned the glass tank on the stage overnight. Jack had no idea how they built the tank or where the parts came from—Mussini had his ways. He probably could get a Trojan horse built if he wanted to. That's how Jack felt, like he was inside the camp of his enemy, hiding in the great belly of a horse, waiting for Mussini to fall asleep before he could strike.

Mussini hardly slept, and the day before Halloween he paced back and forth like a tiger seeking weakened prey. His eyes were all fire, and the sight of a new and dangerous trick thrilled him. Like the dead, Mussini was never satisfied for long. Each show had to top the previous one, and the greatest show of them *all* was rapidly approaching.

Halloween was the most important night of the year for Mussini. All of the towns in the Forest of the Dead threw wild parties with music and food, buckets and bowls overflowing with candy. The dead pulled out their best costumes, and for one night, the streets glowed with twinkling lights and music and laughter. Jack's performance would be the highlight of the Halloween tour—he couldn't disappoint.

"Halloween is a night of celebration, a night of irony," Mussini said. He sat down in the front row and propped his feet up on the edge of the stage. "It's the one night the dead rejoice and run free in the streets. It's their night to *live* again."

Boxer wheeled in an enormous drum that sloshed water onto the stage in sloppy waves. Jack's stomach seized. He wasn't the best of swimmers, and although technically he wouldn't be swimming in the tank, just the idea of all that water made him seasick.

"Today we will see if our Jack is scared of a little water," Mussini said, rubbing his palms together. *Just try and get out of this one.* His dark eyes glittered.

"It's not a little water," Boxer said, rolling another drum of water out onto the stage and filling the tank. "It's a lot." Jack stared at the water. Boxer was right—it was a small ocean.

"I'm not scared of water." Jack sneered at Mussini, trying to convince him that was true.

"I hope you have given up your desire to leave our little family." Mussini put his arm around Jack and began his little heart-to-heart. "I will do anything to make this night a success. After Halloween, we will be the most famous show in the forest."

Jack slipped out from under Mussini's arm, but the man kept talking. "Stars in a starless world, my boy. Are you ready for it?"

"Yeah. I'm ready." Jack grabbed his towel. *Ready to get as far away from you as possible.*

"It's going to be a great trick. Jack's staying with us. He knows better now." Jabber helped Boxer hold the barrel of water as it sloshed into the tank. "Right, Jack?"

"Right. Best trick ever."

Mussini left the boys to practice on their own. This gave them the time and space they needed to plan the trick and the escape perfectly. No mistakes—not this time.

Boxer eased a rickety ladder over to the tank and propped a two-by-four on the edge so Jack could sit down. Wearing swim trunks that Jabber had gotten for him, Jack climbed up the ladder and swung his feet over the edge of the glass. Practice began with Jack holding his breath underwater while Boxer and Jabber timed him. After dropping in, he shot out of the tank gasping for breath. Jabber clicked the stopwatch.

"One minute and thirty seconds. Not bad for a scrawny kid like you." Jabber nodded to Boxer, who tossed a set of shackles onto the stage. "Time to go up-side down."

Jack climbed out of the tank, sat on the stage, and closed his eyes while Boxer locked him up. Sometimes it was easier to see things with his eyes closed. His mind's eye opened wide, and he saw the way the trick played for the audience. Tight metal cuffs closed around his wrists. The cold clasp of shackles gripped his ankle bones. Boxer turned a crank, the chain took hold, and Jack was hoisted into the air, where he dangled over the tank. His body stiffened as he tried to control the slight sway. Boxer let out the chain and lowered him headfirst into the icy water—a black curtain dropped over the box, plunging him into darkness. Jack had to escape the manacles before drowning to death. Torture *was* a good name for the trick.

When he was eight years old, Jack took his one and only trip to the beach. It was fun, at first, running along the sun-baked boardwalk in brand-new rubber flip-flops, eating cotton candy and hot salty pretzels. The sand on the beach was covered in the coolest things he had ever seen—washed-up starfish and iridescent shells. He had only seen sea life in books and on television. The red bodies of starfish littered the beach like small treasures from the sea. Starfish shrivel and die out of the water. So Jack flung them back, one by one, slinging them into the crashing surf, saving them from the impending doom of the scorching sun.

Back then, Jack thought he might be part dog. He had these super-canine senses, like the way he couldn't remember people's names, but could remember their smells. The beach parents smelled like stale beer and piña colada. His big, beer-bellied foster father decided Jack should learn to swim. Jack stood at the edge, ankle deep, while his feet sank into the soft sand. He raced back to where his foster mother sizzled in the sun, drenched in coconut oil, lounging on a bright orange beach towel, reading a steamy romance novel. But before Jack could make it to the safety of the towel, Mr. Big-Belly grabbed him, spun him around, and shoved him toward the water.

Jack's heels dug deep trenches into the sand, but it was no good. His foster dad lifted Jack's featherlight frame up into the hot August sun and tossed him like a starfish returning to the sea.

After the initial crash, mad flailing, and gag-a-thon, Jack stood in the chest-deep water. The suction of the tide pulled against the backs of his legs as the water rushed back out. Slimy seaweed encircled his ankles. Gritty sand stung his calves, and then a massive, greenish peak rose above him. He had nowhere to go. He tried to duck, but the wave crashed onto his head, filling his gaping mouth with salty water. Jack, flung helpless as a starfish, felt swallowed by the ocean. The salt stung his eyes as he tumbled uncontrollably on the wave. He was lost in an undersea world where there was no up or down.

That's what he was afraid of, not having his feet on the ground. Upside down in water was the key to the vulnerability of the trick.

Houdini had invented the upside-down trick himself, so he had a leg up. Jack didn't know how Houdini did it. He was in way over his head, literally, and he knew it. All he could do was to keep practicing and do the best he could. Jabber knocked on the glass tank, returning Jack's focus back to reality. Boxer turned the crank, and suddenly, Jack was pulled back out of the tank, coughing and choking up water, dangling above the stage like a drowned rat.

"How do you feel?" Jabber asked, as water streamed down Jack's body.

"Horrible."

"Good. That gives you an idea of what the trick will be like."

"This trick stinks." Jack's teeth chattered. "Why does everything have to get harder?"

"That's the challenge, the danger. You must create that ache in the audience's heart. Inflict worry."

"That won't be a problem. It's just that I thought I found something I was good at. Handcuffs were my niche."

"Mussini will love it. It's exactly what he's been waiting for." Jabber handed Jack a towel and then realized that his arms were shackled. "Open wide," he said, stuffing the towel into Jack's mouth.

"Fffankss," Jack mumbled as Boxer lowered him down to the stage and helped him out of the cuffs. He sat shivering, wrapped in a towel.

Violet waved at Jack from the other side of the camp. Since water made the dead nervous, Violet screamed her head off the first time she saw Jack get submerged in the tank. Though she agreed to help him onstage, she wasn't about to watch him practice. Since Runt had already betrayed them to stay in the forest, they had decided to keep him in the dark about the escape plan. Violet's job was to keep Runt far away from the theater.

After holding his breath all morning, Jack moved on

to manipulating the handcuffs and shackles underwater. He did all of this right side up—the upside-down part would have to wait while he got used to the water. The heavy-looking locks were actually trick cuffs. One or two good yanks and they easily came free. Then he broke free of the shackles around his ankles, and the chains fell to the bottom of the tank. After a half-dozen tries, Jack escaped his handcuffs and leg irons at the same time, getting his best time yet. Now all he had to do was put the trick together, breaking free from the cuffs and shackles while underwater, hanging upside down. No problem.

The first couple of times he practiced the trick upside down, he bent over and fell face-first into the tank like a pathetic six-year-old diving into a pool. Panic was the problem: The minute Jack hit the water, his body contracted and his knees folded in. Spaz City. He twisted and turned, finally jerking up and out of the tank, gasping for breath. Boxer slapped him on the back when he came up for air the sixth time. Jack coughed, choked, and spit up a mouthful of water onto the stage.

"Sorry," he managed to gag out.

The trick had hit a wall. The control factor was the key. Jack had to control his fear, his panic, and his breathing. Jack sat panting on the board. "We can try again. I know I can do it."

Jabber and Boxer exchanged a glance.

"We can practice more later," Boxer said.

"Maybe one last try," Jabber said.

"One last try," Jack echoed, and braced himself for the chilling descent into the tank. Boxer let out the slack in the rope and plunged Jack back into the water. The trick started out fine. Confident that he might finally get out this time, Jack slipped out of the restraints that held his feet. But then he twisted around and caught himself in the shackles as they fell to the bottom of the tank. Tangled in a sea of chains, Jack couldn't get his bearings. The links twisted and pinched at his skin like an iron octopus dragging him down into the deep. His body felt slow and clumsy underwater. He tried to right himself and dive out of the water, but he wasn't fast enough. Water rushed up his nose. He choked and coughed, inhaling the burning cold darkness. His vision went black.

Jack jerked back. Icy porcelain crashed against his sides. He was in an antique bathtub with big claw feet, just like the one Houdini used to practice holding his breath underwater. He lay flat on his back submerged in a foot of water, air bubbles pouring from his clenched lips. If he could just hold on a little longer. His lungs burned. He leaned up and gasped. It was the night of the show. The theater glowed. The bathtub stood center stage. Jack emerged from the water to the raucous applause of the crowd—a standing ovation, but for what? He stood soaked and shivering. Through the audience, the professor made his way from the back of the theater. He's come to save me, *Jack thought. As the professor approached the stage, Jack noticed the string of handcuffs that bound his wrists.*

Mussini stood, towering above the crowd, and raised his knife. Jack screamed, but no sound escaped his mouth. The knife sliced through the air, driving into the professor's back. The professor stumbled, pitched forward, but kept going. Another knife sailed through the air, hitting the professor, causing him to crumple to the ground. Mussini didn't stop but flung knife after knife with perfect aim. The professor crawled to the stage, leaving a trail of blood in his wake. When he approached Jack, he held out his shackled wrists like a bouquet of steel, a gift that only Jack could receive. Jack held the professor's bloody hands in his.

Pain pinched up the professor's face. "You must escape. You must."

"You're hurt. I'll get help." *Jack tried not to look at the knives cutting into the professor's back.*

"Don't worry about me, my boy. It's you I'm worried about."

"We have a plan. I'm going to do the water torture and make Mussini proud. I'll trick him at his own game."

"You'll die trying, my boy."

"No, I can do the trick and escape on Halloween, Professor. Mussini and the Death Wranglers can't stop us on Halloween."

A calm satisfaction spread across the professor's face as he collapsed at Jack's feet. "Very bright of you, my boy. Halloween."

"Don't go, Professor," Jack held the professor in his arms, his voice choked with emotion. "Don't go."

Jack looked up into the wild eyes of Mussini as he prowled around the back of the theater. He had one knife left, and Jack knew he was saving it especially for him. The audience drifted away, the lights faded, and Jack was alone.

Boxer shook Jack violently, and he vomited a pool of water onto the stage. He coughed and hacked up water and phlegm. Jack leaned up; his throat was raw and his nose burned on the inside.

"That was a close one," Boxer said. "Are you all right? How many fingers am I holding up?" Boxer waved his hand in front of Jack's face.

"All of them," Jack said. His teeth chattered and he curled his knees up to his chest. "What happened?"

"It's called drowning, and turns out you're pretty good at it, seeing as how you almost didn't make it out of the tank." Jabber leaned down and peered into Jack's eyes. "He looks OK," he said to Boxer.

Jack closed his eyes. It was just a dream, but the professor had been so real. He felt like such a sucker. The professor was probably home safe and sound and nowhere near Mussini, just like he planned it. He wasn't going to save him. No one was.

"This sucks. I can't do the trick. What are we going to do now?"

"You have to do the trick—the Chinese Water Torture Cell is the best trick we've got," Jabber said, sitting on the edge of the stage.

"Yeah, and get myself killed."

"Your failure is anticipated. Dying keeps you with Mussini, it's what he expects. So you're going to need a showstopper if you want to get out of here," Jabber said. "Don't worry, I've got an idea."

After they fine-tuned their plan, Jack stumbled off the stage to find Violet and fill her in, and then he made his way to his tent. Every bone in his body ached with exhaustion. Sleep was all he had the energy for, so he threw open the tent flap and made a beeline for his hammock. Jack noticed T-Ray shifting nervously from foot to foot, waiting inside for him.

"What's up?" Jack flopped down into his hammock, which groaned under his weight and swayed back and forth. "Did you get a chance to talk to Jabber? He said he would let you know what's up."

T-Ray fingered the edge of Jack's hammock. "Yeah, it sounds like a good plan. I'll miss Violet and Jabber. I wish there was a way that they could come back. I'll even miss Runt, though he did rat us out. But that's not what I want to talk about. I just wanted to say that it's OK."

"What's OK?" Jack sighed and rubbed his hands over his face. His fingertips were pruned from being in the water for so long.

T-Ray sat down on a trunk and stared at the ground. "It's OK if you want to take off without us. I don't want to hold you back and ruin your chance of getting out of here."

"Why would I want to do that? I told you that we'll get out of this place together." Jack grabbed his pillow and threw it at T-Ray, who caught it with a relieved smile.

"Yeah, I know you did, but you've always been on your own." T-Ray's brow wrinkled. "It would be easier for you."

"Easy isn't my style. Plus, the plan will work. It has to," Jack said, putting his hands behind his head.

"I guess so." He paused. "You know, I'm glad were friends. 'Cause we won't make it by ourselves. We're not like you, Jack. We need you really bad." T-Ray threw the pillow back at Jack and climbed up into his hammock. T-Ray thought for a minute and said, "But you could really drown. And then what are we gonna do?"

"Great, you're gonna give me nightmares now." Jack closed his eyes and rolled over in his hammock. It was strange being needed. He had spent so much time in his life not needing anyone; it never occurred to him that others might need him. It made him feel warm and suffocated at the same time.

"Hey, have you packed up your stuff? We have to be ready to go. Halloween is our only shot."

"Funny how the night of the dead is my last chance to escape alive."

"It'll be fine." Though Jack was not entirely convinced.

"I'm not worried for me. Seriously. I'm worried about *you*," T-Ray said.

"You're not the only one."

Jack barely remembered going to bed. He fell into a deep sleep as if floating on the ocean surface, the waves rocking him to sleep until he sunk deeply to the sandy bottom of his dreams.

The Upside Down

Shackled and bound,
Houdini is plunged headfirst into a deep, dark cell.
Seconds spool like a thread of water down the drain.
Water makes everything harder.
Everything becomes its enormous self.
Breath locked inside his lungs,
blood pounding against thin walls.

We watch transfixed,
pulled down into a dark ocean of worry.
We squirm in our seats.
We have asked for this near-death,
for Houdini to go where we cannot.
We die one by one, holding our breath,
panic racing in our veins.

He is going, faster now, slipping the system,
we want to follow him to that place
where illusion matters,
where we are not alone in our own glass booth.

We steel our nerve,
never letting the fear overtake us

in a race where seconds count,
where the upside is down.

We can't hold it in anymore,
we let out our last burning breath and cry, Wait!

Wait for us.

The devil would say, Come on, that trick's not so hard—
But he'd be lying.

21

Halloween

From backstage, Jack peered through the curtain. Flaming torches burned through the darkness, sending glowing phantom trails into the sky and illuminating the theater with an eerie glow. He shivered. The dead were packed in like sardines; it was a full house. It was the most important show yet, Jack thought—his life depended on it. Literally.

Everyone was in position: Violet's cool arm brushed against his, T-Ray waited with the gear, and Boxer gripped his ax so hard, his knuckles turned white. Jack hoped that Jabber lived up to his end of the bargain. If not, there was no way he would make it out alive.

With his thumbs hooked through his belt loops, Jabber glided out onto the stage, his black hat askew on his head. He stopped dead center, head bowed, and waited. A hush fell over the audience.

"I must warn all of you that what you will see tonight is highly dangerous. The show could be a nightmare realized, or it could be a magnificent triumph. Anything could happen. But then again it *is* Halloween, a dangerous night. Not for the faint of heart, now, is it?"

The audience snickered and bobbed their masked heads while Jabber continued with his speech.

"Tomorrow may be All Saints' Day, but there are only *sinners* here tonight. And tonight is our night. This is the finale you've all been waiting for." The crowd cheered madly. "The one time we can return to the land of the living, if we dare. It will *not* be easy. See there!"

Jabber leaped to the edge of the stage, pointed to the back of the theater, and everyone in the audience turned around, adjusting their masks to get a good view.

"A Death Wrangler has joined us! They will be out in full force tonight to make sure there is fair play if anyone wants to make a run for the wall."

The crowd gasped and clapped. Jack's stomach dropped. Jabber and Mussini failed to mention that a Death Wrangler would be at the show, a minor detail but a *major* blow. The hulking bull head rose above the crowd as the creature stood and snorted an acknowledgment. The mythical beast was twice the size of Boxer, with massive spiral horns curving out of his black furry head.

A thick gold ring dangled from his round snout, and his eyes were pitiless black orbs. The audience gave the creature a wide berth.

The crowd turned its attention back to Jabber, who glanced at the curtain as if he could feel Jack's burning glare on his back.

"There are no warm-up acts tonight. We begin with the best. The Kid will perform his most dangerous trick. In mere moments you will see why we don't bother with life insurance in the Forest of the Dead." Jabber paused, the audience captivated. "Jack just might be one of us when it's over."

Jabber took his position. The curtain rose, revealing the torture cell standing alone on the stage. Silence filled the theater as if the dead had just sucked in their last breath. Jabber pulled a stopwatch from his pocket. Jack hesitated. It was all up to him.

He dropped his towel and walked out onto the stage barefoot and dressed in his swimming shorts. The crowd stared at him from behind their most elaborate feathered masks and bejeweled costumes. The dead were no longer people, but the dream of people who had shed their old selves and slipped into new glittery skins. And there was Jack in the flesh, just a boy, alone in this strangely beautiful, lifeless world.

He didn't need to say a word as the trick began. Violet followed him onto the stage, her cold hands giving him goose bumps as she attached the shackles around his ankles and closed the cuffs around his wrists. Jack lay down on the hard wooden stage as the floodlights danced around him. Boxer turned a crank, and the sound of the chain grinding against metal joined with the excited humming of the crowd. Jack's feet and legs lifted into the air. His body hovered above the tank. He swayed back and forth like a pendulum hypnotizing the audience. Boxer lifted him higher and higher, momentarily hiding him in the curtain above the stage. Jack grabbed the velvet in his hands, hoping the plan would work.

The blood oozed down from his legs to his brain. As he dangled like a worm on a hook, Jack thought about the pathetic choices he had made in life, and how those choices had led him right to his current predicament. He wished that he had made some nicer friends, or done better in school, or not just drifted through life like it didn't matter, like *he* didn't matter. He had stopped caring about his life in the real world—Mildred called it being apathetic. But really, he had given up.

Life was a blur, it was happening so fast. Maybe he was in the middle, too—no longer a kid, definitely not an adult. He still had a chance, and he didn't want to blow it anymore. His whole life, he'd been waiting for someone to believe in him. But fate didn't care that his dad was a selfish jerk who didn't stick around. Destiny had no pity that his mom wasn't there to wipe his nose and bake him cookies. Sometimes there was only one person who was going to believe in a kid, and that person was himself.

The rope was lowering now. He could do this. After all, he was the Handcuff Kid.

Jabber paced around the tank and asked the audience, "Would anyone like to hold their breath to see if they can match the Kid? Just raise your hand and hold your breath if you want to take a crack at it."

A half-dozen hands shot into the air from volunteers in the audience. Boxer took his position on the stage next to the tank; he grasped the ax in his hands, holding it out in front of him, so everyone could see it. The stopwatch dangled from a long silver chain, clasped in Jabber's hand. Tension rose, the audience fidgeting and shifting in their seats as the seconds ticked by. Finally, a person rose from his seat.

"How long has it been? How long has the boy been under?"

Jabber checked the stopwatch and yelled out, "Thirty seconds!"

"That's a long time. A very long time for a young boy," a woman, dressed as a fairy, called up to the stage as she fluttered her wings. A little girl, seated next to her, pulled on her mother's costume. "Mommy, is the boy OK?"

"I don't know, baby," she said, picking up the little girl.

"Let us see him!" another man yelled.

A man from the back of the theater jeered, followed by hoots and cackles, "He's one of us now!"

A long-beaked birdman stood on his seat. "He could be drowning and no one would know." The crowd grew restless. They shivered and recoiled at the water that entombed him in the glass case; they felt the chains that bound him tighten on their own cold wrists.

"Pull the curtain off!"

"Yes! Let us see the boy!"

"One minute!" Jabber yelled. Boxer wrung his huge hands around the handle of the ax—it was all that could save Jack now.

A woman staggered in the aisle, clutching her chest. "Does anyone else feel it? I can *feel* him dying."

Boxer's head jerked toward Jabber. He motioned toward the tank. He gripped and regripped the ax, his palms slick with sweat. Jabber strolled around on the stage, swinging the silver watch, waiting and waiting, the second hand ticking and ticking. The audience was on its feet.

"He's drowning!"

"He's just a boy. For pity's sake, help him."

Jabber slipped the watch back into his pocket and finally snatched the curtain from the tank. The audience could see that Jack had twisted himself around so that he was upright in the tank. Something was wrong. The locks were still locked. The chains hung heavy around his limbs. Jack pounded on the glass with a weak fist. A cascade of air bubbles flowed from his blue lips. His skin was as pale as a fish belly. Jack's eyes rolled back in his head. His limbs sunk to his sides. The shackles pulled him down, and he sunk to the bottom of the tank. His head rested on the glass. His eyes opened in a lifeless stare. Screams erupted throughout the theater. Jabber had waited too long.

"Save him!" the crowd yelled.

"The ax! Use the ax!"

Boxer stood motionless, staring at Jack's lifeless body and then at Jabber. Dread flashed across his face. He held the ax out in front of him, suddenly unaware of what to do. He took a tentative swing at the tank but hesitated. A flood of fear and panic poured out of him. "You said the trick would work," he said to Jabber. "You said I wouldn't have to use it. And now look. He's dead." Boxer swung the ax down by his side, rushed the tank, and slapped the glass with his open palm. "Wake up, Jack! Wake up!"

Jabber raced over to Boxer's side and tried to wrestle the ax out of his hand. "Give it to me. He still has a chance to live. We can save him."

"Look at him! It's too late."

"It's not too late. Give me the ax."

"This is your fault. You waited on purpose. You wanted him dead. Loyal to the Amazing Mussini to the end." Boxer glared at Jabber and then spun toward the audience. Looking out into the crowd, he locked eyes with Mussini. He pointed the ax. "I hope you're happy now. Jack's dead because of you and your show." Boxer lifted the heavy ax and hurled it over the masks of the audience and right at Mussini. The heavy blade struck a pillar above Mussini's head, but he didn't even flinch, and then he rose slowly to his feet.

Jabber pushed Boxer toward the curtain. "Get off the stage now."

Runt rushed up to the tank and pressed his face to the glass, staring into Jack's lifeless eyes. "My new brother is dead!"

Trying to salvage the show and soak in the moment, Jabber returned to the tank and the audience. "Ladies and gentlemen, have no fear. Jack will be fine. The show will go on." He motioned to the tank. "Stand back, Runt."

"Hurry, Jabber! We need to get him out of the tank."

"Since the strongest kid alive has taken a break, may I have a volunteer from the audience?"

The audience hummed with whispers and gasps. No one moved; no one volunteered. Mussini scratched his chin and narrowed his eyes.

"He looks awfully dead." Runt inspected Jack's face through the glass.

Jabber sighed. "Well, if no one wants to help, I guess I will have to empty the tank myself." Jabber walked back to the tank and pulled the drain plug. Water gushed from the drainage hole, which had been positioned to face the audience. Gallons of icy water poured out of a drain, gushing over the edge of the stage and into the crowd. Screams rose up from the struggling masses as they tried to get away from the water. Panic spread through the shoving and clawing crowd. Masks and feathers flew from shredded costumes up into the air. The dead ran for the aisles, charging the doors.

Mussini tried to push his way past the fleeing crowds to the front of the stage. "I want to see the boy! Get him out of the tank, Jabber. Bring him to me."

The Death Wrangler thrust his weight forward to block the crowd, but he was trampled in a stampede of terrified audience members. Finally, the creature shoved the dead aside like dried corn husks and barreled toward the stage. Mussini followed in his wake.

If Jack had learned one thing in the Forest of the Dead, it was that death was all about perspective. Magic was all about tricking the eye. Jack knew the trick was too hard for him and that if he attempted to do it, Mussini's plan of killing him would definitely work. So he and Jabber decided it was best to give Mussini what he wanted, and let Jack die in the tank.

Or so everyone *thought.*

When Boxer raised Jack above the stage, he was momentarily hidden by the curtain. That's when the switch was made, and Skimmer was lowered into the tank in his place, though he charged Jabber extra for submerging him in water. Seeing as Skimmer was already dead, it didn't matter how long he was under, and Jabber took his sweet time building suspense. Once the trick began, Jack climbed down the side of the curtain and waited backstage for his dead alter ego to be revealed. Mussini wasn't dumb. He would soon discover that he had been duped, but in the minutes meantime, they would make their getaway.

"Mussini never saw it coming," Jack marveled as he watched the magician react to seeing *Jack* dead in the tank. "He never expected me to fail. He thought I could do it."

"He may have wanted you to die, but he's a great magician, and he wants you to be one too. And succeeding at the torture cell would have made you one," Violet said.

"But I failed by not even trying to do the trick."

"And your utter failure just saved your life," Violet reminded him.

"No one was expecting it," Boxer said, rushing backstage. "Jabber's a genius."

"The dead hate water." Violet wrung her hands and turned away from the screaming masses, now drenched. "They're going wild to get out of the theater."

Jack looked up at Boxer and smiled in relief. "Nice

throwing. See how Mussini likes having a knife thrown at him."

"That was a big knife," Violet said. "Very theatrical."

"I hate to break this up, but we've got to go," T-Ray said. "Mussini will be after us. We can't wait any longer."

"One second." Peering through the curtain, Jack saw a frantic maze of masks and spotted the Amazing Mussini trying to shove his way through. A dark rage twisted up Mussini's face—his skin turned scarlet red. Mussini reached for his belt—for the knives—and in a second a blade sliced though the air, barely missing Jabber as the knife bounced off the glass of the tank. *He knows!* Mussini crashed into an audience member who had foolishly headed right for him.

"Get them! Get out of my way!" Mussini bellowed and pointed toward the stage. "Don't let those kids escape!"

The kids rushed behind the theater to where the horses were waiting, packed with gear. Jack turned to say good-bye to Violet. She brushed his hair out of his face. Jack had to leave her. It was his only choice. Was this how his mother and father felt? Was it possible to love someone so much and still have to leave her?

Violet's hands were cold in his hands. Her violet eyes were like nothing he had ever seen. He threaded his fingers through hers; it felt like running his fingers through feathery snow. Violet was staying in the forest, and so were Jabber and Runt, but this was not the fate of the others. It was time to ride.

"Thanks, Violet. For everything," Jack said. "We couldn't have done it without your help." Jack's heart ached. He never could have saved her. "Tell Jabber thanks, too." He wondered if Jabber would end up like Mussini one day, rotting and twisted, caught in the choke hold between life and death. He hoped not—maybe he'd move on to the river one day like he should.

"I will. But please go. Hurry. Mussini will make a last-ditch effort to stop you. Remember, he's a magician. He'll try and trick you. Don't let him win." Violet gave Jack one last look before turning to help T-Ray and Boxer mount their horses.

Jack positioned his wrist out in front of him and commanded the magic compass to appear. "The North Wall!" The mark of Mussini sprung to life, the arrow spinning on his wrist and then stopping as the North Wall appeared off to the left, directing them where to go. Jack realized in that moment as he stared down at his wrist, this was their last chance. He gave his horse a kick and they took off into the woods.

Jack held on as the horse galloped through the trees. Mussini and more Death Wranglers would be in quick pursuit, but he didn't care. He was leaving, running away from the best family he had ever known, leaving it all behind and letting go.

Halloween

A full moon hung overhead, illuminating the trees
as impenetrable as prison bars. The horse ran faster and
faster, dodging through the trees, toward the wall. A rush
of wind blew against Jack's face. He was so close, but
he could feel the urgency of pursuit building all around
him. Jack could feel Mussini gaining on him with every
second.

And then, up ahead something flashed, bright and
burning. The sudden brightness reminded him of his first
night in the forest, when they all sat around the campfire
and Mussini waved his hands over the fire and held the
flame in his palm. A warm wave of air hit Jack right in
the face. Flames reached up into the darkness. The North
Wall was no longer just a wall. If Jack wanted to get
out of the forest, he would have to walk through a wall
engulfed in *fire*.

Death Defying

Jack never would have thought stone could burn. But sure enough, crackling, hissing pops filled the air. A fiery crust replaced the thick layers of moss and climbing ivy. The raging inferno was so high it was impossible to see over the top. And to make matters worse, the massive iron gate had been left wide open, mocking them. Flames formed a wall between the metal gap, as high as the regular wall.

Sure, anyone could leave the forest, as long as they were fire retardant or at least dead. Mussini was always one step ahead, no matter how perfect Jack's plan. No one was leaving tonight, not if the amazing magician had anything to say about it.

"What do we do now?" T-Ray asked.

Jack shielded his eyes from the gust of heat that hit his face. "Can we jump through where the gate is open?"

Boxer dropped his pack. "I can't see anything through the flames. It could be too deep."

Jack jumped down from his horse and walked as close as he could to the blazing curtain that stood between him and his freedom. "It's no use going through this way. We can't walk through fire, and it's too high to climb over."

T-Ray fell to his knees. "We're so close and yet so trapped."

"There's always a way out." Ideas raced through Jack's mind. There was no way *through* the wall, and there was no way *over* the wall, so that left only one way: the Houdini way. One of Houdini's tricks was walking through a brick wall. He did it by going *under* it, through a trapdoor in the stage floor. Jack scanned the woods for a torch. When he found one he ran to it and searched the forest floor, desperately shoving aside leaves and dirt. After a minute his foot struck metal—he had found one of the hatches to the labyrinth.

"Look, come on." He pulled open the hatch and started climbing down.

"I'm not going down there. The Death Wranglers will be on full alert." T-Ray and Boxer stared down into the pit of the underworld as Jack jumped down from the ladder.

"I've got an idea. T-Ray, toss me the pack. How are you at digging?" Jack asked Boxer as he climbed down.

"OK, I guess."

Jack pulled two small camping shovels out of the pack that Boxer had insisted on bringing. "This is all we've got. It will have to work." He held one out to Boxer.

"What do you expect us to do with these?" T-Ray asked, joining them reluctantly in the labyrinth and taking one of the shovels.

"We've got to go under the wall. Start digging."

"A tunnel!" T-Ray and Boxer both tentatively chipped away at the wall of the labyrinth with their shovels, not fully accepting the idea. "That's a lot of digging."

"It's our only chance. We can take turns keeping watch above so the Death Wranglers don't sneak up on us. The tunnel is perfect cover."

"There's no stone covering this section of the wall." Boxer ran his hand over the rough dirt surface. "It might work. But it might also cave in halfway there."

"Let's do it." T-Ray gouged the wall with his shovel.

Jack alternated between digging and keeping watch while T-Ray and Boxer dug out the tunnel. It was a long shot, even with all of them digging, but Jack wasn't about to say so, especially with T-Ray so close to dying. Mussini and his Death Wranglers were searching the woods at that very moment for them, and it wouldn't be long before they made it to the North Wall.

Jack clawed at the ground with his hands, clearing out piles of dirt. He had no idea how much time had passed when he climbed up the ladder from digging to check the woods. Through the darkness of the forest, he saw a flicker of light moving slowly and steadily toward them, a burning torch sailing through the trees. A flash of gold winked at Jack, causing him to leap up from the ladder. It looked as if a hawk were flying right at him with its sharp gold beak, a cape flapping behind it like dark wings. Mussini was on horseback, racing through the trees. Mussini didn't need the Death Wranglers to hunt them down—he had come for them himself.

Jack looked back at his two friends, frantically digging the tunnel that would lead them under the fiery wall and back to the land of the living. If Mussini reached the wall, there was no way they would make it. Jack had to stop Mussini; he was their only hope. He yelled down to T-Ray, "I'll be back. I promise."

"What's happening?" T-Ray asked, but Jack didn't need to answer, because T-Ray's eyes widened as he spoke. "Mussini. He found us."

"Just keep digging! And if I'm not back soon, both you and Boxer get out of here."

"We won't leave you."

"Please, T-Ray! Please just do it. I'm the one Mussini wants. Just don't let it all be for nothing."

"OK, but hurry. Boxer's a fast digger."

Boxer had already dug a five-foot tunnel, burrowing through the earth. Jack didn't have much time. He grabbed his duffel, jumped up into the saddle of his horse, kicked her haunches, and was off, charging right toward the golden hawk. The only way to give Boxer and T-Ray more time at digging the escape tunnel was for Jack to lure the Amazing Mussini away from the gate. Jack made great bait, and he had one trick left just in case.

Jack barreled toward Mussini. He focused on the gold hawk mask. Tree limbs slapped at his arms and legs. The distance between them grew smaller. His stomach twisted, his nerves sharpened. He stayed straight, until finally swerving out of Mussini's path at the last second.

Mussini never flinched. Jack looked over his shoulder and saw that Mussini had pulled up his horse and was coming after him. It had worked!

Jack flicked his sleeve back. "The river!" Jack yelled, knowing the mark would show him the way. The arrow rose up on his skin, spun wildly, and stopped as the Black River appeared on the compass. Mussini's pursuit continued, and he was gaining on him, so Jack leaned into the horse's neck, urging her on. Racing through the tangled woods, Jack finally heard music and saw the city lights.

Jack slowed as he entered the city, and jumped off his horse. He was engulfed in crowds of the wildly costumed dead. He hid among them and waited for Mussini to catch a glimpse of him before taking off down one of the docks. Jack was pretty sure that Mussini knew that he was setting a trap for him, so he had to be ready. How was he going to defeat a person who was bigger, stronger, and meaner than he was? Then he remembered his first day in the Forest of the Dead and how the gang had trapped the pig.

Jack ran for the bridge, but he stopped short and climbed up a rickety rain gutter that leaned against the old tavern. He scurried up the side and perched on the rooftop.

From up there, he could see Mussini pushing through the crowds of dead. Music filled the streets, and the dead whirled and danced. A highly annoyed Mussini was swept up in a jostling current of dead merrymakers spinning to the flow of music.

He forced his way through the crowd and strode toward the building where Jack was perched. It was just like catching a pig, Jack told himself. A large, muscular pig that could kill him, but still.

He reached into his backpack and pulled out his secret weapon, his only chance: the devil's handcuffs. He had kept them after the show and was surprised that no one, not even Mussini, tried to take them from him.

Mussini yelled his name over and over. It was Jack's cue to get ready. Mussini was coming, the gold mask thrown from his face, exposing the desperate man behind the magic.

"Come out and show yourself!"

Mussini stepped into place. Jack's mentor and nemesis was right beneath him. Something shifted inside him. Jack was the hawk now—the predator taking control. Magic took guts, but it also took control. After stepping onto the stage every night, he knew that he was capable of more than just tricks and magic. He had become a believer in his own bravery. He was worthy—fight-worthy, trick-worthy, magic-worthy. All he had to do now was jump.

Jack threw his legs over the side of the roof and leaped onto Mussini's shoulders, sliding down the front of the magician, easily getting one cuff on. As it snapped around his thick wrist, Mussini went wild, bucking like a bull. The magician knew what Jack was trying to do and kept his other hand out of reach; no matter how hard Jack struggled, he couldn't clench Mussini's wrists together.

Mussini pulled at Jack with his one hand, holding the other high into the air. They spun and struggled. Jack's body ached; his muscles shook. He wasn't strong enough to topple him, so he pulled Mussini along, dragging him toward the bridge.

The two stumbled as Mussini tired of the game. He reached his free arm toward Jack and muttered a magical phrase. At his command a half-dozen snakes poured from beneath his sleeves and wove their slender venomous bodies around Jack's arms and legs. Jack thrashed wildly, flinging and shaking himself free of the deadly reptiles.

"You aren't scared, are you? Would you prefer rats or spiders next?" Mussini taunted. "I've still got better tricks than you!"

"And you're still trapped in one of them." Jack wrenched on the devil's handcuffs, refusing to let go.

"Hold still, or I'll tear you limb from scrawny limb!"

Jack faltered, sweat-soaked and exhausted. Size and strength were not on his side, neither was experience or skill. Courage and bravery were not enough to stop the magician.

Jack struggled to his feet and edged his way closer to the bridge. The pulsing crowds of dancing and laughing dead had grown around them, sweeping them up until they were halfway across the bridge.

When he was in position, Jack stopped struggling and fell to his knees at the feet of the giant magician. Mussini raised his huge arm, the golden handcuff attached and Jack still hanging on to the other end.

"You little weasel, slapping my own cuffs on me. You're lucky I'm a patient man, but it's wearing thin."

Mussini twisted Jack's wrist until it seared with pain. He winced and squirmed in Mussini's grasp. As Jack hung on to the handcuffs, dangling and staring up at his sweat-stained armpit, he realized one thing: Mussini really stunk. Then he realized something else: Mussini had a weakness. He still had a beating heart. Maybe Jack wasn't defeated after all.

Jack grabbed for the ledge and leaned over the stony side. The Black River roared and crashed beneath him like a raging, living thing. Jack breathed in the cool night air and let the music of the dead wash over his face. His mind spun. He steadied himself. Ready.

"Stop it. Stop this blasted game!" Mussini yelled, but it was too late. Jack was too close to the edge. Holding on to his half of the golden handcuffs with one hand, he stepped over the side and let gravity take him.

He fell. His body rushed toward the water and suddenly stopped in midair as Mussini's weight and strength kept them from both going over. A burst of agony shot through Jack's arm, burning in his shoulder as his arm bore the weight of his whole body.

The devil's handcuffs sprung to life; the golden metal tightened around Jack's fingers as he tried to hold on. The metal tore into his skin. The Black River licked at his heels; splashes of icy coldness stung his hot face. Jack screamed as he dangled beneath the bridge.

"Help me!" Jack yelled. "Please, Mussini! I don't want to die!"

Instinctively, Mussini reached for the boy and grabbed him with both hands and pulled him to safety. Jack knew that deep down Mussini liked him and cared for him, maybe even like a son. He wouldn't let him fall, and that simple act of kindness was his undoing. Jack groped for the ledge, and through the haze of pain in his arm he slapped the other cuff on Mussini's empty wrist. Jack had tricked Mussini with the man's own kind heart.

Mussini pulled the boy up by his shirt and tossed him to the ground with both hands. Jack fell on his back and scrambled to his feet, clearing Mussini by a few arm lengths.

"You little punk. You think you're so clever, don't you?"

Jack leaned on the bridge, gasping for breath. "I learned a lot of that cleverness from you."

"The game is done. Come back to camp. I can offer you everything—fame, fortune, and eternal life. You will be the star of the show—the greatest magician ever—greater than me, greater than your Houdini." Mussini held his hands out to Jack, begging him. The golden cuffs cinched around the magician's wrists shined like an offering. He dropped to one knee. *Very convincing, very theatrical,* Jack thought. Mussini was always a showman, always laying a trap. Jack hesitated.

Mussini caught his eye. "The mark is the first of many gifts that I can offer you. I will teach you everything I know. You can follow in my footsteps and run the show. You're a special boy. No one on the *other side* can offer you what I can."

Jack stared down at his tattoo. He could learn so much from Mussini, for whom magic sparked and flowed so easily—a powerful magician, respected and awed. He would finally have his mentor, teacher, and dad. He could learn to do magical things, not just handcuff tricks. He could stay with Jabber and Violet and be a real magician, like Mussini. More importantly he would have a home and a family.

But trust was a labyrinth Jack was still learning to navigate. And though Mussini offered him many wondrous things—fame and adventure, magic and a family, in the end the magic was just an illusion, the family was stolen and forced. Mussini's world wasn't real, but half-alive, barely breathing. Jack couldn't bring himself to trust the magician—a man whose whole life and death was based on a lie, no matter how beautiful and magical the lie may be. Jack knew that if he stayed, he would die, and he didn't want to end up like Skimmer, stealing pretty things from the dead, seeking fool's gold to feel valuable.

Mussini had one thing right—it would be much easier to stay. The real world was tough, and Jack didn't have a Mussini out there to take care of him and encourage him. He would have to brave the real world on his own. But if the best magic was man-made, then so, too, was bravery, and he knew that he would have to trust himself. He didn't need a magic compass to get through life.

He thought of T-Ray and Boxer frantically clawing

their way through the earth to escape the forest. Maybe he would never be like Houdini, but one thing he could achieve was to be around people who cared about him. For the first time Jack had true friends, and he wasn't about to let them down.

"I can't stay. I won't. I don't believe in you or your magic." Jack swallowed. It was the worst thing he could think of to say to the magician. "I won't fall for your tricks. Your word is as real as your magic. You promised Jabber the show first, and now you promise it to me. If I stay with you, I'll end up with a knife in my back. No thanks. I want to go home to the real world, where I belong."

A dark cloud of anger passed over Mussini's eyes. "I'm sorry to hear that, because I've got a vindictive streak in me, bordering a bit on the obsessive. If you step one foot out of the forest, I won't rest until we meet again. And as you can see from the mark, there is nowhere in the world you can hide from me." Mussini advanced, blocking Jack's path to his horse.

Panic pulsed through his tired body. Jack thought fast. "There is only one way out of those cuffs. You know it, and I know it. And it's with the key."

Mussini struggled in the grasp of the golden manacles. "Do I look like a fool? I helped design these handcuffs." His body tensed. His biceps bulged against the twisting magic.

"Then you'll be lucky to get out of them by morning." Jack pulled the golden key that fit the golden handcuffs from a chain around his neck. Mussini winced, his eyes trained on the key. Jack rubbed the key between his fingers.

"Don't you think I kept a spare?"

Jack had to risk it. There was no way Mussini had the key, especially on him. He was bluffing.

"If you have a key, then you won't need this one." Jack held it high into the air. He dangled the key over the side of the bridge. Mussini's whole body jerked toward him. Never trust the dead. Jack smiled and loosened his hold on the chain, letting the key slip a few more inches toward the rushing water. The look of fury on Mussini's face slowly relaxed. There was only one way out for both of them, and they both knew it.

Sink or swim.

Jack cocked his arm back and threw the key high into the air. The key soared toward the Black River. Mussini barreled down the bridge and dove over the side.

Jack stood back and watched as the Amazing Mussini plunged into the river. The crowd that had gathered around them erupted in applause; they probably thought it was part of a street act. Mussini was a magician to the end. If there was a trick to the devil's handcuffs, Jack didn't know it, but if *anyone* could beat the cuffs, it was the Amazing Mussini.

Jack knew that Mussini would make it. He would find the key at the bottom of the river. He would survive in this place. For whatever reason, Mussini was not ready to move on.

When Mussini didn't surface from the river, Jack ran back to his horse and rode out of the River City. It was nearly dawn and so Halloween was ending. Death Wranglers would be after him now, but he didn't care. He had done it. He tricked the Amazing Mussini.

The horse raced back toward the wall as the air grew colder, and thin black shadows raced alongside him. Spirits flew through the sky like dark winged birds, and Jack thought he saw something chasing him. He urged the horse on. The wall glowed with fire ahead of him. He was so close. But then the horse spooked, rearing up on her hind legs, throwing Jack to the ground. He tried to grab the reins but the horse bolted, pulling Jack a few feet before he let go. He was facedown in the leaves. Alone.

Jack crawled to his knees and saw what spooked the horse, and the sight took his breath away. For standing a few feet in the distance was a shimmering, magical beast. At first glance, he thought it was a horse, but then he saw its body and face. It was a woman with long golden hair cascading around her upper body, which was attached to the body of a horse. A centaur! Was this the beautiful, magical gift that Mussini traded to the Death Wranglers?

The horse moved closer to him and she spoke, "Run, human. My master comes for you."

Jack was tired of running, tired of being strong, and tired of resisting. The magic of the forest was so amazing. He wanted to collapse right there and stare at the beautiful beast. But his friends were counting on him. Jack struggled to his feet and started to run the rest of the way. It felt like he had already run for miles. Suddenly he froze. Torchlights approached like fireflies, hovering closer and closer—Death Wranglers, swarms of them, in between him and the wall. Jack was trapped.

23

Into the Labyrinth, Again

The wind stung Jack's face. The Death Wranglers closed in. There was only one way out: He had to go down into the earth, into the labyrinth. A torch burned off to his right, indicating a trapdoor in the forest floor. There was no time to think about what might be down there. Jack had to take the gamble that on this night there were more Death Wranglers above ground than below.

He dove for the open hatch, and the gaping mouth of the tunnel swallowed him. He clung to the metal rungs of the ladder and climbed down. An unsettling quiet washed over him. The cold unknown of the underside seeped into his bones. Jack pushed back his sleeve and whispered, "Show me how to get to the North Wall."

The tattoo compass pulsed to life, only this time he was shown the maze; the narrow corners of the labyrinth appeared hovering in the air and an arrow directed him on which turns to take.

Jack navigated through the maze of stone, darting around tight corners, getting closer and closer to the North Wall. His heart raced, and his confidence grew as he fled through the labyrinth. He pretended that he was playing a game, a challenge he accepted and was winning. He could tell by the change in temperature that he was almost to the spot where Boxer and T-Ray were digging the tunnel under the fiery wall above them. He was going to make it. He could feel it. And the next second, Jack slammed into a wall. Not a brick wall, but a muscle-bound, bull-headed, highly agitated wall—a Death Wrangler.

Jack bounced off the creature's chest and fell backward onto the ground. The creature roared and snatched Jack up off the floor, holding him one-handed in the air close to his hairy snout. His black orbs narrowed. Jack's own face stared back at him in the reflection of the bull's eyes.

"Looks like it's my lucky night," the guard said.

"You can't stop me from leaving. It's Halloween."

But the creature just snorted and slung Jack over his shoulder. "Not for long," he said.

"Hey, put me down." Knowing how close he was to

the North Wall, Jack yelled, "Boxer! T-Ray! Help! Help me! Boxer!"

The Death Wrangler carried him through the maze, and his screams faded into the darkness. Jack checked the tattoo; they were headed toward the Death Wrangler lair and the terrible fighting pit. Once they reached the lair, the Death Wrangler dropped him on the ground and tossed his duffel bag beside him. Another Death Wrangler approached. Jack recognized the creature as the smaller guard that he had seen fighting in the pit weeks before. "Tie him up and throw him into the pit. I will alert the others that a prisoner has been caught."

"No, I will alert the others. You will stay and mind the child," the guard said arrogantly, obviously considering the other guard to be his subordinate.

"Put him in the pit. Or you will end up there yourself." The smaller guard pointed to the great hole in the ground.

"I would gladly fight in the pit, especially if you were my opponent," the guard said.

"We can make that arrangement."

Jack clutched his duffel and tried to think of a way out. He felt his heavy stash of handcuffs through the canvas fabric. The larger guard stood near the side of the pit, turned his back on the smaller guard, and peered over the edge. With the guard standing so close to the edge of the pit, Jack saw his one and only chance to escape. He choked up on his bag and slammed it against the back of the creature's legs at the knee joint, causing the Death Wrangler to lose his balance, windmill his arms frantically, and fall into the pit. A loud crash followed as the Death Wrangler tumbled into a pile of shields and weapons. He was knocked out cold.

Relieved that he now had only *one* hideous horned creature to face, Jack turned and saw Boxer peek his head out of the maze behind the smaller Death Wrangler. A flood of joy and pride flowed through him. T-Ray and Boxer must have heard him calling to them and had come to his rescue. The remaining Death Wrangler approached Jack, laughing as he came. Puzzled, Jack asked, "What's so funny?"

The beast peered down at his comrade. "I never liked him. Too arrogant, too confident, and even for our kind, he was annoying. I can't wait to tell the others how a mere mortal took down a ferocious Death Wrangler. No wonder Mussini wants to keep you."

Jack glanced at the creature, looking for an opportunity to make a run for it, but the creature sensed his intention. He snatched Jack's duffel bag and threw it into the pit.

"Hey, why did you do that?" Jack stared down at his duffel. His handcuffs and straitjacket were lost for good.

"Because I can't let you leave. Tell your friends to come out of hiding, and I won't hurt any of you. I'll just return you to Mussini."

Boxer and T-Ray emerged from the maze. Their

clothes were covered in dirt and sweat. Boxer motioned for Jack to move away from the Death Wrangler. He held a machete, one of the creature's weapons, in his hand. T-Ray held a shield. Jack swallowed hard. What were they thinking?

"Halloween is the one night that we're allowed to leave the forest. You can't change the rules just because Mussini says so!" T-Ray yelled. His eyes blazed. He was done. Done with Death Wranglers. Done with being afraid of his own death.

"You're right." The Death Wrangler faced T-Ray. "I can't stop you from crossing the North Wall, but I can keep you from reaching it until Halloween is over."

"What did Mussini promise you? Did he bribe you with magic?" Boxer asked to antagonize the guard, distracting him so that Jack could move closer to the exit where Boxer and T-Ray stood.

"We came to get Jack and get out. No more games, no more rules, no more forest," T-Ray said.

During the speech, the Death Wrangler uncoiled a long leather whip and snapped it in the air. Jack heard the crack of the whip; it was so fast it broke the sound barrier. The whip snapped again, inches from Jack's head.

Boxer ran to Jack's side and blocked the Death Wrangler. The whip bit through the air, sending chunks of sediment from the ceiling cascading down on them. A bright splotch of blood appeared on Boxer's arm where the whip had torn a hole in his T-shirt. Boxer turned his back on the Death Wrangler, shielding Jack from the whip. Jack and Boxer ran for the cover of the labyrinth. The whip cracked over and over. Jack winced for his friend, the whip tearing into his skin, but Boxer was the strongest kid alive, his heart the size of an elephant's. Nothing was going to stop him.

The Death Wrangler roared. Boxer turned and faced the beast. The whip clipped his arm. Blood appeared instantly. The whip snapped again, but this time Boxer snatched the thin leather strap from the air and yanked, causing the Death Wrangler to stumble. A tug-of-war followed as the two tried to claim the whip. Blood dripped from Boxer's clenched fist where the whip cut into his hand. His muscles tensed and the whip flew from the Death Wrangler's grip. The beast staggered and bellowed, but still advanced.

In a burst of courage mixed with temporary insanity, T-Ray grabbed a torch from the wall, held up his shield, and charged the Death Wrangler. When he came within a few feet of the creature, he used the torch like a spear and drove it at the Death Wrangler's face. An explosion of sparks filled the air as the creature batted the torch away.

The beast roared. Bits of fur smoked. Furious and blinded by the flame, the Death Wrangler lowered his huge head and wildly charged at T-Ray with his sharp horns. T-Ray darted out of the way and threw Jack the shield. Jack drew the Death Wrangler toward him, moving at the last second, causing the Death Wrangler to plow headfirst into a stone wall. The beast slumped, staggered, and kneeled. Finally, he fell to the ground in a heap of charred and matted fur.

The boys raced out of the lair and back toward the North Wall.

"We've got some bad news." Boxer sighed; his shoulders slumped, the weight of the underworld becoming too much, even for the strongest kid alive.

"Are you serious?" Jack asked. He couldn't take it anymore. "How much worse can it get?"

Jack skidded to a halt in front of a huge mound of dirt. They had made major progress in the tunnel. The hole was deep under the wall. Jack ducked his head inside to get a good look, and that's when he noticed the problem. Thick, black metal bars blocked the tunnel. They must have been buried under the wall when it was constructed, making the forest a literal prison, even from underground. There was no escape. Hopelessly, Jack grabbed the bars with both hands and rested his head against the cold metal.

T-Ray grabbed his shoulder and shook him out of his trance. "Come on. We have to go. He'll be after us when he wakes up." T-Ray led the way out of the tunnel back to the surface.

Jack climbed out of the labyrinth, turned around, and stared at the flaming wall. It was over. There were no Death Wranglers, no Amazing Mussini, no Jabber or beautiful Violet. The blazing wall was hypnotic. There was no way through, no way out.

Suddenly, a hand clamped down on his shoulder. Jack jumped and jerked around. His heart skipped a beat. Standing before him was a criminal kind—Shepard. "Out for a stroll in the woods?"

"No, we're trying to get home. What are you doing out here?"

"Don't worry, kid. I'm not going to stop you," Shepard said. "It's every man for himself tonight."

"I thought you said that you've never been across the wall?" Jack was relieved that Shepard wasn't under Mussini's orders to bring them back.

"There's a first time for everything. Ain't that right, kid?"

Shepard walked toward the wall and then turned back to Jack. "Don't waste your last chance. Don't end your life with regrets." And then Shepard walked right for the burning wall.

"No, Shepard! Don't do it!" Jack yelled, but Shepard kept going and stepped right into the fire. His screams filled the night sky. His body spun and his arms whirled around, his dark image igniting into a stunning blaze of fire. And then as quickly as he went in, Shepard stepped back out of the fire. His long leather coat was smoking from the heat but otherwise he was fine. He laughed and pointed at the wall. "This ain't real, kid. It's just a trick." Shepard demonstrated again by reaching his hand into the fire. "I guess Mussini gets the last laugh."

"Brother." Jack just shook his head. Shepard waved and stepped through the wall.

"That proves that the dead can walk right through the fire, but what about us?" T-Ray asked. "It's blazing hot. I'm sweating just standing here. It feels real."

"It feels like fire," Jack said. "Mussini is the master in real illusions." Jack rubbed his arms that only hours before were crawling with snakes.

"What are we going to do now?" Boxer asked.

"We've come this far, we can't quit," T-Ray said.

"Maybe Shepard's right and it's a trick," Jack said. "Violet said that Mussini would try to trick us. He's a magician. It's all he knows."

"An evil magician," Boxer said.

Boxer coiled the whip he had taken from the Death Wrangler. "One of us could make a run for it?"

But none of them wanted to be the one. Jack closed his eyes. The fire felt like a warm lake of water luring him closer. He took a step toward the flames and then another one, tentative, but certain. He could do it. His insides felt twisted like his gut was full of hot metal tumblers twisting in his stomach. It was time to find out what was real in this world and what was fake.

Boxer grabbed his arm, but he kept going, walking into the flames, into the last trick of the Amazing Mussini. He was so hot at first, he thought the flames would lick the skin right off his bones, but suddenly the flames cooled.

In his elation, Jack hardly noticed a figure approaching from the other side. Jack jumped out of the flames back into the forest. A tall, thin man in a long coat walked out of the fire. Jack could hardly believe his eyes. It was Professor Hawthorne.

"Professor?" Jack reached out to him. "Is it really you?"

"It's really me. I knew you would make it. I knew you were the one. But I'll admit I was worried for you."

"Yeah? If you cared so much about me, then what took you so long?" Jack glared at the professor and dug his hands into his pockets. Anger seethed through him, the fresh cut of being abandoned reopened. "I've been here for weeks on my own with no help from you. You sent me in your place and left me there. So you can quit your worrying."

"Jack, believe me when I tell you that I studied the laws of magic for fifty years, and all roads led me to the same conclusion. I needed to beat Mussini on his own turf, with his own tricks. But by the time I knew, I was too old to do it myself. So I went looking for a boy like you. I knew you would figure out a way to escape."

"Why should I believe you? You threw me to the wolf to save your own skin."

"I'm here now. I came back. I can only ask for your forgiveness, my boy. And ask you to come home."

Jack winced inside when he heard the old phrase *my boy*. Maybe the professor did want him back.

He had done it on his own—well, with his friends' help. He had escaped the Amazing Mussini. He hadn't needed the professor or anyone else to rescue him. Maybe his destiny wasn't something that he ran aimlessly toward, but something he claimed and grabbed hold of with both hands. He wanted to go home, back to the way it was before. But things would be different because now he knew for sure that no matter what happened, he would be OK—he would survive. He wouldn't waste anymore of the time he had.

"If I go home with you, you're not going to sell me to any more magicians, are you?"

"No, I promise no more tricks." The professor motioned toward the fiery wall. "I see Mussini has added his usual flare."

"Can we really walk right through it and not get burned?" T-Ray asked.

"Yes, this is one of Mussini's many tricks. Can you forgive me, Jack? Let me take you back to the land of the living." The professor held out his hand and Jack took it.

Jack's shoulders released; the effort of holding a grudge was too tense.

"We're really going home?" Boxer asked.

"I think it's safe to say, you boys made it."

Together, they followed the professor through the fire and out of the forest.

Halloween

Houdini didn't believe in ghosts.
Maybe he saw the spirits as pitiful,
their act riddled with mistakes,
wringing their ghostly hands
as they pounded on the glass window of life
trying to get back into a world that was done with them.

Halloween is a myth owned by the dead.
The living slip on masks and inch closer to the thin skin
that separates two illusions—life and death.
One we know by touch, one we know by word of mouth.

Houdini takes a sucker punch.
But he still goes on,
performing till the end folds in on him in pain.
Entire lives can be fit into small increments of time.
Even in the bleakest hours,
through hunger, poverty, and disillusion,
he never loses faith in his own destiny.

He dies on Halloween,
on the one day that he could turn around,
look over his shoulder,
return one last time
to prove that the world of spirits is real
or just a beautiful illusion,
to tell us how the big trick is done.

But Houdini has already gone.

Jack held perfectly still and took slow, shallow breaths. He closed his eyes and shifted slightly in his seat. He never heard of anyone actually dying from eating too much, but he didn't want to be the first. Ever since they arrived back at the professor's house, Concheta spoiled the boys rotten, cooking all of their favorite foods.

"*¡Mi chico!*" Concheta patted his cheek. "Wake up. Ms. Mildred is here."

Jack sat up, carefully placing Little Miss B. on the floor. Boxer and T-Ray were sprawled on the settee, watching a movie.

"Right this way, Ms. Crosby." The professor escorted Mildred into the room. Jack leaped up to greet her, throwing his arms around her and squeezing. Mildred brushed his hair back from his face and placed her hands on his shoulders.

"Let me get a look at you." She examined him up and down and then glanced over at Boxer and T-Ray. "Those two the ones?"

"Yes. I found them." Jack didn't know what else to say.

"Where?" Mildred asked. Jack's phone message to Mildred had been completely incoherent.

"Purgatory." Jack shrugged. He might as well at least continue trying to tell the truth; when he told her on the phone what had happened, she accused him of making up a Halloween story to scare her.

"I know, baby, life is hell. Now tell Millie what you've been up to."

He knew Mildred would never believe him. Who would? It was an unbelievable story. And as angry as Jack was at the professor for selling him to an evil magician in the Land of the Dead, it had been the adventure of a lifetime. For a brief moment he was his own hero. He got to be a real magician and a star. He faced down Death Wranglers and survived through impossible odds. "They were in a forest. Just lost I guess."

"Come on, pack your friends' stuff. We've got to go. I've been on the phone all morning with social services." Mildred scanned the room with hawklike precision. Jack knew she was suspicious, but for now she saw no reason to take him away from the professor, mostly because she didn't believe the story about the Amazing Mussini—not one bit. At least Jack's conscience was clean, and he got to stay in his first real room and with the best, if a little odd, family he had ever had.

Though it was hard to say good-bye, both T-Ray and Boxer were eager to get home and see their families. They made a pact to stay in touch and visit over the summer. And the professor promised to do all of the driving—said it was the least he could do. Mildred herded the boys out of the house and settled them into the car. Jack waited on the porch with the professor.

"I wanted to give you this." Professor Hawthorne handed Jack his Houdini book.

"Where did you get it?" Jack took the book, secretly thrilled to get it back. He thought it had been lost forever.

"As I have previously mentioned, my boy, I have otherworldly connections."

"Thanks." Jack smiled. They hadn't discussed Mussini much, as the professor still felt guilty, but Jack had an important question. "Professor, do you think we will ever see Mussini again?"

"I have tried not to think about it. But it is a very real possibility. Mussini is a man of revenge, and though I don't want to scare you, he could find a way. You should beware, my boy."

"I'll be careful. I've always got Mildred. I would hate to see him try anything with her around." Jack made light of the subject, but Mussini's final words of revenge stayed with him. Did Mussini have a plot for revenge? In the end, Jabber had helped Jack escape for the chance to one day be like Mussini and inherit the show. Jack could only hope that Mussini wouldn't punish Jabber or Violet if he ever found out they helped with the escape plot. He wished that they all could somehow make peace with their lives and move on—take the Black River to its end—but it wasn't up to him, and only they could decide for themselves. Runt was probably thrilled to have Skimmer as a new brother. In some ways he hated leaving them behind, but they had each other and made up their own family.

Mildred settled into the driver's seat. Jack ran into the yard and waved one last good-bye to his friends. When he raised his arm, he felt the metal slide down his wrist, but this time it wasn't a handcuff, but the professor's gold watch, which he had given to Jack to wear to hide the tattoo. The last thing he needed was for Mildred to see it and start asking questions.

The shiny gold watch sparkled in the sunlight and was a constant reminder of his ordeal. It even reminded him a little of the devil's golden handcuffs that Shepard had made. But mostly it reminded him, proudly, of the amazing and terrifying magician who had given him the tattoo in the first place, and whose grasp he had escaped. He slipped the watch back down and tried not to think about the mark etched into his skin, linking him forever to the Land of the Dead.

The professor stood on the porch, somberly dressed all in black. The professor reminded Jack of the old priest who'd been his foster father and given him the Houdini book. He would never forget those men, the ghostlike dads that drifted in and out of his life. They weren't ghosts at all, but real people, and he connected them all, even Mussini. Jack knew that they would remember him, too.

Jack wondered what he owed the world. As Jabber said, no debt went unpaid. He couldn't add it up. He thought about his life, about the gift of being alive. He felt indebted to the universe, the sky, the stars, and to the invisible air. How would he ever pay it back?

All he could do was live his life. Hold on to it, every lousy card and every hard-learned lesson. He didn't let the kids fool him, the ones dressed up in pointy hats or long black robes with wands and magic dust. Jack knew the secret that every magician knew, and that Houdini knew. And that was: Real magic was man-made. Everyone could do it.

Mildred started the old car, and as she pulled away, she scraped the tires against the curb like she always did. Jack laughed and waved. It felt strange to see his friends and Mildred drive away, but he knew that he would see them again. For once, Jack was staying put, and it felt good to finally be home.

Acknowledgments

I am grateful to many people for their help, guidance, and support in bringing this novel to life. One day while bemoaning the demise of a less-than-stellar manuscript, I had a flash of inspiration to write a book about Houdini. I quickly discovered that it is impossible to simultaneously research the life and magic of Houdini while feeling sorry for oneself or remaining complacent. Magic was hard work. But I didn't want to write a novel about Houdini; I wanted to write a novel about a kid who cared about Houdini and was inspired by him the way that I was inspired by his tireless effort to fool the eye, to rise out of his circumstances, and to be great at something as fleeting as creating illusions. I thank Harry Houdini, who showed me that, especially through life's hardest moments, creating illusions is important.

I would like to thank my family, especially my nemesis—I mean, loving and caring sister—Jen, who never tires of listening to me talk about how the book is going. Also, I would like to thank Nadja and Bob Muchow for their unwavering support, and Steve for his endless supply of calm and assuredness. I have a great critique group, No Vampires Invited, and I would like to thank Robin Galbraith, Elizabeth Buck, Farrar Williams, and Joan Silsby for their kindness and support. I must also thank Ted Malawer for finding a wonderful home for the manuscript.

I am grateful to everyone at Abrams, particularly Susan Van Metre for her early support of the project. I am especially lucky to work with editor Maggie Lehrman. Her insightful edits pushed me to be a better writer and storyteller, and the novel benefited greatly from her effort. And lastly, I would like to thank Maria T. Middleton for the great book design and Brandon Dorman for the gorgeous artwork for the cover.